A WINTER WAR

TIM LEACH is a graduate of the Warwick
Writing Programme, where he now teaches
as an Assistant Professor. His first novel,
The Last King of Lydia, was shortlisted
for the Dylan Thomas Prize.

Also by Tim Leach

The Last King of Lydia
The King and the Slave
Smile of the Wolf

A WINTER WAR

TIM LEACH

HEAD
ZEUS

9 7 5 3 1 2 4 6 8

A catalogue record for this book is available from
the British Library.

ISBN (HB): 9781800242869
ISBN (XTPB): 9781800242876
ISBN (E): 9781800242951

Typeset by Divaddict Publishing Solutions Ltd

Printed and bound in Great Britain by
CPI Group (UK) Ltd, Croydon CR0 4YY

Head of Zeus Ltd
First Floor East
5–8 Hardwick Street
London EC1R 4RG

WWW.HEADOFZEUS.COM

For Ness

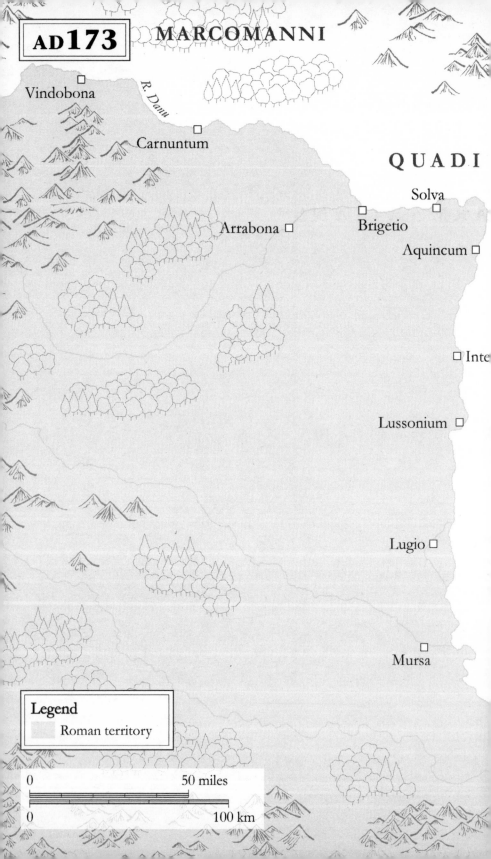

AD**173**

MARCOMANNI

R. Danu

Vindobona

Carnuntum

QUADI

Solva

Arrabona

Brigetio

Aquincum

Inte

Lussonium

Lugio

Mursa

Legend

Roman territory

0		50 miles
0		100 km

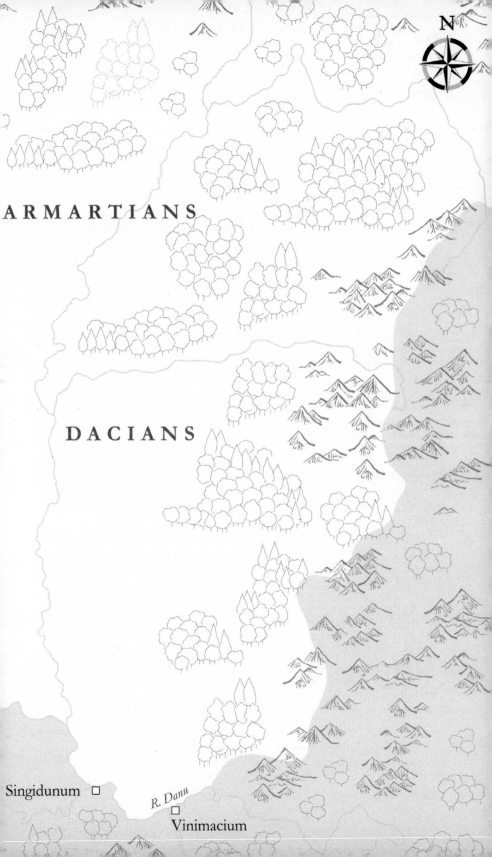

N

SARMARTIANS

DACIANS

Singidunum ◻

R. Danu

◻
Vinimacium

Part 1

THE RIVER OF ICE

1

From a distance, it might have been an army of statues, or of the dead.

Six thousand riders upon a plain of ice and snow, in a land where it seemed that nothing might live. The wind rattled against tall spears like a gale passing through a winter forest, but the horses did not stir, and under close carved helms and thick furred hoods, the men's eyes seemed hollows with no glimmer of life. Seen from afar, one might have thought them a great monument carved to a forgotten king, or an army from a long forgotten war struck down by curse or spell, doomed to stand in place for eternity and wait for a command that would never come.

It was only if one drew close that one could see the little whorls of their breaths frosting before their lips, here and there see a horse toss its head and stamp at the snow. Closer still, and one could hear the impatient whicker and mutter of the horses, more eager for the battle than the men who rode them. They thought only of the rush and joy of the charge, the surge of muscle and hoof, for unlike men they could not imagine their own deaths. Their riders were silent as they looked on

3

the frozen river before them and waited for the Romans to come across the ice.

One spear tilted down in the line, as a warrior laid the weapon to rest across the neck of his mount. The horse gave a snort of protest, for she bore a heavy weight, she and her rider glistening with scales of horn and bone fitted like a second skin. Yet when the rider laid his palms against the haft of the spear and rolled it against the beast's neck, the horse's protest went silent, and she leaned into the touch and gave a shiver of pleasure.

The rider beside them shook his head. 'I think you love that horse more than my wife loves me, Kai.'

The first man answered. 'And why not? My horse is more worthy of love than you are. She's braver. More handsome, too.' He pushed back his hood as he spoke, baring his teeth in a friendly smile.

Laughter then, to break the silence – soft, and half choked, but it was there, scattering down the line. Even some of those who could not have heard the jest grinned for a moment, patted their horses, lifted their spears to stretch frozen muscles. For a moment, the army lived once more.

The second rider, Bahadur, cuffed Kai about the head, a slap of leather against bronze, but he answered Kai's smile in kind. He leaned forward to speak, close enough for Kai to see every mark of the tattoos on his cheeks, the streaks of grey in his beard. 'Keep the laughter going, if you can. The others are frightened.'

That last word was like a spell, for when it was spoken the air seemed to grow thin and cold as the air of a

Carpathian pass. Amongst his people there was nothing worshipped like warriors, no trade thought noble but that of spear and horse, no death counted as sweet save the one found on the point of a blade. Yet only a madman would not be afraid in that moment, for the Sarmatians all knew what was coming across the ice of the Danu.

Kai looked out across the frozen river in front of them, shading his eyes from the spindrift with a gauntleted hand. Little to be seen there, even if the mist had cleared. In summer one might see boats on that river, merchants coming to trade wine and perfume, furs and amber. Or fishermen seeking some blessing from the river god that might feed their families. But the merchants came like thieves across the water, and the fishermen did not care to linger long. For the Danu was a border, and it was more than another country that lay across the water. It was another world.

On the other side of that river, the Roman Empire. A chieftain's gold dripping from every woman's neck, a prize of iron in every warrior's hand. But more important than that, enough wheat and cattle to feed the clans twice over. For the Sarmatians, winter-starved by sickly herds and blighted crops, it was life that was over the water, life that they could almost reach out and touch.

Almost. For across the ice the enemy waited for them. An enemy whose name was spoken as a warning to children, a bitter curse to a rival clan.

Kai had seen that enemy broken in battle, their general cut open while he still lived, left pinned out and screaming for the carrion birds to butcher as a warning to his people.

5

Still, they had come back. Another tribe, the Marcomanni, had burned fort and city and carried the fight almost to within sight of Rome itself, and the Legions had returned undaunted. A few years before, the gods had cursed the Romans with a plague that had piled the corpse fires high, had murdered entire armies, murdered so many that it seemed there could be no man left alive west of the Danu. Yet they were there in their forts, scarce two miles away, somewhere across the ice. For those were the men that it seemed not even the gods could kill.

'We are the last ones left,' said Kai.

'What?'

'The last people still fighting Rome. The Marcomanni are kingless. The Quadi pledged to Rome after the miracle of the rain. The Dacians...' Bahadur muttered a foul curse at that name, and Kai had no need to speak further of them. 'There are none but us left to fight. What do you think that means?'

Beneath his cloak and helm, Bahadur's face was unreadable. The touch of light on his eyes – was it anger or grief at the words that Kai spoke, words that danced at the edge of doubt?

'That we shall have to win here today,' the older man said, 'if we are to eat this winter. If we are to be free. What do you think that it means?'

'That our grandfathers should never have left Scythia. That our people should have stayed upon the Sea of Grass to the east.'

'They would have come for us there, too. A little later, that is all.'

'Better that we fight them now,' said Kai. 'Or our children would have to fight them instead.'

A little cry at that – not from Bahadur, but from the rider behind him, a boy who huddled on his horse and shivered and wept. Too young for the warband and drowning in his armour, it should have been another summer at least before he was asked to set his spear in the charge. But the ranks were filled with those like him – greyhaired men who could scarce hold their spears, boys who should have been herding sheep out on the steppe. It was Bahadur's son, Chodona, who shamed himself with those tears, and Bahadur put his arm about the boy and drew him close, whispering the wordless charms against fear that father might speak to his child.

Watching them, Kai felt the coward's hope that the Romans would not come. Let them stay in their forts across the water, so that the boy might live to become a man.

But already, it was too late. For a sound was echoing across the river, coming through the mist. At first Kai thought it the bark and chatter of the ice, the echo of a distant storm that boomed and blew across the open land. But soon there was no mistaking what it was.

Mothers whispered stories of that sound to children around the campfire at night. Warriors spoke of hearing it for the very first time, as though a great monster had crawled up from the pits of another world to scuttle across the ground on ten thousand feet. And everywhere that it moved, it left the dead piled high, too many to honour and send to the next world with iron and gold. And for those

7

that lived, a different kind of death. A death of submission, and slavery.

The stamping tread of an army moving as one. The sound of the Legion on the march.

It struck the horsemen like a curse. The quiet words of encouragement, the boasts and the black-humoured jokes – all went silent. The riders hunched their cloaks about them, and even the proud horses fell quiet. They had heard that sound many times before. Hard-fought victories, bitter defeats, retreats that had scattered them across steppe and plain. And in victory or defeat, nothing changed. Still the Legion walked on.

Beside him, Kai heard Bahadur shift, the scales of his armour clinking against each other like chimes in the wind. The hood slipped from the older man's head, and the helm was in his hands, his thinning hair exposed to the wind, the white of his skin shockingly bright in the midday light. Bahadur turned his head to the side, listened as closely to that terrible sound as he might have listened to the whisperings of a lover in the night.

And then, he laughed.

'You can laugh at that?' said Kai.

'Listen. You are young. Your ears should hear it better than mine.'

Kai slipped the hood from his head, pushed his helm up onto his forehead. The wind drew still for a moment, and he could hear the fell tread of the Legion. Yet he heard other things, too – a rattle and clatter, an echoing curse spoken in a foreign tongue, sharp scrapings from the ice.

He felt the smile stealing over his face, too. For he knew what those sounds meant.

Other sounds too, then – the rattle of hooves, moving fast, coming close. Shadows in this mist, as spears tilted forward and the captains barked to ready a charge. A moment later, the spears lifted once more, and calls of greeting filled the air. For it was no enemy that emerged from the mist, but a scattering of Sarmatian horsemen. A few dozen and no more, some of them holding the reins of a second horse with an empty saddle. Here and there, a bright spear dulled with the touch of blood.

They broke to different places, returning to their clans. And some of those riders came towards Kai and Bahadur, beneath their own banner – a twisting creature, armoured with scale and brandishing tooth and claw, for it was the mark of their clan that they rode under, the River Dragon.

'They have stuck the boar of Rome,' Bahadur said. 'But it shall be for us to kill it.' He turned in the saddle to the rest of the company. 'They shall be here soon. If there is anything you have left to say to each other, say it now.' And once more, he leaned in close to Kai. 'That goes for you, too.'

'Bahadur, I—'

'Not to me, fool,' the older warrior said as he tipped his lance and pointed down the line.

For everywhere about them, one could see feuds being settled. Kai saw two men of different clans, the Wolves of the Steppe and the Shining Company, men who had quarrelled and feuded for the better part of ten winters, standing with companionable arms draped about each other. In another place, a father and a son, not a word spoken between them since a knife fight over a woman, were in a firm embrace, the son's head cradled against his father's shoulder. Everywhere there were warriors breaking from the ranks, trotting up the line to exchange some quick word and exchanging gifts, handing over carved belt buckles, leather knife sheaths, and sometimes, where a particularly vicious feud must be settled, some precious little piece of iron. For it was the Romans that had brought the five warring clans of the Sarmatians together, a common enemy to undo all other feuds for one winter at least.

Bahadur was pointing to a figure on horseback, standing a little apart from the rest. The champion of their clan, wrapped in a cloak of wolf fur, the spear trailing tassels of red felt from it, reminders of all the blood that it had spilled. He saw many warriors – young boys mostly, the occasional older man in particular need of luck – coming up and asking a blessing from the champion. A touch of a spear, a clasp of a hand, a single word, an occasional small token for them to take away to bless those particularly marked with favour.

'I shall not beg,' said Kai.

'You do not have to,' the older man replied. 'Just keep that tongue of yours in check.'

Kai touched his heels to his horse – perhaps she felt his reluctance, or a grudge of her own that she did not wish to answer, for she moved sluggishly, dragging her hooves, turning her head and casting a look back at Kai. There was an almost human light in her black eyes – *Are you sure?* she seemed to say.

'No, my friend,' Kai said, 'but we shall have to try.' And he stirred the horse forward once more, moving alone upon the ice.

Voices called to him as he passed. A few wished him good fortune, others muttered curses under their breath, those whom he had ridden against in one feud or another, or where words had been said, once the wine had run thick, that could not be unspoken. But most spoke even softer words that could barely be heard above the crack of the ice and the rattle of armour. Prayers they spoke as he passed them. Wards against ill luck.

He did not slow his horse to answer those who greeted and cursed him. He kept his eyes upon the rider they called the Cruel Spear.

Even in the dim light of the winter morning, he could see the glitter of gold on the belt and broach of the champion. Once, all their warriors had gone to war clad in gold. The tombs of even the most humble warriors had been marked with grave gifts that shone under the funeral fires. Now only the champions and chieftains rode with that touch of gold about them, and even their tombs were dulled with gifts of clay and bone.

The fear returned at that thought – not a fear for his own life, for the battle to come, but a fear for a whole people, a nation, a world. He stirred his horse a little faster. It would not be long before the Romans came.

The champion gave no greeting as Kai came forward, and it was the horse that first marked his arrival – its

left eye had been taken by a Roman spear many winters
before, and it was forever tossing its head back and forth,
seeking an enemy on the blind side. As Kai drew close he
saw the beast tilt its head to fix him with its one forbidding
eye. Lips curling back, ears flattening, the scrape of hooves
against the ice like that of a blade against a whetstone.

Kai brought his own horse still before the champion,
gave a bow from the saddle and made the ritual greeting.
'Good fortune to the Cruel Spear. May I swallow your
evil days.'

Beneath the helm, the grey eyes glittered at him. A
wordless silence.

Kai pulled the gauntlet from his hand, felt at once the
chill wind cutting at his skin. He took a bronze ring from
his finger, and it slid away easily – poorly fitted, for it had
not been made for him. He offered it up, trying to keep his
hand still as he did so.

At last, the champion stirred. First a twitch of a gauntlet,
then an arm raised slightly, moving forward, before the
hand dropped back and reclasped the spear once more.
And then, the warrior spoke.

It always surprised Kai, how soft her voice was. When
one had seen how she rode on the battlefield, or had her
wild gaze lock against his like sword against shield, the
softness of the voice would always come as a surprise.

'You seek a blessing?' she asked. 'Some guidance for
your unlucky spear?'

'No.' He hesitated. 'I would settle our feud.'

She cocked her head to the side. 'You fear to ride to the
Otherlands with such a shame hanging over you?'

'I do not feel shame,' Kai said, even as he felt the blood pulse beneath his cheeks. 'I wish that it had not come between us.'

'And yet it has.'

'Bad blood brings ill fortune to the warband.'

'No. Just ill fortune to you.'

Laughter then, from the pack of riders behind her, and a madness stirring in his heart and on his tongue.

'I have always heard it takes a brave spear to start a feud, but a braver one to end it,' he said. 'I did not take you for a coward.'

'Oh, you would speak of bravery? A braver man with your tongue than with your sword.' She favoured him with a hideous grin. 'Hoping to be my third man, Kai? You'd earn some fame with that honour. But I shall not darken my spear on you.'

'You had best keep it bright for the Romans. Even you might have your share of blood after this battle.'

'I doubt that.'

'Laimei...' he said, risking her name.

A turn of the wrists, too quick for him to see until it was done, the spear cutting through the air towards him. He leaned back and away, but he had misread her – that was always her art, some trick of the arm or eye, for the attack never came from where one thought it would be. One guarded against the blow of a phantom, only to take the stroke from a warrior of flesh.

She aimed not for him, but for his horse.

The spear came from above like an eagle plummeting to the mark, and his mount staggered beneath him. He thought it a killing blow at first, but the dull crack that sounded in the air told a different story – she struck with the flat of the blade, and not the edge.

A sharp snort of anger, a toss of the head, and Kai's horse made to rear and strike, to beat to death this enemy who wore the smell and garb of a friend, for a horse hated a traitor just as much as a man would. For one terrible moment Kai wanted to let it happen, for the feud to be over in a flash of hooves and blood upon the ice. But he bore down with his knees and wrenched the reins to the side, while her warband jeered and hooted with laughter.

'Ride on, little boy,' said Laimei. 'Have that touch of the spear as your blessing, and well may it serve you. Or rather, well may it serve your horse, that she may find herself a better rider. I shall waste no charms on you.'

'This will be the last battle you ride in. Even you shall have had enough blood after today.'

'When the grey is in my hair, and I can no longer mount a horse or steady a spear, then it will be my time to die. But I shall ride and live longer than you. My spear is cruel, but yours is cursed.'

There were words – he knew there were words that might break the feud. He dreamed it sometimes, as they embraced in forgiveness, raced each other across the plains as they had done when they were children. When he woke he could remember every dancing turn their horses had taken, the pattern of the clouds in the sky, the sound of her laughter. Everything he could remember of that dream, save for the words that had been spoken, the words that might silence the feud.

But then from all about him, the song began. The war song of their people, sung for generations, since the time when they had ridden across the great plain that spanned half the world. A song of victory. First, the deep voices of the men, speaking with the tongues of the ancestors. And then another set of voices joined them, higher and sharper and sweeter. The voices of the women.

For there were other women among the warband. Wrapped thick in furs and armour, an unpractised eye might have mistaken them for young men. Yet they were there, the grandchildren of the Amazons and Scythians, the young women who had not yet earned the three kills that might free them from the warband, and they too sang of war and victory. And when Kai looked back towards the river, he saw what it was that had stirred those voices. Shadows at first, a line of black figures. Then there were the red cloaks dancing in the wind, the great shields and narrow spears, the golden eagles swooping above them in the mist. The Legion had come.

Before he went back to his place, he cast one last look back at Laimei. He thought of the face that lay beneath that helm, the coppery skin marked with nicks and cuts, black hair rough-cropped, chopped away by a dull bronze knife. It was a face that he could see himself at any time, were he to look into a polished copper mirror. A face just like his own.

For what else would one expect, from a brother and a sister?

★ ★ ★

The battle line was forming, the captains shouting their last orders, riders leaning forward and whispering words of love and encouragement to their horses. Somewhere, there was a speech from Fearless Banadaspus, chieftain of the River Dragon – a distant figure who rode back and forth before his clan of the Sarmatians, bellowing and exhorting and answered by cheers. From that distance it was barely a whisper on the wind. Later, if they won, Kai would learn what had been said. If they lost, it would not matter.

As he rode back to his place, Kai saw the riders passing skins of wine and drinking from them greedily, marking beard and chin with red. Kai had heard tell that his people were thought of as cannibals abroad, the eaters of the dead – surely those stories had begun from a shaking hand that lifted the wineskin before a battle. Here and there, he saw a god-touched man draw a hare from a writhing bag at his waist, slit it open and cast its entrails on the ice, looking for some favourable omen from the gods.

Beneath the banner of the River Dragon, the battleline was forming, each veteran paired with one who had not ridden a charge before. A one-eyed warrior next to a trembling boy, a greybeard whispering words of advice to a woman who had yet to claim a kill. Kai nodded to the rider he had been paired with, a heavy-set girl of sixteen summers. She seemed steadier now – earlier he had smelled the mix of bile and wine on her breath, the sweet and rotten scent of a frightened warrior.

Bahadur was giving last instructions to his son, shifting his grip upon the spear and tightening the ill-fitting armour as best he could. When Kai rode up, Bahadur asked a silent question with his eyes, and Kai answered with a little shake of his head. The older man sucked air through his teeth and tapped his spear against Kai's weapon, metal ringing on metal. There was nothing to be said.

Out upon the ice, the Romans came not as a wandering horde but in the precise lines and columns that their people seemed to love. Warriors who walked rather than rode – a shameful thing by the code of the Sarmatians, for only cowards and madmen would go upon their own two feet. Many of them were beardless, an army of children so it seemed, though they were children the Sarmatians had learned to fear. Red cloaks, plumed helms, and everywhere, the cold glitter of iron. On the links of the mail that they wore, on the thin spears, the rounded pommels of their swords and the curves of their helms. A fortune in iron, out upon the ice, and above them, the standards almost obscured in the mist, the golden eagles flew.

The Legion drew still. No war cries or death songs rose from the Roman ranks, for that was not their way. They fought in near silence, save for the sound of drum and horn and whistle to signal a change in formation, to advance or retreat. They were passionless killers.

The speeches of chieftains and captains died away, the last words of advice and command fell silent. The horsemen waited, the Romans waited, the only sound the calling of the wind and the chatter of the ice.

Against his palms, Kai felt the weight of the spear, the feel of the wood. A memory came, of finding his way through the forests of the northlands, one hand pushing past the trees, the other twined about the hand of a lover. He felt that ache, that longing for love that only the warrior knows before a battle, that last moment when life is at its sweetest.

Then a sharp, clear image came to his mind, of a child. A carved toy made by Bahadur in her hand, a half-toothed smile, as she looked up and caught sight of him. His daughter, Tomyris, somewhere far to the east. A greater love, then, to look upon her, the mad urge to stir his horse forward and sweep the dream figure from the ground, to hold her close and never let her go. She seemed to call to him, but her words were not her own – it was the chanted roar of those soon to kill and to die that he heard, that brought him from his mind and back to the ice.

No telling from where the chant began – somewhere to the right, from the Wolves of the Steppe or from the clan of the Grey Hand. It was not one of the old songs, no song at all, nothing but three words, spoken again and again.

Iron and gold. Iron and gold.

The treasures that would be theirs if they won, that would make them whole again. Iron to give them their freedom. Gold to honour their dead.

No signal was given, no horn blown or command sounded out. But like a flock of birds wheeling together in the sky or a pack of wolves who spring from the snow as one, the Sarmatians knew that it was time and stirred their horses forward with a rattle of scale and blade. Five clans, riding together as one, perhaps for the last time.

The riders stepped from the snow of the bank to the ice of the river. A moment when the horses should have gone tripping and tumbling to the ground, the line broken before it had even begun. The ice was clear and slick to the touch, and yet the horses moved upon it as carelessly and easily as if it were the tall grass of the steppe.

For this was the wager. They had gambled their entire people upon this one cast of the dice, with all the odds against them save for one – that the Sarmatian horses knew the dance of the ice, and the Romans did not.

Iron and gold. Iron and gold.

Imagination, perhaps, but Kai thought he saw the Legion – the undaunted, immovable Legion – give a shiver of fear at the ease with which the cavalry moved. They must have understood the trap that closed about them, at the sight of that death that walked calmly towards them. No need to gallop or trot, not yet.

Iron and gold, iron and gold.

Before them that Legion formed the square as they must, their only chance against the charge that would surely come. Shields as big as men locked together, but there was a tremble across the line as the Romans struggled to hold a steady footing. For the first time that Kai could remember, there was weakness in the shield wall.

Iron and gold! Iron and gold!

The taste of sand was in Kai's mouth, the blood beating in his ears like the hollow strike of hand against drum. Sharp points of cold across his flesh at all the places that a blade might cut – a stab into his belly, a raking coldness across his throat, a pain that seemed to stitch his legs together. The first time he had ridden to battle, in a bloodfeud against the Wolves of the Steppe, the fear had been so strong that it seemed as though he would go mad. The fear was still there, as strong as it always was. He had only learned that it always passed at the very last moment.

Iron and gold! Iron and gold!

Then all words were lost, as the cry went up that belonged to all languages and to none. The cry of the charge.

Like falling through the sky – that was how it felt as they sprang forward. As though the entire world had tipped sideways, and they fell screaming towards their enemies.

The cold wind struck tears from Kai's eyes, and all he could hear was the crack of hooves against the ice. He guided his horse with his knees, both hands on the spear before him, one to grip and the other to guide, holding it high like a fisherman about to thrust into a river.

The line of shields trembling before them. The horses charging perfectly. The Legion trapped upon the ice.

And then the horns began to blow.

Roman horns, all calling at once. They did not call a pattern that he knew from battles before, to advance or retreat, to form a square or a wedge. He saw the men before him raise up their shields as one and as one bring them down. An echoing crack that he heard over the beating of the hooves as the shields found their home, anchored in place and part buried in the ice.

The world seemed to hold still. That torrent of motion brought to a stop, as though by the touch of a god or the spell of a magician. And in the stillness of that moment, he could see the faces of the Romans. Peering over their shields, half masked by the helms they wore, but even so he could see them.

They looked afraid.

The spear wrenched from his hands, the sky was tumbling and turning about Kai as he fell screaming through the air, until he slammed back first into the ice and the world was struck into silence.

From where he lay on the ice, half stunned, he watched the charge fail.

The horses trying to turn away at the last moment, flinching from the shield wall. The second rank of riders driving into the back of them, a mass of men and horses that rolled over the shields like a wave, the Romans reaching up to pull the riders from their saddles.

It should have been a butchery, riders pulled from their mounts and carved open on the ice. But dark shapes loomed high, a line of monsters it seemed in the mad whirl of the battle, standing tall against the Romans. For it was the horses who held the line – standing tall on their hind legs and breaking shields and helms with their hooves, or turning and kicking out behind. Riderless, undaunted, the battle fever upon them, bloody foam flying from their lips and their eyes rolling wild as a berserker's.

No time to think, to remember any of the finer arts of killing. No time even to take a weapon in hand as Kai scrabbled from the ice to his feet and launched himself at the nearest Roman bare handed. All about him, the dismounted Sarmatians did the same, diving into the Roman ranks like swimmers into white water. Slipping, stumbling, fighting their way through the press, seeking throats to close and hearts to still, and all around there was the rip and tear of hand and tooth against flesh. And even the Legion was screaming now.

Kai fought by touch and feel more than by sight. He reached out, felt a beardless face against his skin – the face of a woman or boy of his own people? No, for he felt the scrape of stubble and knew it for a Roman. He rolled a thumb into an eye, heard a shrieking scream, and closed that scream with his gauntlet. Lifted up into the mob, hands pulling at him from behind, he kicked out and felt the crack of teeth beneath his heel.

Back into the roiling mob once more, barely room to breathe, much less to swing a sword, his vision filled with flesh and metal. It was only occasionally, when the mob broke open, that he caught a vision of the battle – an eyeless Sarmatian, blinded by the cut of a sword, tearing the throat from one of his companions with his teeth, mistaking him for a Roman. A horse dragging its entrails beneath it like a fallen rider, still kicking out against all who came near. The golden eagle dancing in the sky high above them all, twisting and swaying as the mob swirled upon the ice, but never coming close to falling.

Space opened up around him as suddenly as it had been stolen away, and Kai was on his hands and knees, scrabbling and scratching against the ice, trying to get to his feet. A blow cracked off his armour, then another. Kai lashed out with a fist and sent one man spinning to the ice, snatched a Sarmatian axe off the ground and faced the second man. No time to try and wear the man down, to use the tricks of footwork, and so Kai swung at once.

The stone head of the axe broke and shattered against the mail, and the Roman answered with a thrust of his sword. Kai threw up his arm to block it, felt the line of cold pain across his wrist as the iron blade cut past the scales of horn and bone.

The Roman bared his teeth, a smile of relief. He came forward but the ice took his feet from underneath him. Kai stamped down once, twice, a third time, snatched the sword from the twitching fingers, and all around he saw Sarmatian stone breaking against Roman iron. The line of Roman shields reforming, the swords flickering out like claws from a crawling monster, and above them, the golden eagles steady in the sky.

A screaming voice nearby – Chodona, Bahadur's son. He was there upon the ice, tiny it seemed amongst the tall men of the Legion, pinned by a fallen horse. In his high child's voice he was screaming at them to stop, to wait, that he surrendered. But they could not understand what he spoke, and as the swords fell Kai heard a high-pitched squeal, like a hare in a trap.

Kai looked elsewhere – for Bahadur, or the Cruel Spear, his sister's name upon his lips. Yet the only familiar faces about him were those of the dead.

'Kai!'

A call, piercing through the air. A singer's voice, that cut through the howl of battle. What it meant to hear a name, in a place such as that. Kai turned to answer it, and saw Bahadur, somehow still mounted, the long spear running red in his hand. He rode forward, sure footed, one hand on the spear, the other reaching forward, beckoning.

Something flickered past Kai's head. A little line of darkness, the shadow of a spear.

There was something wrong with Bahadur – grey faced and still, as though some witch's curse had aged him a decade in a moment. Then he turned in the saddle, and Kai saw the spear in his side, the wicked point buried deep, just as Bahadur fell backwards into the mob. The whirling mass stealing him away, the wave of swords falling over him bright and coming back up red.

All about, the spears flew from the Roman shield wall, and men and horses died upon those points, and Kai could hear the horns of his own people, calling the retreat.

The circle of iron closed about him – no horse for him to mount, no path to safety off the ice. The stillness then that comes with the certainty of death, the chill touch of omen and fate that removes all fear. A gladness, of sorts, for who would wish to outlive one's people? Who would want to be the last one left, when all had been lost?

Others were coming – they were all around now, dancing shapes upon the ice, grey death in their hands. Everywhere he looked, they were about him. His breathing came fast in the close-fitted helm, his vision obscured and narrowed through the eyelets. He turned his head from side to side, trying to see who came closest to him, to see which man he might take with him to the Otherlands.

But there was another shape coming with the Romans, moving closer, moving faster. Crawling over the ice, back legs dragging, front legs scrabbling at the ice. It drew close to a man of the Legion – a hoof flickered, and the Roman was bowed in half, clutching at his side. A second strike, a ring of metal like the striking of a bell, and the Roman was on the ground, eyes rolled back white, blood pouring from the staved helm.

Bahadur's horse moved forward again, and Kai felt the terrible joy of one who no longer has to die alone. But too late he saw the madness in its rolling eyes, the bloody slather chanting from its lips. It was trapped in some last command from its master – Bahadur had sought to save Kai, to keep him safe, and so did the horse. It bore down upon Kai, rolling him to the ground, lying upon him with a smothering love.

Kai screamed out, pushed up, fought to lift it, but it only moved further upon him, shutting out the light.

The weight bore down. He could not breathe.

2

In the darkness of the dream, a circle. A circle of men and women, dressed for war, watching and waiting.

The land warped and shifted, in that impossible, changeable way of the dream. Sometimes it seemed they stood upon the green sward of a grazing ground, at others in a clearing of the forest fringed by leafless trees. Or ringed by the huts of a Sarmatian village, where it seemed he could hear but never see the daughter he had left behind. Every place and none, that was where the circle stood.

The faces changed, too. Some were the living, and others the dead. He saw the first man that he had killed, a tall and soft-faced Dacian – jawless, tongue lolling and slobbering on his throat from where Kai's clumsy axe stroke had hacked away half his face rather than splitting his skull. His mother was sometimes there, though she wore a changing face. She had died giving birth to him, and the face she wore was one he had made of stories he had been told.

The faces changed – all except one. For there was a man kneeling before him, there at the centre of the circle. And that man was always the same.

The hilt of the sword was slick in Kai's hands as he held it beside his head, his breath frosting on the iron of the blade. A broken weapon, half the blade lost in a battle that had been fought long before Kai was born, yet it was still a rare treasure for a people reduced to fighting with weapons of bone and stone.

The stench of sour, fermented milk was in the air, wet upon the beards of the men in the circle. A drink of the old times, for this was a ritual of the past. They rapped their weapons against scale mail and shield – a sham battle, war music for what had to be done.

Kai raised the sword higher still, his arms straight and the sword reaching towards the sky. His vision spun and danced, and not just from the workings of the dream. When he had stood in that circle in the waking world, his vision had wavered too.

The chant stopped.

In that dream he hoped to strike fast, to make his kill in the single beat of a heart. As always, he swung too slowly. For the man on his knees raised his head, locked eyes with Kai. Those eyes – bright and kind – that looked back at him with love.

The sword swung and bit, the dream turned and swirled, and darkness was all.

He was not certain, at first, that he had returned from the dreamlands. Blackness and stillness, an unseen weight that seemed to pin him in place – all familiar sensations of his dreams. But the air was filled with the stench of blood, that hot, coppery smell that never found its way into sleep. It was no invisible force that held him in place; there was something of weight and flesh that covered him. And then Kai remembered the horse.

He could not seem to breathe, his lungs half crushed, and the panic made him gasp too hard, driving him from consciousness for a moment as the blackness stole back across his sight. He breathed again, shallow and careful, and felt the chains of the dream slip from him fully.

He was beneath the horse, pinned in place. He could turn his head but a little, and when he did so a sliver of light crept to the edge of his vision. He could see the ice, marked black with blood. He could see the still shapes that lay upon the ground.

Kai listened for the sound of a battle still being fought – the death songs of surrounded, doomed men, the panicked, high-pitched screams of routing warriors being ridden down. Or for those sounds that come after, the heavy tread of those who wander the battlefield, cutting rings from fingers and scalps from heads, opening the throats of the wounded left behind.

There was only silence, and the wind.

Gradually, Kai worked his way loose, crawling like a snake from beneath the body of the horse. There was pain in his side, a stabbing three-pointed pain, but he could not think on it until he was free, and he crawled and wept and cursed his way slowly across the ice until he was out from under the weight of the corpse. He tried to stand, but his legs shivered and gave way, and he fell back to sitting, looking upon the silence of the battlefield.

A fortune in iron lay about him. There were tales that the elders told around the fire, of men cursed with useless wealth, starving and weeping in a world of gold and iron and praying for meat and milk. Had he the wagons and horses to cart the treasure away, if he were to live beyond the coming of the next day, he would have been a great man of his people.

But it would not be. For there was nothing that moved on the field of ice, only the familiar dead remained, friends and companions. Padagos was there – Kai could remember a hard winter's night spent curled in that man's arms, scouting for a cattle raid, too close to the Dacian border to risk a fire. Now Padagos was curled up once more, almost sleeping it seemed, pillowed with red blood. Kai could see Galatus as well, not so far away. Always quick with a joke, and now he lay with his face carved into a permanent smile. And Mada – she had been so frightened before the battle. He could remember the rattling sound of her hands trembling on the spear, stilling as Kai and Bahadur had told her the old lies of war. No need for fear now, for her hands were brave and still around the spear that had split her tattered armour. Even run through, she had hoped for the impossible, fought for the impossible, to live against the odds.

The dead lay all about him. The Romans were many. The Sarmatians and their horses, uncountable. And somewhere amongst them was Bahadur.

Kai went to his feet, and gasped at fresh pain. His hand was at his side, searching for shattered armour and open wound, but his fingers remained unmarked, and when he spat upon the ground there was no blood. Three cracked ribs, even spaced and piercing into his side. But it was a pain he knew – kicked by a frightened horse after a raid on the Dacians three summers before, he had known it then, and the familiar pain came to him as a comfort. And so, stumbling forward, one hand to his side, he began to search for Bahadur.

A hopeless task, but he had to try. Bahadur had ridden back for him, and now Kai was filled with the mad longing to find him, to lie there beside him and return to the sleep, to the dream. And why not? The sun was rolling through the sky. It would soon be night, and a killing wind would come with it. He could already feel the cold biting deeper, the short day mostly spent and no shelter that he could reach on foot. He would walk until he could walk no more, until he felt that caressing, seductive sleep that comes to those who wander lost in ice and snow.

But then a sound, close by. A scrape against the ice, the clatter of arms and a whisper of flesh, frighteningly loud in the silence of the battlefield. Something stirred from one of those mounds of corpses, as though the dead themselves were returning to fight once more, and Kai snatched up a spear from the ground to face it.

A monster it seemed, a creature of meat and hoof that bore a human face. Until it shook its shoulders and a corpse tumbled from its neck, and Kai understood the trick his eyes played. A horse – a great Sarmatian horse, its armour half hacked away and the blood black upon its flanks, buried as Kai had been by the dead. As the horse stood he could see the frost blooming from the wide lips as it snorted and gasped, tossing its head like a drunken man. The horse tilted its long head to the side, gazing on him with one familiar eye. His sister's horse.

The beast looked on Kai – weighing his life, or so it seemed, thinking to finish the feud on behalf of an absent master. It lifted its head and whickered into the air, calling for companions, the warband, the herd. Only the wind answered, and it stared back at Kai once more.

One step after another, Kai moved across the ice. He stooped, let the spear fall to the ground. The horse stepped back at the sound, snapping its head about to watch for enemies on the blind side, and Kai stepped forward again. He was close now – close enough to smell the sour stink of the horse's breath, close enough to see within the hollow of the blinded eye where sinews and fibres still twitched. He held one hand up by his chin, ready to parry, and laid his other upon the dangling reins.

The horse bared its teeth and flattened its ears, and he heard the scratch of a hoof drawing back across the ice. Kai laid his other hand against the horse's forehead, let it rest there. He waited, for a time, and was quite certain that, in that moment, the horse and he thought of the same thing. That they both thought of Laimei.

She was dead, then. He only knew at that moment, with his hand upon her horse. He could not imagine her being parted from that great beast any other way.

'Laimei,' he said, as though the sounding of her name had the power to bring her back. He had heard of men who might do such a thing, warlocks and sorcerers of the Sea of Grass, masters of the old ways now lost.

Perhaps that was why the horse did not fight him. Perhaps it knew, somewhere deep in that soul of a horse, the soul all Sarmatians knew to be wiser than that of men, that she was dead, and the feud ended.

'Revenge,' said Kai. And the horse bared its teeth again, and he thought that it smiled.

Kai picked at the treasures on the ground – a pair of Roman swords, a coat of mail half hacked from its wearer, one of the long thin throwing spears that the Legion favoured. No time to take any more than that, and he tied them to the horse's side as best he could. The horse stamped at the ice, impatient, but gave no sign of pain at the extra weight.

Had he more time, Kai would have walked with the horse for hours – the long, slow courtship of a rider with a new mount. But there was no more time.

Kai placed both hands on the horns of the saddle, his teeth tight against each other, his eyes half closed. He took a breath in, held it, then leapt upwards, throwing himself into the saddle, gasping at the stabbing pain in his side as he landed.

The horse tossed its head, danced sideways across the ice, and beneath him Kai felt the great muscles of back and flank twitch, ready to buck and rear. If it threw him, he did not know if he would have the strength to mount again. He would lie broken upon the ice until the cold took him.

But at last the beast went still, an uneasy truce between them. Kai stirred the horse forward, and read the tracks as best he could, reading the story written down in ice and snow.

3

Five days' ride to the east of the Danu, one might have thought to have found a campground rather than a village. Viewed in the half-light of a falling sun, shadowed by the foothills of the mountains that rose above that place, a traveller would see a collection of rounded huts that might have been tents, the snow that gathered on them making them seem like pale horseskin over a wooden frame, not the mud and reed that they truly were.

But this place was no fleeting campground, a circadian city that would be packed into wagons and placed elsewhere on the steppe at the rise of the next sun. For Iolas was one of the winter villages of the Sarmatians; the ground furrowed into paths between those huts that a generation of footsteps had carved out, where children had wandered and old women tottered. Around the village, where the marshy ground would allow it, there were a few fields cut and marked for the planting. The claylike soil offering little promise – the farmers here were stubborn, it seemed, if not wise. They tried to learn the art of grain and coin, the tricks that had made their neighbours rich, that might feed them every winter without raiding across the Danu. But they had come to it too late. They were no longer a people of plain or city, but lost somewhere between the two.

In the west of the village, there was a gathering. Women and those children too young to yet hold a lance, staring towards the setting sun as though in worship. Even the children were quiet, carved wooden horses and branch-swords hanging limp in their hands.

Amongst the women there was no mark of a chieftain, no sign of rank in the long dresses and tall headscarves. But there was one who seemed to act as a leader of sorts. Like many of them, the woman's face and hands were marked with little white scars, remnants of wars fought long ago, her braided hair twining gold and silver together. Not the eldest amongst them, for there were many there whose hair was painted fully white and whose skin was deep-furrowed by years spent under the sun. But this woman had chosen, or been chosen, to watch over them. She spoke to many – a touch of the arm here, a whispered word there, a sharp command to a woman who stood with her head bowed in grief, ensuring that all kept their eyes to the west.

The sun fell and kissed the horizon. It was said that a queen from the old times once wished for but another moment of light to look upon her lover, and so the gods always held the sun still before it fell away completely. And the woman who led the village whispered to herself, and asked for another miracle. That they would see silhouettes in the distance, framed against the sun. That they would see the warband riding home.

The last sliver of the sun fell below the horizon, and no riders came. In answer, a little sigh from those gathered at the edge of the village, nothing more than that at first. But as though it had been a horn calling them to war, the children were off, giving little yips and hollers as they formed bands and chased one another round the huts and under the carts. Slower, more reluctant, the women followed them.

One woman lingered at the edge of the village, eyes fixed to the absent sun, still as one in a trance or struck by a spell. The older woman hurried to her, the snow crunching beneath her boots, and said: 'Best to get home. No more use waiting out here in the cold.'

The other woman turned her head slowly, her eyes dull. She was young, the war scars still fresh upon her skin. 'They should have returned by now, Arite,' she said. 'Shouldn't they?'

'Not if they won,' Arite answered. 'They will be raiding far beyond the Danu, if they put the Romans to flight.'

The younger woman returned her gaze to the horizon. 'Sometimes I think we should not watch for them. A bad omen.'

'Think of when they return – that will be a fine day.'

'If it could stay this way… it would not be such a terrible thing.'

Arite grinned, a wolfish flash of teeth in the twilight. 'You would not miss the young men about the village? I know I would.'

'I would not miss the killing.'

Arite's smile fell away at once, in its place a sharp set

of the jaw. 'Get home,' she said, 'and do not let the others hear you speak that way.'

The crunch and patter of quick steps in the snow, and the younger woman was gone. Arite lingered a moment longer, giving one last look out to the horizon. Then she was back amongst the huts, picking restlessly at the long, loose ends of her dress with one hand and holding the collar close with the other against the fell wind that blew in from the west.

The children were still circling and brawling, though their numbers were fewer now, many of them picked off by their elders. Without breaking stride, Arite plucked a small figure from one of the tumbling warbands. It was not a girl whose face resembled hers, but that was not such a strange thing in this place. Everywhere, children went with women who were not their mothers.

Snatched from the games, the child sulked and whined like a kicked dog for a moment. She went limp, and a moment later Arite permitted the child to walk back to their hut rather than be carried – an honourable courtesy given to the captive.

Their home was a crude one, a life half learned. A poorly cut chimney let the smoke fill the room, and the bedding was nothing but a pile of blankets. There were well-fashioned tents that might have been warmer than that hut, for the wind cut through little cracks in the walls and went against the skin like a knife.

Arite cursed and muttered to herself, trying to fashion some crude blockades against the fingers of wind that worked their way into the room. The child flung herself

into a pile of blankets, but at once there was a click of the
fingers, and the child fell to mixing the grain, stirring the
pot over the fire.

They busied themselves with their tasks for a time, the
child keeping half an eye on the woman, looking for a
response. At first, Arite feigned not to notice the slackness
with which the child worked the grain, the deliberately
clumsy strike of spoon against cooking pot. She strode
around the room straightening and correcting as she went,
her fingers straying across the little mementoes scattered
about it. A broken arrow with russet red fletchings. An
image of a dragon carved into a horn. Last of all was the
greatest treasure – folded into three separate pieces of
cloth that she carefully unwrapped one layer at a time.
She shook into her palm a tiny oval gold coin, a relic of
some long dead empire, tossing it in the air to watch the
firelight wink against the turning metal, before snatching
it back.

She tilted her head to the side, and saw the light of the
fire in the child's eyes.

'Do you ever dream of that coin, Tomyris? In your
hands, impressing the other children, perhaps? It would
buy you a good sword and lance, on the day you join the
warband.'

Tomyris sat up stiffly. 'It is not mine,' she said, for a child
she was, but she already had the nomad's pride. Out upon
the steppe a thief was nothing but a slow and cowardly
murderer, for to take a horse or bow or bag of grain was
to take someone's life as well.

A twitch of the lips at seeing the child so haughty, but

39

Arite covered it with her hand. 'Quite so, and well spoken. Kai has taught you well.'

'Bahadur gave it to you, didn't he?'

'He did. Did he tell you the story of how he found it?'

The child wrinkled her lip. 'He told me *lots* of stories of how he found it.'

'And what was your favourite one? The one with the ogre and the golden sheep?'

'No.' She paused and thought it over. 'I like the one with the apple tree, the people under the sea.'

'That is a good story,' said Arite. 'Now tell me, why do you sulk more than usual? Speak. And stop rattling my bowls. If you break them, we shall be eating from the floor like the hounds.'

The child stared at the ground, covered with their one fine furnishing. A well-woven carpet, where tigers ran after stags in endless looping forests. It was faded and marked by generations of footfalls – a treasure from the old times, when their people had lived in wagon and tent and wandered all across the plains.

'They did not come back,' she said.

'We should not expect them back so soon. Not unless there were some disaster.'

'Saka says they're not ever coming back.'

'Who is not?'

'All of them. My father.' A pause. 'Bahadur. Or Chodona.' And those last two names were spoken with a child's careful desire to wound.

The woman looked evenly at the child across the fire.

'They may not be. You may have lost Kai. I may have lost my husband. My son.' Her voice had held steady, but gave the faintest crack on that last word. 'What would we do then?'

In the light of the fire, a glaze of tears on the girl's eyes. But only for a moment, before she wiped them away. 'Avenge them.'

'Well spoken. Kai would be proud of you. That is one choice. Another?'

'What do you mean?'

'What if their enemies were too many to face? Or too far away to fight. What then?'

The child shook her head, curled her lip in irritation. 'I do not know.'

Arite leaned forward and sampled the stew. She sat back, and said: 'We would remember them. Could you do that, if you had to?'

She nodded.

'You remember your mother, don't you?'

Again the child nodded. For a moment a ghost was in the hut with them, a woman who made the air ring with raucous laughter as she chased her daughter round the campfire or when she leapt on Kai from behind when he returned from the hunt. Then she was gone, and it was just the two of them once more.

'It is just like that,' Arite said. 'We remember them, and tell the stories. And so they live forever.'

Tomyris was still and silent for a time, staring at the dancing of the fire. Turning that thought over and over in her head, like a trader studying a finely glazed pot, searching for the flaw.

'And if there are none left to remember?' she said.

Arite gave no answer. For there was none to give.

The girl was weary then – not the tiredness of a child worn down from field and herd, but that of the rider on a long campaign, or the heartsick woman spurned by her lover. One who grows tired of the hard business of living. Arite had seen it many times before, but seldom in a child.

Arite reached forward and stroked the child's face gently, and Tomyris leaned into the touch. They sat there together for a time, and it was Arite's turn to look into the fire. How many generations of her people had lived upon the steppe, none could say. All the way back to the birthing of the world, Scythians and Amazons, and their children the Sarmatians. How many thousands of years had the horsepeople stared into fires like that, remembering their songs and those they had loved? And what would it mean, if this was the last generation?

But everyone thought that way, she told herself. That they would be last people. It would be true one day, but perhaps not yet. She held the child close, and walked her to the entrance of the hut. Together they looked upwards, at where the first few stars were gathering into constellations above them, the legends of their people. The trickster Syrdon, two matching lines of stars marking out his liar's lips as he whispered to Tabiti. Pkharmat stealing fire from Sela, a wheel of stars showing the wheels of the chariot as she rode across the sky. Arash,

plunging a sword of stars into a gravemound of black sky
to seal an oath.

Arite looked on those stars, and prayed to any gods who
might be listening. She prayed for the warband to return.

4

F ar to the west, close to the banks of the frozen Danu, Kai
watched the same stars break out across the sky, the same
stories retold in points of light amidst the darkness. And
beneath them, beneath them all, out upon the plains, ringed
by the shadows of the Carpathian mountains, a second set
of stars came into being. For there were none who would
live upon the plain without fire on a winter's night.

First, a great constellation of light – a new city, a fortress
that had sprung up in a single day and would vanish at
dawn like a dream. No mistaking it for a camp of the
Sarmatians, one of those conferences of the shepherds
that would sprawl and wrap about plain and river and hill
like a lover's embrace, for every line of the camp was as
straight as a blade, each tent precisely laid in place, each
fire marked and measured and positioned carefully by the
Roman Legion. Claiming their ground beyond the Danu,
ready to harry the defeated Sarmatians.

That was the first fire he saw, but soon there were others,
little points of light that sprang up across the plain. At
each one, Kai knew, Sarmatians would be gathered around
fires made of bone and dried dung, huddled together to

45

survive the night. Scattered bands, spreading back to the lands of clan and kin, the great alliance of their people broken upon the ice.

He tried to judge the fires from a distance, even as he shivered upon his horse. Some were made too openly, made by men too sick or stupid or careless with their lives, shamed by defeat and longing for death – too close to the Romans, and the night hunters would find them long before dawn. He could see other fires that were already fading, too weak to last until dawn, and no doubt when the sun rose it would show a ring of dead men like a circle of stones, already part entombed by the ice. But here and there, the fires burned strong, where some captain had held order, where the riders had been fortunate or careful with their fuel. It was to one of those that he made his way.

As he travelled towards it, he wondered if there were others like him – shadows moving across the plain between those points of light, men wandering like the ghosts of the dead, moving along the unseen paths back towards their homes. Perhaps even some who had died upright upon their mounts, held in place by the care of the horse beneath them who did not know that they faithfully bore a corpse towards the fires. He hunched up beneath his cloak, offered a prayer that he would live to see another dawn.

As he drew close to the fire, he slipped from the saddle. Even at a distance, he could see the light of the fire shining upon the horn armour of the Sarmatians, see the tall horses tied to a line of spears thrust into the ground. A longing to call out, to rush to them and embrace them as his own. But there was a silence in the air, the sharp kind of silence that is dangerous to break. None of the Sarmatians were speaking, their tongues stilled by the shame of defeat, and even the horses were quiet – leaning and nuzzling against each other for comfort, for they too had suffered in the battle, and sought comfort in silence, the embrace. In their own particular way, they too knew shame.

Only a low moan of pain broke the silence. A boy in blankets, his beardless face white with agony, hands clasped around a wound in his belly, red coils pulsing beneath his hands. Even at a distance, Kai could hear him speak.

'Water. Please,' said the boy.

None moved.

'Water. Please.'

Slowly, one of the men about the fire placed his head in his hands.

Nearby, a fair-haired woman carefully nursing a wounded wrist said: 'We can make the lands of the Shining Company in a few days. And then…'

'Then what? You forget the feud between our clans.' This from a dark-haired man on the other side of the fire.

'You think any care for such a thing now, Gaevani?'

'What else is there to do now, but settle feuds? It is the end. Even the gods shall pay what they owe, at the ending of the world.'

'You think it is the end? Is that why you—'

'You shall not speak of that.' Kai saw the man called Gaevani lay a hand on the axe at his side. 'We are too many mouths beside the fire already.'

The fair-haired woman looked about – seeking allies, perhaps, in those men around her.

'Where do you say we go, then?' she said.

Gaevani scratched at his jaw. 'We go south tomorrow.'

'That is towards Dacian land.'

Silence, then. But it seemed there was no need for words – the little defiant smile on Gaevani's face spoke enough.

'You cannot mean to...'

'Ride alone, if you will,' he said. 'But those that want to live, ride with me. There's always a place for a good man with a spear.'

Silence again, the crackling of the fire. The voice of the dying boy: 'Water. Please.'

'Quiet lad!' Gaevani snapped. 'Die quietly, will you?'

And at that, Kai spoke at last: 'Why not give the boy water?'

The men around the fire started, stumbling to their feet like drunkards, pulling weapons and staring out into the blackness beyond the fire. Only Gaevani did not stir.

'Be still, you old women,' he said. 'The stranger speaks our tongue, does he not?' He turned his head towards the newcomer. 'Come on. Let us see you.'

Their eyes were upon him as he walked forward, and Kai knew that they would see the metal first, catching the light of the fire. The curved pommel of a Roman sword slung in his belt, a few plates of metal sewn into the armour, the glint of a spearhead and a salvaged coat of mail upon the one-eyed horse that he rode – a chieftain's weight in black iron.

Kai raised a hand in greeting as he came close, his eyes dancing from one man to another, reading the markings that were etched into their gear, searching for a sign of their clan. Wolves of the Steppe, for the most part, though he saw a man or two of the Grey Hand and the Serpents of Jade amongst the dozen or so who were gathered about the fire. Not a face there that he knew; no people of the River Dragon.

He swung down from the horse, clasped the hands that were offered to him. They gestured to a place close by the fire, for they could see the frost that laced his beard, hear the rattle of his armour as he trembled with the cold. But before he sat, he went to where the boy lay in soiled blankets, poured the water onto a rag and wetted the boy's lips. A hand rose from the blankets, and Kai took it in his, knotted the fingers together.

'Shame to waste water on a dying man,' said Gaevani. 'But then, I have always heard Kai of the Dragon was soft-hearted.'

Kai looked over to the fire. 'You know me, then?'

'Aye, I know you. Stories of you. Stories of your father, too. He should have taught you better.'

Kai gave a quick look about the circle, but saw no recognition on their faces. 'Did your father teach you to leave your camp unguarded?' he said.

'I did not think that it mattered. The gods are against us – there is no setting a watch against them.'

'You are of the Wolves?'

'Most of us are, aye. A few from other clans.'

'No time to think of the Five Clans now. We stand together.'

'No doubt,' said Gaevani. 'Just a question of who leads.'

'No doubt.'

Silence for a time. Beside the fire, Kai saw a map carved

crudely into the ground by the edge of sword and knife. The boundaries of the five clans of the Sarmatians, marked as best they could be, the vague, unseen lines by which his people lived and died. For they had fought against each other long before the coming of the Romans, only the most desperate famine bringing them together against their common enemy.

The fair-haired woman spoke then. 'How did you get away?'

'What is your name?' Kai asked.

'Tamura.'

'I was left for dead on the battlefield. Buried beneath a horse.' Kai glanced towards his mount, standing apart from the rest of the herd and staring at them, one-eyed, with lordly contempt. 'He was left for dead, too.'

'A lucky man!' she said. 'And a lucky horse. We need a little good fortune.'

'He's no lucky man,' said Gaevani. 'None of us are.'

'I think we may all be counted lucky,' Kai answered. 'To live as we do.'

'To live shamed. You are hurt?'

Kai quickly took his hand from the wound at his side when he saw how the firelight shone in the other man's eyes. 'Not much. I was lucky.'

'So you keep saying.'

'How did you all get away?' said Kai, looking about the circle.

Their eyes slid to one another for a moment.

'After the first charge, we tried to circle back for another. It was too late by then,' Tamura said.

Kai did not answer. He merely thought of how long they had fought upon the ice.

Gaevani tilted his head back towards the horses. 'Looked like a good bit of a treasure you found for yourself, picking at the corpses.'

The others about the fire followed his gaze, and Kai heard them sigh as they saw once more what he had brought from the battlefield. A spear, a few swords, a coat of mail – it was still enough to make him a rich man amongst the people.

'Gifts for the rest of us?' Gaevani said.

'They are mine.'

'We are friends here.'

'Yes. And not thieves.'

The fire burned low. A creak of leather and scrape of horned armour as the men shifted around the fire.

Kai looked about them, slid back just a little from the fire. He tapped the ground where the map was marked. 'Where do you go now?'

'We were just speaking of this,' Tamura said softly.

Gaevani cut her off. '*We* are—'

'I shall be heading to the east,' said Kai. And he laid a finger onto a place unmarked on their map – a little to the east, in the lands of the River Dragon. 'I have kin here, in a village called Iolas. Beyond the swamplands, but it is not so far from here, if you know the way as I do.' He looked each of them in the eye, one by one. 'All who want to are welcome to ride with me, no matter what your clan. I know you are far from your own country.'

Gaevani shook his head ruefully. 'Making choices for

us? You think to be a captain? A chieftain, with all that iron dripping from your horse?'

'I make no decisions. I am no chieftain or captain. I ride to the east.'

'You ride alone then. We are not of your people.'

Kai looked at them again, one after another. 'On my honour,' he said, 'you shall find safety with my kin in Iolas. This truce between our people, it shall hold a little longer, until the spring thaw at least. It is no time for Sarmatians to be killing each other.' A moment's silent debate. Then, by the light of the fire, Kai could see the others nodding. 'It seems they will ride with me,' he said to Gaevani.

'Is that so?'

'It is so.'

'A shame. That is a shame. On your honour, you say? If only they knew how little that honour was worth.'

They stared at each other, across the fire. Kai saw the man smile then, his lips twitch as he made ready to speak. Kai knew the words that would be coming next – the words from his past, the story to shame him.

But it was Tamura who spoke, starting and staring into the darkness. 'Did you hear that?' she said.

'Quiet,' Gaevani said. 'You would jump at the wind if it blew hard enough. We still need to settle this. There are things you need to know about this man you would follow.'

But he spoke no more. They all heard it then – the rasp of shifting armour, the heavy tread of footfall in the snow, the rattle and gasp of a blown horse. A shape in the darkness, a rider leading a horse towards the fire. Clumsy, staggering steps – the horse's head bobbing up and down, the way a horse moves when utterly exhausted, the man's steps crossing over one another like a drunkard's, for it seemed the horse was no longer strong enough to bear a rider.

Closer now, and they could see a Sarmatian who seemed aged by wounds. Closer still, and they could see the man's armour was almost ruined, the plates of horn and bone ripped and torn away. A thing of blood the figure seemed, though how much was his own and how much that of others they could not say.

Another sound – from behind, a tearing sound, like blade through flesh, a dark shape moving at his side. The one-eyed horse was loose, the tied reins torn apart, the beast rushing forward to stamp the life out from the stranger who came towards them. Kai waited for the horse to rear and strike, that great murderer of men that had left so many dead behind it.

But the horse stopped short, stood still and trembling before the newcomer. The bleeding man raised a hand and gave a gentle touch to the horse's face. For the horse came to greet, not to kill.

The warrior's face was half covered by the helm. Blood ran from the mouth, and there was something wrong with the jaw – dropped low on one side, fixed in place. That was why Kai had not recognised that face at first. That was why he had not known her for who she was.

Laimei pulled the helm from her head with shaking fingers, her close-cropped hair matted with blood and dirt. She leaned her head against her horse, and the horse gave a great cry of joy and grief. Then, slowly, Kai's sister sank to the ground and painted the snow with blood.

5

Her jaw was cracked and swollen – perhaps by the edge of a Roman shield, the pommel of a sword, or the kick of a blinded horse. But Kai knew that there would be a worse wound than that. So many times before he had helped to search a bloodied body, thinking it almost whole, only to find the flesh spilling its secrets from a ragged slash in the belly, the life pulsing away from a cut in the thigh, a great blackish bruise that bloomed into some deep and hidden wound.

Kai did not check the throat or the thigh, for if she had been cut there she never would have made it to the campfire. He pushed his fingers past the hacked plates of armour and searched the belly and the low sides of the back, seeking those slow wounds that bleed but do not knit, that stink of rot from the moment they are opened. He ran his fingers over her skull, feeling for a shifting softness, the kind of wound that would slowly drive a warrior mad before it killed them. And she twitched at his touch, little jerks of hand and foot, for even unconscious it seemed that she fought against him. Even in dreams, she remembered the feud.

He found it then, as he pushed aside the armour that guarded her arm – a hack at the shoulder, half clotted, still oozing blackish-red blood. But perhaps it would not kill her. He ripped cloth to rags, bound and packed the wound, and as soon as he had finished her horse batted him aside with its head and began to nuzzle at Laimei's face once more. It was only then that Kai remembered the others.

They stood in a circle about him, as solemn as men before a funeral pyre. And from them he could hear the whispers, as they spoke her name like a prayer. Not the name their mother had given her, but her war name – the Cruel Spear.

On a cattle raid into River Dragon lands, a warband might turn back in a heartbeat if one of the men thought he saw a rider on the plains bearing her sigil. Whispered stories passed around campfires at night, of clans with the odds in their favour breaking and running before the charge of the Cruel Spear. And it was not just stories around those campfires, for every clan had a survivor to look on, and to pity. Men with cut spines who had to be tied onto their horses, women left blinded or handless from their time in the warband. For it was a trail of the maimed that she had left behind her on the battlefield, and so she was feared more than death. To see her so broken seemed a final omen of defeat.

'Will she live?' It was Gaevani who spoke, picking at his teeth with his thumb.

'If anyone can live through that wound, she will,' said Kai.

'And what does that mean?'

'Only the gods can tell.'

Gaevani hissed, and shook his head. 'No. What does that mean for us?'

It was then that Kai understood. He rose carefully, and faced the other man down.

'She will be our captain, if she lives. Not you, and not me.'

'And where will she lead us?'

'Not to Dacia, that is for certain. Not to sell our spears to our enemies.'

The crack and spit of the fire, the clinking of armour as men shifted in their place. Kai could not before have said that shame had a scent, but he could almost smell the stink of it upon them.

'It is said that you speak too much, Kai,' said Gaevani. 'I did not know that you heard too much as well.'

'I told you that you should have set a sentry.' Kai half-turned to speak to the other men, his voice raised in command. 'Help me with her. We need to—'

It was quick, so quick that Kai could not say how he knew. Some whisper of a god in his ear, perhaps, that made him drop his shoulder and twist away, to feel the crack of a blade glancing from his armour. But he knew, and the Roman sword was in his hand and cutting at the air as he slid back and went into a low stance. Gaevani stood before him, the chipped stone axe weaving before him. There was surprise on his face, for perhaps Gaevani had not known what he meant to do until the moment he struck, had not known that he could be a traitor until the axe sang in the air.

57

But there could be no turning back now. Kai could see the others broadening the circle, making no move to step between them. They stood with their hands clasped before them, for much had been broken that day, but not the warrior's code. A challenge made and answered – this was a matter for Kai and Gaevani alone.

They had no shields, and so they carried their left arms high, looking to block with armour and bone. It would be no fight like the old stories, where men leapt and danced and gave half a hundred strokes of their weapons before the end. They still wore their horseman's armour – weighted and balanced for a man in the saddle and not one who walked upon the ground. Exhausted from the battle, they took little careful steps on the icy ground, gave slow and testing jabs with the weapons. Like two men fighting underwater they seemed, or practising the moves of a dance. Barely moving, offering only little flickers of the blade, a slight shift in stance or position that was countered by just as subtle a movement on the other side. But it did not take Kai long to realise the danger that he was in.

Gaevani was taller, heavier, and his axe longer than the Roman sword that Kai carried. Half a hand of height and reach, and it would be enough. Quickness was the only answer, the hope that the thrust of the sword could be faster than an axe swing, but every time that he moved and breathed Kai could feel those daggers of pain pressing into his side once more.

A shift of weight, his feet pressing into the ice, the sword darting forward. But Gaevani saw him coming – a turn of the body and the axe was moving in the darkness, cracking off the arm that Kai threw up at the last moment.

So it went – thrust and counter, thrust and counter. Kai feinted and tried to cut at the axehead instead, but Gaevani was ready for him and almost took his head off with the return swing. If things had been but a little different, Kai could have pressed him, driven him to the edge of the circle where his reach would count for nothing. If he had a shield, if they fought in daylight, if he did not bear his broken ribs like a spear in his side. If.

The weight of the armour burning in Kai's legs, his steps stumbling like a foal's. Gaevani, too, was breathing hard, his face grey with exhaustion, but there was lightness in his feet as he paced across the snow. The lightness of a man who knows he is winning.

But he was a little too light – the snow had been worn away by their circling footprints, and his foot skated against ice. Kai was forward without thinking, crossing the distance in a single beat of the heart, the iron singing in the air. But he did not strike with a thrust, for already Gaevani was guarding against it and turning his body to the side. Kai moving closer, hearing the little sigh of fear from one of the men who watched as he came to the killer's distance – close enough to cut rather than stab, swinging at the unprotected throat to spill the life upon the ice.

And as he swung, he felt a wrist close about his. Almost a gentle touch, like a lover taking one's hand in the dance, as it guided his sword arm aside.

For Gaevani had seen that, too. What a warrior he was, Kai thought, as the axe fell towards him.

The haft of the axe was in Kai's hand – jarring, bruising to the bone, but he had caught Gaevani's swing in return, the two of them standing together like a carved statue cut from a single piece of stone. Close enough to smell the man's breath, sweet with wine, to feel it on his face.

A twist of the hands, a surge of weight, feet scattering across the snow and ice, and the two of them were parted. Parted, yet still close enough, the axe turning through the air. But Kai saw a chance of his own and knew he would not get another.

They swung and cut at the same moment.

Then they were away, leaping back, gasping and hunched over, each watching the other for some mark of weakness, for some sign of a wound. For there was fresh blood upon the snow.

Kai's sword ran dark, the blade seeming black in the darkness, and Gaevani's hand was at his side, the blood pulsing through the fingers. But Kai saw something else, too. Blood upon the tip of the axe and dripping onto the snow. And it was then that he felt his own wound.

A cold line across his thigh, the hot blood pulsing down his leg, into his boot, spilling out and steaming on the snow.

He felt it then, a sensation he had known before. Practising the swordsman's craft with his father on the fields to the east, when the old warrior had seemed to know each of his moves before Kai even thought of them. A duel over a woman, fought to the first blood against a man too fast for him. A tournament on horseback fought with blunted spears – against his sister, before the feud – her laughter surrounding him as she tumbled him from his mount. The weary sadness of the fighter who knows he cannot win.

He hoped against hope to see Gaevani's wound break open like a riverbank in flood, for the lifeblood to pour swift and hot upon the snow. But it ebbed slowly, as slowly as Kai went to one knee, his wounded leg unable to take his weight any longer.

They stared at one another, heavy breath frosting the air.

'Will you yield?'

Kai started at the voice. It seemed that they had fought for so long that they had gone to a place beyond words, regressed to creatures who had lost their language. He had forgotten that they were still men who might speak to one another.

'Yield,' Gaevani said, 'and swear an oath upon my sword, to ride at my command. And you shall live.'

Kai looked to the men in the circle, though he knew he would find no assistance there. It might have been a trick of the firelight, but he thought he could see sadness on their faces, and a silent pleading. They had wanted him to win. Now they wanted him to live.

Then his eyes fell upon his sister.

She lay beside the fire, still in the way that the dead are still. But her eyes were open – little slits that shone in the firelight, closed over briefly, and opened once more. No lifeless stare, but one of the living as she watched him to see what he would do.

'What of my sister?' Kai said.

'She cannot ride, and we cannot wait for her.' A muttering

then, from the men in the circle. Gaevani tossed his head and spoke louder, speaking to them. 'We must ride south tomorrow, before the Romans close the way.' He hesitated. 'If the gods mean for her to live, then she shall live.'

Kai shook his head. 'Then no. I do not yield.'

'You will not save her by dying.'

'I know.' He got to his feet, one hand pressed to the flowing wound, balanced on his good leg.

Gaevani's lips parted – there was more he wished to say. And a face which had been like stone softened a little, and Kai thought that he saw a sadness there. No killer's pleasure, but the call of the iron had been too strong. Gaevani offered a warrior's salute with the axe, and Kai answered it. What he would have given to know that man in a different time.

They were treading the familiar steps now, enacting the weary ritual that had come to pass countless times before. The end of a duel that can have only one outcome. Gaevani circling around him, Kai turning with little hops of his good leg, the blood trailing on the ground. Kai swinging freely, off balance, the other man shifting away and waiting for an opening.

Kai's sight was trimmed with black at the edges, the snowplain swimming before him as though it were a rolling sea. He could see nothing of the circle of men, the fire beyond. It was Gaevani and him. The last two men left in the world, or so it seemed.

It was time then for the last chance, the reckless thrust that every man gives at the final moment. Gaevani knew it would come, and was ready. He batted it aside, hooked and looped the axehead about the blade and sent it spinning from Kai's grasp.

But from somewhere close, the rattle and scrape of armour, and Gaevani did not move forward for the killing blow. He froze still where he was, looking beyond. And when Kai risked a glance himself, he saw his sister standing at the edge of the circle.

She was leaning against the horse that stood beside her, for it seemed that she did not have the strength to stand alone. Her wounded arm hanging useless at her side, the other now clutching the horn of the saddle. Wordless, her bloody jaw slack, she stared at them both with grey, murderous eyes.

A moment where all was still. Kai drew out a dagger, though he barely had the strength to lift it. Gaevani was backing away across the snow and watching both of them. A murmur from the circle, uncertain what to do. For this was beyond the warrior's code.

Laimei took her hand from the saddle and levelled a finger at Gaevani. A wordless curse, it seemed. The mark the dead may give to the living, a last defiance.

Then her horse began to move.

It did not canter or trot. It walked forward as Laimei sank back to the snow behind it. Calm, almost careless, except for the one eye that it fixed upon Gaevani.

That man backed away, looked set to run. But even at a walk the horse had closed the distance and now loomed above him, the murderous beast that seemed to kill for pleasure, that had left a trail of the dead behind it on every battlefield it walked upon.

He called at it to stop, a crack in his voice, but the horse only had ears for one master. Gaevani drew the axe back, but the horse was too fast for him. It danced up onto its hind legs, sent a flickering touch forward, too fast to be seen in the light of the fire. A snap like dry wood breaking, and the axe was in the snow. Another hoof drove into his belly, folding him over. A third blow struck his head and sent him to the ground, blood washing across the snow.

The horse dropped back down, half raised a foreleg again as it watched to see if the man would rise once more. Then, seeming satisfied, it dropped the hoof to the ground, turned a half circle and walked away, returning to Laimei's side.

She remained on her knees, reaching up to stroke the horse's face as it came to her. She watched Kai – they were all looking at him now, it seemed, the men and women of the circle. None spoke.

The blood still pulsed against Kai's hand, but his sight was clear. He limped forward, but in a moment an arm was circling about his waist – the fair-haired woman, Tamura, helping to take his weight. Others were at his side, offering him a captain's escort. They had come back to life, brothers to him once more now that the duel was over.

Almost over. For when they came to where Gaevani lay upon the ground, he yet lived. Part of his scalp torn and hanging over his face like a cap, his eyes like beads of glass as he looked up at them, waiting for death.

Kai extended his sword towards him, the jagged tip steady.

'Swear on it,' said Kai. 'Follow me to the east, to Iolas. And you shall live.'

A guttural sound behind him from Laimei. He ignored her, and did not take his gaze from the man at his feet.

Gaevani did not hesitate. His fingers trembling like an old man's, he laid them to the blade and spoke the words that would save his life.

Deep within the fortress at Aquincum, the fires burned brightly in a stone chamber, hot air shimmering above the braziers. Yet the man inside still hunched and shivered with the cold as he sat behind the carved wooden table. A glimpse of a cloak, dyed in Imperial purple, was visible for a moment, before he pulled the furs tighter over it and returned to his work.

Silver marked his hair and beard, and his left hand rubbed at his side, an aching illness or an old wound that he worried and nursed incessantly. The right hand shifted between a map, unfurled and marked with tokens of wood and brass, and a sheaf of papers. A great curving line cut across the centre of the map – the Danubius, the great river that marked the edge of the Empire. On one side of that river, precise markers denoting Legions and Auxilia, the comforting linear paths of the roads that led to the west, the forts and towns that guarded the border. Aquincum itself, tucked up against a turning of the Danubius – the last outpost at the end of the world. Beyond the river, great swathes of uncharted land, a scattering of known settlements. The names of barbarian tribes – the Quadi, the Marcomanni, the Sarmatians. Tokens that marked armies across the water, their numbers more a matter for folklore than fact.

From time to time, a finger extended to push and

pull those tokens before returning them to their original positions, to trace the lines of rivers and roads, tap at the bridges and fords. Then the hand would move, curl about a metal pen, dip it into an inkwell, and slowly scratch at the papyrus, each stroke of the pen an act of stillness as much as of movement, pausing halfway through the scribing of each letter to be certain it was as he intended.

When he had been a man, the Emperor had been called Marcus Aurelius, but there were few that could speak that name to him now. For he was not a man any more – not quite a god, but as close as one could come to being one on this earth.

Yet a god in exile. From time to time, his eyes would stray from the map of the Danubius, wander down and to the left. Across the marked and pitted surface of the table, to a scratch he had placed long before. If the map had extended that far, that scratch might have marked Rome, marked his home. The place he had not seen for many years. Precious little time left to him, he thought. So much that he could have done. Yet he spent the twilight of his life here upon the borders of the Empire, fighting a war against the barbarians, a war that it seemed would never end.

One by one, his generals came in, saluted, stood. Some he acknowledged as they entered, others he did not seem to notice as he sat absorbed in the writing, in his meditation over the map. They remained in silence – respectful, almost worshipful.

A messenger came. A sealed wax tablet handed to the Emperor, broken open, and then the tokens were marching across the map, gathering upon the Danubius itself. The Emperor no longer shivered and fidgeted, though the chamber had grown no warmer. He grew still, closed his eyes to slits, and stared down at the map. He waited.

The generals tried to mimic this stillness, though here and there one could see a line of sweat carving across the skin, a head tilting at some imagined sound. For they were not far from the place on the Danubius where they knew a battle was being fought. Countless times had the barbarians come crawling against their borders, and always they had sent them back. Yet always there was the fear that this would be the time unlike the others – that this would be the moment when the Empire fell. That they would hear the calling of the horns, the barbarian war cries, and know that their world was ending.

At last, another messenger entered the tent, one quite unlike the others. Bone weary, the wild eyes of a man who has traded one horse for another on a desperate journey. A man coming from battle with urgent news, with a steady hand he passed the sealed message to the Emperor.

The crack of a seal, a scraping of wax, the Emperor reading with an unhurried focus. The generals straining to read him, to interpret some sign of victory or defeat from a twitch at the corner of the mouth, the slightest furrowing of the brow. He let them try for a time – a quiet pleasure in keeping that knowledge from them.

At last, he lifted his head. 'We have defeated them on the ice,' he said.

A moment of release, as men clasped each other in arms, shared the proud words of the victorious. One hastily wiped tears from his eyes, for he had a mistress in the border towns and had not known if he would see her again. For a moment, they forgot that they were before a god.

Only the Emperor seemed unmoved. He watched the men with a quiet impatience, a schoolmaster watching unruly boys at play. And they saw it, one by one, and came once again to attention.

'Forgive us, Caesar,' one of them said. 'We are glad to see the end, that is all. They shall not be back for many years. They shall starve on their side of the river.'

The Emperor wagged a pale finger at them. 'No. Not this time.'

He made the generals wait to know his meaning as he sent for the captains of his cavalry. And when those men arrived – breathless, flushed, stinking of horse sweat – the Emperor had another moment's hesitation. One captain in particular caught his eye – reddish-gold hair touched with silver, a certain sadness to the eyes. A man close to the end of his time in the Legions, and it was hard to send such a man to die.

But there was to be no turning back. The Emperor lowered his finger once more to point at a place on the map, and with an open hand he swept the tokens of wood and brass forward, past the river and into a place that they had never been before, not in a hundred years of war.

An intake of breath amongst the generals, a light in the eyes. For they knew then what the Emperor meant to do.

6

From the mist and the marsh, the figures came. Shadows at first, that might have been mistaken for the ghosts that were said to haunt the mire, or the witch-fires that lured men to join the dead. But soon those shadows resolved into men and women, leading their horses through the swamp. Black mud, a layer of ice over stagnant water, clumps of grass that seemed to offer solid footing, leading only to the choking mire. In winter, at least, it did not carry the stink of rot in the air.

They moved slowly, carefully, but from time to time a horse or rider still plunged deep into the mud, others gathering to wrestle them free. Their armour was tattered, their weapons hacked and broken, limbs thick-caked in mud and washed with stagnant water. The defeat was written upon their bodies, but they stood tall as they walked, trading songs as they picked their way through bog and tussock. They did not carry themselves like the defeated. And at the head of the company, wearing the crudely scratched mark of a captain on his armour, the sign of sword and circle, it was Kai who led them from the swamp.

Three days since the duel by the fire. Their numbers were changed – they had found others as they fled across the land: the half-dozen riders who had ridden to their fire on the third night; the lone boy trying to bury a dead friend in frozen ground; the pair of women mounted on a single horse whom they found camped at the edge of the swamp.

Others they had lost. The wounded boy at the first campfire who died, with a strange silent courtesy, before the dawn. A pair of brothers who had crept away in the night, taking their chances alone. A young woman stolen away by wound fever, who had been laughing around the fire one evening and was found dead in sweat-soaked blankets the following morning. Yet Kai counted more riders now in his company than at the start of the journey, and there was no captain who could ask for more than that.

He listened to the songs rise high as his warriors came to the edge of the swamp – they were hurrying then, horse and man, for the horses seemed to long for dry ground even more than their masters, to feel their hooves beating against the steppe. They had struggled and fought through the muck for days on end, miserable as falcons bound to a perch. Now it was time for them to fly once more.

Kai saw a number of the riders break ranks, their horses surging forward and tearing across the plains with all the reckless love that a horse has for speed. With the slightest smile on his lips, Kai watched them scrapping and squalling like a colony of sea birds on the cliffs, the restless testing of idle warriors.

Beside him, Tamura looked out at the riders who had broken away, restless as a mother whose children are ever proving elusive.

'Should I call them back?' she asked.

'Let them ride free,' said Kai. 'There shall be no Romans here. Not yet, at least. Why not join them? You have earned a little freedom.'

The young woman flushed with the praise, her hands fiddling with the reins in her lap.

'No. I should... I do not want to.'

'Go, it is my wish.'

She hesitated a moment longer, as though waiting for some trap in his words. But then she was away, her heels to her horse and whooping like a child. And for a moment, Kai rode alone.

The firm ground had been beneath his horse for no more than a hundred heartbeats, but already the crossing through the marsh had taken on the quality of a fever dream, something he could not quite believe to be true. Back at the fire, after the duel, when he had first told them he intended to ride through the mire, he had not thought his captaincy would last the hour. It would have been much to ask of a fresh company hungry for battle, let alone men and women half broken by defeat. But though a few faces had paled at the suggestion, there was not a voice that spoke against him.

And so they had followed him, retracing the secret paths taught by the mothers and aunts who had learned the secrets of that labyrinth, following cairns and totems that marked the way. Days spent sleepless, for to be still in that place was to die swallowed beneath the muck. Walking dismounted like shamed men, dragging fearful horses through the mire. Yet now they were on hard ground and beneath the open sky once more, and there would be no questioning his leadership. He had risen from the dead of the battlefield, had a horse save him in a duel, found a path where they thought none to be. He had earned his place through luck and omen.

Not for long. He had only to look back, to where Gaevani rode sullenly at the rearguard. Or forward, where Laimei rode, silent and white-faced with pain. One was bound by oath, the other by a cracked jaw. But one of them would speak a story soon, a story of Kai's past. When they did, he would be captain no longer.

But that was for the future. At that moment he could feel the careful pride of one who rides at the head of a warband, of one who speaks and is obeyed. Unknowing what lay before them, certain of the death that rode close at their heels. But the sweetness still lingered, that particular sweetness of a life lived between strokes of the sword, each day a passing treasure. He could see their eyes that roamed restless across the horizon, searching for the curl of smoke from a cooking fire, the round shape of gathered huts, the gentle motion of a herd wandering across the grazing grounds. That longing to cast the spear upon the earth, and to see the sights of home.

He felt his horse stirring restlessly beneath him, a new steed taken from one of the men who had died along the way. They were still learning to trust one another, the patient courtship of horse and rider. It would not do for the captain to break ranks entirely, but he stirred his horse forward and moved up the line, giving it just a taste of the speed it longed for. He rode towards one horse in particular, careful to stay on the right-hand side of the company. For it was his sister's one-eyed horse that he drew near, even more foul tempered now it had been reunited with its rider.

He had thought at first that it might be days before she could ride, that they would be waiting patiently by their fallen champion as Romans closed about them like a noose around a neck. But she rode the first day after the duel by the fire and made no sound of complaint. By the time they reached the marsh, she had strength enough to walk, leaning on the arm of one of the women left in the warband (she would take no aid from any of the men).

With her wounded jaw, she spoke only by sign and gesture – most frequently, with an impatient tipping gesture of her unwounded arm, calling for wine. A black and wordless rage hung over her, and always there was a gap around her in the ranks, the other riders staying well away. Always before had she been an omen of luck, and victory – in this new world it seemed they did not quite know what she meant.

He leaned over in his saddle to offer her a waterskin, and she shook her head, gave a little hiss of pain. There were no words at all for a time, just the gentle footfall of two horses side by side, syncopated like a drumbeat. He thought of days long ago when they had ridden together on the plains – children herding cattle, playing at war with branches and horsewhips, sleeping out under the stars that told stories and sharing secret stories of their own.

'I thank you,' he said at last. 'For what you did in the duel.'

She snorted in response, and tapped her fingers on the neck of her mount.

'I thank your horse, then, for saving my life twice that day.' He studied her for a moment, as he had many times in the day since the battle, looking for the signs of fever and infection – the touch of fire at cheek and throat, a yellowish stain to the wrappings on her shoulder. He did not find them.

'I shall not lead them for long,' he said. 'Back to our village. There will be an elder there to lead us, and tell us what will be done.' He hesitated. 'I know it shames you to ride under my command.'

She gave no gesture that he might read, offered only the cold eyes of a knife fighter.

'But I welcome your counsel, if you would give it.'

A twitch of her lips that might have been the start of a smile, then a finger laid across her broken jaw.

'I think you may find a way to say what you mean to say.'

She pointed back behind them, and when Kai turned he saw her finger levelled at the rearguard, at Gaevani. She clicked her fingers to draw his attention, and pointed to the sword on Kai's belt.

Kai shook his head. 'He swore an oath.'

She spat, bloody phlegm falling like rain upon the steppe.

'He had won the duel against me. Then your horse defeated him. His life is not mine to take.' Kai grinned, and pointed to the horse beneath her. 'And it seems that he at least is inclined to mercy.'

Once more, there was murder in her eyes. Answering some invisible signal, her horse danced around to face him and half lifted a foreleg from the ground. But another sign was given, by a touch of the knees, a twitch of the reins, a thought from the mind, and the horse returned to its place.

She managed a word – her first since the battle. Low and hissed, for she could barely move her mouth. But he understood the word that she spoke.

'Weak,' she said.

Then a scream in the air – no warrior's call, but a cry of terror from one of the boys that broke out across the plain. It was behind them, and Kai was turning, giving his horse the gift of speed, was at the back of the line in moments.

At first he thought it might be a false alarm. Xobas, the boy who called out, had barely spoken a word since the battle and screamed his way through each night. But it was no phantom of the mind that the boy had seen. For the mist had cleared, and there were shadows on the horizon, on the other side of waterlogged ground. A company of riders, the shapes melding into one another at such a distance. Half again as many as Kai led, perhaps more.

Kai heard a horn blow close by – Tamura, calling them into ranks, two lines forming behind him. Then she was at his side, skin grey and eyes darting.

'My thanks,' he said. He glanced at the cavalry, arrayed for battle, and could not help but smile. 'Though I do not think we'll be charging them across the swamp.'

Laughter then, from the others, Tamura's cheeks flushing red, and at once Kai regretted his words.

'Forgive me,' she said. 'I thought it best—'

'A jest only, pay it no mind. How good are your eyes?'

'Fair, I would say.'

'That makes them better than mine. Who are they? Our people?'

Tamura leaned forward in the saddle, shaded her eyes against the sharp winter sun.

'I cannot say,' she said, after a moment.

Another voice, then: 'I can.'

It was Gaevani who spoke, slouched sullenly on his horse. He was in the line beside the frightened boy, Xobas – he too had been given the rearguard, for he was thought unlucky.

'What do you see?' Kai said.

'The man who leads them wears too much iron to be of our people. And there is a red crest on his helm.'

A change in the light, as the sun broke a little through the clouds, and Kai saw that man a little more clearly – the iron armour, the red crest that Gaevani had noted. And Kai even thought he saw the light upon the pale skin, the reddish gold of the beard. The colour of Roman kings, it was said.

The wound in Kai's leg ached. For a moment the fear was rising like bile in his throat, his vision dancing before his eyes, his skin cold with shame. He blinked and breathed, and the sensation passed. 'Romans, then. You think they are scouts?'

A shake of the head. 'Too many. Raiders.'

A chill touch, then, that started at the nape of Kai's neck and danced down his spine. This time, a sensation not of fear, but of hate. 'Come to hunt our people, after the battle on the ice.' He turned his horse away, to speak to the warband. 'They cannot cross the swamp here,' he said, 'and we shall be long gone by the time they have made it round.'

One of the riders spoke, a man Kai did not know well: 'We let them go?' For the first time since he had taken the captaincy, there was a mutter of dissent.

Kai could not help but smile. Three days through mud and mire, wounded and with barely a spear for every three riders, and still they thought only of the hunt.

'I think we may have mercy on them for now. But let them know what you think of them.'

And at once the warband were alive with noise – cheering, jeering, screaming insults. It was a far distance to the other side, but those horsemen must have heard something, or seen the movement at least. For they were in motion, seeming to shout back, and the wind brought the Sarmatians something of their reply – the barest whisper of a curse.

With a few last choice insults bellowed through the air, the riders broke from their ranks and began to wander back across the plain once more. Only Laimei lingered behind.

Kai watched as, with a little sigh of pain, she lifted her wounded arm. There was a sword in her hand, a Roman blade that he had gifted to her. She lifted it high, then levelled it down towards the riders in the distance. Towards their leader.

To Kai's surprise, he saw the spear lifted and pointed in response. The challenge seen, and answered.

For the first time in as long as he could remember, he saw his sister smile.

Later, when night had fallen on the plain, Kai let them have a fire.

No roaring blaze, but a smoking, smouldering thing of bone and dung and wet grass. To them it was as good as a chieftain's fire stacked high with precious wood and burning clean through until the dawn. They huddled close to it, lying down together like packs of dogs.

Most collapsed into sleep at once, taking all the rest they could before it was their turn to stand guard. Those unlucky men and women who had drawn poorly in the lot remained on horseback, doing slow loops of the camp and singing to themselves to stay awake.

Still, there were those who were not on guard and yet did not sleep. They gathered close to the fire, passing around what little koumiss was left, staining beard and chin with the stink of fermented milk. They did not sing, or read the stars for the stories of old heroes. They did not speak of what might come to pass, or tell of the victories of their youth. For they had left thousands of their kin upon the frozen water, to be swallowed by the river when the first thaws came. No barrow dug, no fire lit above or sword placed to mark the place, no grave gifts to take with them to the Otherlands. And so that night, they buried the dead with words.

So many to speak of, spirits clustering unseen about the fire, pleading for the story that would set them free. And only one way that the speakers might choose from those ghosts, to speak of the one that mattered most.

It was an older rider, one they called Saratos, who was the first to talk. In the circle of dozing warriors, his voice sounded cleanly out.

'My cousin. Opoea. She was so frightened,' Saratos said. 'Never could do much right. But I remember how she was with the horses. How they were with her. She'd have liked to be one, I think. Perhaps the wrong spirit wandered into the wrong body when she was born.' He drank deeply from the koumiss, then let his head sink into his hands. 'Her own horse kicked her to death when she fell in the mob. He was frightened too, I suppose. She should have ridden a braver horse, but she loved that one above all others.'

A muttered chorus about the fire, of sorrows and memories, and the consolations of the next world. Then silence, until the next voice to speak broke out into the night.

'Pideis. My friend.' It was Gaevani who spoke, his fingers picking restlessly at the shaft of an arrow that he held in his hands, turning it over and over and over again. 'We grew up together. We shared everything. He did, anyway – anything he was given, half of it he gifted to me.' A pause. 'Sometimes I hated him for it. We had not spoken in a long time. I thought that there would be time.' And with that, he took the arrow, broke it in half, and laid a piece of it down next to him. He lifted his head, and spoke to the circle, as if in defiance: 'I loved him, once.'

Silence, for a time. Around the fire, there were men who held their companions a little tighter at those words. And women, who looked with longing at faces across the fire.

A voice came from the darkness, one that Kai could not place. 'How did he die?'

'Rode at the front of the pack – too far in front,' said Gaevani. 'Perhaps he wanted me to see.' His eyes drifted out of focus, into memory. 'A thrown spear put him down. And the rest of us rode over him in the charge.'

A toast was given, prayers sounded out. Then other voices, one at a time. Each spoke a name, a memory of the dead, and then the way that they had died – the mistake they had made. A slackly tightened saddle, a reckless thrust of the spear, a poorly trained horse. That knowledge a last gift from the dead, so that the living might not meet the same end.

They had spoken long into a changing of the guard, and there were few left around the fire still awake. Kai was at the borderlands of the mind, where the dream and the real intermingle, when he heard his name spoken. He was not certain at first whether it was from the waking world that he heard the voice, whether it was the living or the dead who called to him.

But it was Tamura who sounded his name. 'Will you speak, Kai?' she said, and the eyes of the circle were upon him.

Would it be right, for the captain to speak of what he had lost? Or should he be a man without feeling to them? Kai tried to think of the old stories, whether those heroes had never spoken a word of grief or wept at every fireside, but they all seemed to tangle in his head, the heroes weeping and silent all at once like the madness of a dream.

The skin of koumiss came to him once more, and as the thick, bitter taste settled on his tongue he found that he did not care what others had done, only what he would do. He knew that there was someone that he had to speak of.

'Bahadur,' he said.

A murmur round the fireside. For a man as good with song and spear as Bahadur had been was known beyond his clan.

'A second father he was to me.' Kai lifted his head, looked about the fire. 'You have heard how he sang?'

One voice said: 'Aye. I have.'

Another: 'He could call the spring birds down, or so I heard it said.'

'No idle tale, that,' said Kai, 'for I saw it happen.'

A mutter of disbelief spread around the circle, and Kai knew that he would have to answer it, as he would have answered a challenge to a duel.

'Five summers past, we rode north,' he said. 'Further north than I have been before. I had heard there was good grazing beyond the mountains, back towards the Sea of Grass. That we might leave the swamplands behind, raise tall horses and fat cattle.

'Well, we did not find it. We did not go far enough, perhaps. But there was a forest we passed, and I have never seen a place so alive with birds. It must have been a place where the hawk did not hunt, and no boys came with arrow and sling.

'And Bahadur sang at them as we rode, trying out one

birdsong after another – the high trills and the quick chatter. And at last, there must have been one that he perfected. For one of those birds came down – darting, confused, singing its answer to the question he must have asked it.' Kai raised a hand, extended a finger. 'Right here is where it landed.'

The circle broke into laughter at the thought, and they were turning to each other, sharing memories of their own, singing scraps of the songs they had heard from Bahadur, long ago. Children around the fire – that is how they seemed in that moment, wanting to believe in heroes and in fate.

So he did not tell them the rest – that Bahadur had snatched the bird and smashed its neck against the saddle, bitten into it at once. For they had wandered north starving, bellies hollow with hunger, for the crops had failed and the herd was blighted with plague, and the dead of the clan were countless. He did not tell them how he and Bahadur had taken their bows and shot down every bird they could, while they sat there dumb upon their perches and waited for their lives to be taken. The men returned to their clan, sacks filled with wet treasure. Some of their people had lived.

He did not say how they had returned there again, a year later, and found the forest empty and still. It had been a blessing of nature. Now, it would always be known as a place where no birds sang.

Kai spoke, to drive away that memory. 'He brought the bird back as a gift to his wife, Arite. I never heard a voice so sweet as his. And none of us shall hear it sing again.'

'He was a fine man,' said Saratos. 'You are certain that he is dead?'

Once again, Kai could see the man falling from the saddle, pierced by the spear, into the arms of the Romans.

'Yes, he is dead. And his last son too, Chodona.'

Another voice from the darkness: 'The son met his death well?'

Kai heard once more that piercing shriek from the battlefield, the panicked cry for mercy. 'Yes,' he said. 'A brave death.'

'His wife still lives?'

'Aye. Arite. Brave and beautiful.' A lump grew in Kai's throat. 'May she find another man as good as him.'

The silence thickened then, grew heavy. At last, it bore fruit with words.

'How did he die?' Gaevani said. 'Bahadur, I mean.'

'I saw him struck down myself. Speared from his horse.' Kai heard his voice crack, as he spoke the next words. 'He had come back to rescue me. That was his mistake.' And Kai tossed his head, as though hoping he might shake away the memory. There was a great longing for sleep, though he knew the memories would find him there. That the dead would, too.

Tamura spoke once more. 'You said he was a second father to you, and so you were a second son to him.'

'Kind words. I thank you for them.'

Another voice asked: 'Your own father, he died in battle? Tell us a story of him?'

From the corner of his eye, Kai saw Gaevani smile sourly.

'That is a story for another time,' Kai said.

And on the ground nearby, Laimei shifted. He had thought her asleep, and perhaps she had been for a time. But at that moment her eyes were open, and glittering in the dark. If she could speak, and if she chose to, he knew whose story she would tell.

'Come,' said Kai. 'We have buried enough of the dead. Tomorrow we may make Iolas, if we ride hard enough. Sleep now. Think of those you love.'

'And what if those we love are dead?' said Gaevani.

'Think of them even so. You shall still see them soon enough. But not tonight.'

7

Once more in Iolas, the waiting at the edge of the village, a ritual akin to worshipping the sun. The women and children gathering and looking towards the west, waiting for the warband to return. And once more, the sun fell from the sky, and the warriors did not return.

This time it was Arite who lingered after the others had gone, waiting until she stood alone. Let Tomyris roam free a little longer, she thought; let her watch the stars and feel the cold night air on her skin. And the dream, the dream of those they loved returning – that could stand to live a little longer, too.

As she stood there, a memory came unbidden to her – a memory of the last time she had seen her husband and her son. Once more, all about her she heard the calling of men and women on the march to war, preparing for the great gathering by the Danu, to face the Romans on the ice. Once more, she saw her son, Chodona, the last child left to her, the others gathered to the gods by sword and fever.

He had been so small standing beside his horse – he should have been heading to tend the herd, not joining the warband, yet he was smiling at her, brave and proud and brilliant, so eager to go towards a war that he knew nothing of. And in her memory, she saw Bahadur before her, his temples touched with grey and his beard silvered, but still the beautiful singer and warrior she had loved for twenty years. No laughter or song from him then, for his voice was raised against her. She heard him saying, again and again, that Chodona must stay behind, that he was too young to go to the war. And again and again, her hand cutting at the air like a blade in front of her, she told Bahadur that their son must go.

At last, it was over. She had got her wish, as she always did in the end. He had taken one of her hands in both of his, raising it to his lips. Then he called to the boy, and for a moment they were all together in an embrace. Then they broke apart, and the memory broke with it.

Waiting at the edge of the village, the cold wind did not cut her as deep as the shame of that memory, the shame of sending her son away. She offered a prayer to the gods, as she did every night. Her life for theirs. Let the fever take her, let her starve to nothing that winter, if only her son and her husband came back from the ice.

Arite had heard many stories of the way in which thoughts might be made flesh by the whim of a god, unspoken prayers answered at once. And so it was, just as she was about to turn away and return to her hut, that she thought the gods were listening to her. For she heard a dog barking, somewhere out beyond the village, out where the half-feral packs roamed as sentries.

Alone, it was a sound that was as much a comfort as the singer's voice around a night fire, the whoops and hollers of a hunting party returning home to safety. For a single voice meant a dog calling to one it knew, an old master returning home. And so perhaps it was that the warband was there, out in the dark, pressing on to reach them, not willing to wait another night out upon the steppe.

Then another dog cried out. Another, and another, and another, until all of them were rising with one voice. Dozens howling together at the western border of the village, the voices rising to a crescendo and then softening as they moved away, moved beyond the borders of the village and out into the night. And there was only one thing that might mean. Enemies at the border. Raiders, coming in from the darkness.

Arite felt it then. The coldness that finds the palms of the hands first, then dances around the heart. The warrior's coldness, before the killing begins. And there was another sound. Echoing above the sounds of the village coming to life, of panicked cries and barked, contradictory orders, there was a sound that stilled all others. From somewhere near the centre of the village, the sounding of a Sarmatian war horn.

It was a quavering, uncertain tone – blown by one long unpractised, yet who still half-remembered the war calls of old. And Arite knew it too, the sound that had been the music of her youth, the call to arm and mount that every Sarmatian knew from the first time they could ride.

The fear was gone, banished by those three notes of the horn. Arite was hurrying to the horses and found Tomyris there already, for she had been raised for this moment, when death rode across the steppe and came for them.

The horses knew it too, were already giving the little snorts and stamps that a cavalry horse makes before the battle. They were old, too old for war, cut and scarred and limping like many of the women in the village. But even so, they too remembered the sound of the horns from their youth.

As she mounted and pulled the child up behind her, Arite risked a look out to the west, in the half-light of dusk. Shapes moving in the darkness, the swing of a sword, the cry of a dog cut short. The hounds had been there first, waging a hopeless war, but they had held long enough. For there were enough mounted and armed now, and again the horn called – the familiar notes, from a lifetime ago. *Form line, prepare to charge.* And from the ground, someone passed her a lance. How long it had been since she had held a spear in her hand, but by the way the weapon felt against her palm it could have been but a day since she rode in the warband. Killing, like any practice of the heart, is not forgotten.

They were in the line then – greyhaired women who had not ridden to war in decades, young women who had fought their way from the warband just a few months before and thought to put the spear aside forever. And everywhere there were children mounted in front of their mothers. They did not have enough horses and ponies to mount the children separately, no time to hitch wagon and cart.

The good spears had all gone to the west, and hers was a crude, curving thing without even a true spearhead to it, just a sharpened wooden point. What she could have done with a spear of black iron, she thought. She would make it count for what she could.

'Do not be afraid,' Arite said to the child who shivered against her. 'They will remember us.' And she was grateful there, at the last, the child was too frightened to question the lie.

For if the raiders were here, the battle on the ice had been lost. There were none left to speak the names and bury the dead, and she felt the last of the fear wash away and be replaced by something else. Not the cold joy of killing, nor the feeling of hatred that is like embers scattered across bare skin. But that reckless longing that comes at the very end of hope, and all about her she could see the signs that the others wore too – the dull glazed eyes, the little half-smile, the gently nodding head. That longing to fight, and join one's beloved in the dark beyond.

Figures in the darkness, drawing closer. The calling of the horn once more, the rattle of lances dipping down and pointing forward. No time left to speak anything but a name before the charge, and all around her she could hear the whispers as the women spoke, a muttering like prayer as they spoke the names of those that they loved.

'Bahadur,' Arite said. And then, just before the charge, she spoke another name. Soft, the barest whisper, as though she were afraid that then, even at the end, Tomyris might hear her.

'Kai.'

★ ★ ★

In the nameless hours long before dawn, they woke him.

Kai had tumbled through one dream after another, of drowning and smothering, water pressing at his lips and hands closing at his throat. At first, he could not seem to hear their voices – the words came to him deadened, as though he were still under the waters of his dreams. But he followed where they pointed, and on the horizon he saw fire.

Something was burning in the distance, the smoke rising in a great column towards the sky. No funerary or sacrificial fire, but an artless scattering of smaller blazes that had joined together to form something greater.

It was when he looked up for a moment at the stars that he understood. For in this place he had looked on the night sky many times before. Coming back from cattle raids or riding beside a trading caravan, spending one last night under the open skies, reading the stories written in the stars, following the lines of the constellations. And now, as before, they pointed him back towards Iolas, his home.

For that was the cruelty of the steppe – how far one might see on the flat open ground. Disaster could always be seen at a distance, it seemed. He was too far away to see his village, but not too far away to see it burn.

Kai did not move for a time, watched the fire burn. For it was a sacred thing, that fire that took all forms and none. The holy fires of the old ways, where the smoke granted visions. The funeral fires, where a sword plunged into a burning barrow. And with all fires there was one thing they all held in common. They were a place to take oaths.

He looked about the warriors – *his* warriors – and found them watching him once more, waiting for a command. They had camped that night with a hunger – not for food or warmth, but for memories of the dead, and hope that the living still waited for them beyond the horizon.

That was gone, now. There was a different kind of hunger in their eyes.

The wolfish twitch of the lips, the glitter in the eyes.

They were not of his clan. It was not their kin that lay beyond the horizon. He had been their captain for but a handful of days, and already he knew they would take his feud as their own. That his loss was theirs.

He pointed to the fire in the sky, and there was no need for words. With barely a whisper, they slipped onto the saddles of the horses, and made their way to the east.

The fires were long dead when they got to Iolas, killed fast by the winter air. A little smoke still rose, like the aftermath of a harvest festival, or the morning after the great fires with which their people greeted the spring. It was as they drew closer that they saw where that smoke rose from – the burned out huts, the black skeletons of the wagons and carts. And the dead who lay in the fields.

As they approached – no longer hurrying, but idling along listlessly, like shepherds herding in the height of summer – Kai knew that he should have issued commands. To search, scout, gather the dead, to do something. He found that he could not speak. For one never knows quite how much strength one has until one comes to the end of it.

Without his command, the riders drifted through the village, looking for some sign of a survivor, hoping that they might find some building untouched and its people spared. Others circled back around the edge of the village, searching for the dead, and the story that their still lips would speak.

He dismounted, wandered on foot through the ash and snow. The hut he had once called a home was a circle of black ashes, a witch's circle. He found nothing there, could only let the fine ashes run through his fingers like sand. Nearby, Bahadur and Arite's hut had not burned fully, but had been cut in half as though by the stroke of some great flaming blade. He pawed through the ashes, searching for some lost relic of the dead. The arrow that had saved Bahadur's life, the drinking cup they had all shared around the winter fire. He took up the half-burned woven rug that he found, rolled it up and slung it across his horse, for it seemed that he had to take something from that place.

A calling of his name. Tamura, who came towards him, her eyes eagle bright. For she alone seemed not to have been lost to the still madness that had taken the rest of the company.

'Kai. You have to get them out of here.' A hesitant hand reached towards his shoulder, but she did not quite touch him. 'They shall go mad, staring at all this. At you. Get them out.'

He nodded, an uneven tilt of the head like a drunkard. 'Gather them at the far side of the village. We'll find what we can and move away.'

'Come with me?'

Kai shook his head. 'Not yet,' he said, for he knew that there was something he still had to see. He made his way out towards the western fields, out to where the dead lay.

There had been few in the village itself. A handful, speared and burned in the huts, or crawling in the paths between them. The sick, it seemed, a few of the truly old, those who had not been able to rise in time. The rest had fought and died on horseback. There was a gathering of them, out in the fields to the west. Horses and women laid on the ground, as though in silent ritual.

There was only one of his riders out amongst the dead. It was Gaevani – dismounted, circling around the corpses, one hand scratching at his jaw and picking lice from his beard, looking up as Kai approached. He was smiling.

'You can smile at this?' said Kai. 'If you have touched them, I shall kill you.'

'I am no vulture.' Gaevani inclined an eyebrow towards Kai, dressed in the armour and bearing the iron blade he had taken from the dead. 'I do not pick at those that I do not kill,' he said. 'But I do smile, because I know what to look for, and you do not. Look with me, and tell me what *you* see.'

Kai swung down from the horse, and as soon as he had dismounted it stamped the ground, unsettled. He stroked its mane and whispered to it words of courage – words he needed himself, before he made himself look upon the dead.

The dogs first. All of them white, or nearly so, bred so as not to be mistaken for the wolves that always haunted the borders of the villages in winter. Many of them left faceless from the long sweeping blades that had swept down like scythes, or folded in half by the kick of a horse, backs broken.

Then the raiders – Roman cavalry, bearing red shields and the mark of the eagles upon them. Men of many nations, who had traded their honour for iron, sworn service to Rome. More poorly armed than the warriors of the Legion, but wearing in iron scales and bearing long grey swords that would have made them chieftains amongst the Sarmatians.

At last he looked upon the Sarmatians themselves, the familiar dead. The women who fought their way from the warband, many long before he had been born, who had thought they had left a death by the blade long behind them. Old and young, those who had not fought for half a lifetime, and those just free from the killing, women who had believed that they had so much time left to live and to love. The bile hot in his throat, he looked for his daughter amidst the corpses strewn upon the ground, but saw only a handful of children there, none with her black hair and coppery skin.

And yet something was not right. He felt it, but could not say what it was. Like a splinter of a spear beneath the skin, too small to be seen, but that seems to catch at every touch.

Beside him, Gaevani waited. 'You see it, don't you?' he said.

'A part of me does, but I do not quite know it yet.'

'Count the Romans.'

Kai thought he saw the other man roll his eyes as he counted hesitantly upon his fingers.

'Very good,' Gaevani said, once he had finished. 'And now count—'

'The horses.' For he was there now, and began to understand. 'More Roman horses dead than men.'

'That's right. And now look at our people.'

'A simple thing for you to say. They are not of your clan.' But he did so once more.

'Notice anything about them?' Gaevani said, as he tapped his hand to his own temple.

'Greyhaired. Most of them at least.' He made himself look closer still. 'They all bear their wounds on their front.'

'Yes. You see?'

And he did see it then, in his mind's eye – a story told in images and moments. A warning given in time. A line of women forming at the edge of the village, mounted for war and greeting the invaders with iron and stone. A horn sounding, riders fighting their way to the front ranks. Not the young who believe that they cannot die, but the old and greyhaired, their horses shouldering past the others and leading the charge. Many of them who could not have walked half a mile but could still stand tall in the saddle, who could not have gathered the wheat from the fields but could still hold a spear one last time. And when the riders levelled what few long spears they had, they did not aim for the Roman riders, but for the horses.

'I see it,' said Kai, 'as you do.'

'They did well.'

'You almost seem impressed.'

'I am,' said Gaevani. 'I never thought much of your clan.' His gaze flickered to Laimei, a still sentinel at the edge of the village. 'But perhaps it is as some say. That your women fight better than the men.'

'Where are the tracks?'

'There is hope for you yet. And the tracks lead north. Not back south and west. They head for the hills.'

'All tracks lead that way?'

'Yes. The Romans have not gone home. They are still out there, hunting those who got away. Think we can catch them?'

Kai nodded, as solemn as a priest before the offering. 'Oh, I know that we can.'

After they left the burned village, they rode wordless, communicating by gesture alone, vigilant for any un- necessary sound – the necklace that clicked against a cuirass, the loose plate of armour that scraped against others, the low-slung sword that jumped and clattered with every strike of the horse's hooves against the ground. They moved like shadows across the steppe, for even the horses, great brutes that they were, had learned to run softly when they had to.

They rode as one. No advance guard, for they would have no time to scout and return if they made contact – they would meet and strike as one action. If they encountered some greater force, a Roman wide patrol or raiding warband, they would have no chance to get away.

That was how they passed the first day. Dancing their lives on the edge of a blade as the sun passed across the sky, until the twilight came and even the keenest of their hunters could follow the tracks no longer.

Thickly wrapped in furs and flanked by the fire, the Emperor waited, one hand picking at the Imperial purple of his cloak. The tall walls of the Aquincum fortress behind him, an open field ahead, where the Legion gathered in line and square, watching and waiting.

In Rome, after the great victories, there would come the Triumph. A parade of soldiers and treasure through the streets of the city, a festival for bloody victory and the fortune of war. They were as far from Rome as they could be, beside the frozen Danubius. But here on the frontiers of the Empire, in the depths of winter, they were to have their own little Triumph.

The trumpets sounded out and the carts came forward, filled with the pickings of the battlefield. In the torchlight the Emperor saw the faces of the centurions and tribunes, and thought he could read the touch of fear there. As the carts drew closer still, he could see why. They were few, shallow-piled, and there was no shine of treasure there.

This Emperor was not one of the madmen of old, those who might have a man tortured to death or ripped apart by wild animals at a whim for a single misplaced word or the slightest mistake. Still, he had little tolerance for failure, seemed to remember every fault. There were those who had languished in the ranks until their hair was *grey, marked down by some mistake that they had long forgotten but the Emperor had not.*

One by one, the carts were brought before him and emptied at his feet. No order given, no careful presentation of treasure, for this too was part of the theatre of victory. The broken remnants of a broken people, scattered before the master of Rome.

Banners and clay-stamped tamgas bearing the mark of one clan or another. Broken spears, headed with flint for the most part. Hacked cuirasses, dressed in plates of horse hooves, and only here and there, when one of the torches sparked and flared, did the Emperor see the occasional glimmer of iron or gold.

He eyed it as though he were a canny merchant in the markets of the Greek quarter, and found it all wanting. Had it been a Triumph in Rome, they would have showered the crowds with stamped silver coins, piled silk and gold and statues of bronze high before the Temple on the Capitoline. There would be no such glory in these offerings – the crowds in Rome would laugh and throw dung at such a display. But there was something in those offering that the Legionaries might respect, those who knew what it was to go to war. That a people as poor and wretched as this, armed in this fashion, had thought to stand against Rome.

If only they had captured the horses – that would have made for a worthy prize. For this was a pitiful people, scratching out their living on the borders of the Empire. But the Emperor had never seen horses like the ones these barbarians rode. Impossible to catch them, it seemed, for

*they fought like monsters even after their masters were
slain, all the way to the last.*

*Still, it was not all a loss. They had won something on the
battlefield that was worthy of celebration. Some particular
prizes of flesh. He knew his people well enough, that they
would keep until last the finest treasure.*

*For here, at last, was iron, the deep hard grey of the
manacles. And there, too, was gold, for many of the
prisoners were golden haired, those wild-eyed children of
the steppe.*

*They held themselves with pride, even as they swayed
and stumbled on their feet – wounded and half-starved,
unused to walking on their bowed horsemen's legs. There
were some who carried others, entire ranks of prisoners
who all leaned against one another to stay upright. The
Emperor's eyes danced across their ranks, noting the
greyhaired men, the frightened boys amongst them. And
women too – he had thought them myths, when first he
had been told of them.*

*At the sight, hoots and jeers from the ranks, quickly
silenced by the centurions. Other emperors had favoured
the leering soldier – the first Caesar, himself a famous
lecher, had made a sport of such a thing. But the men knew
that this Emperor was not such a man.*

*As if in answer, words rose from the ranks of the slaves
– not curses or empty boasts, but some sweet, sad song
of death. The guardsmen raised their cudgels, looking to
centurion and Emperor for the sign to beat the music out
of them. No signal was given, and they let the song wind
around to silence.*

The Emperor spoke.

'Some of you have fought at our side before. Years before. And I am certain that amongst you, there are those that learned our language. For it was a long campaign we fought together. You have forgotten that fellowship, it seems. That is a shame. But I think some will still know the words. Speak, then, and live.'

Silence answered him. It did not matter.

He strolled beside the ranks – a safe distance, for he could see the twitching hands, the manacles that were wrapped into clubs and garrottes, the killing hunger those men and women had in their eyes.

The Emperor looked for the older men, those old enough to have fought in the last war. The ones who had the look of command, the light of intellect, who might have once been quick with laugh and song. He beckoned those men forward. Shoved and pulling, they came.

He spoke to each in turn. Stories of his son, Commodus, of the miracle of the rain that had defeated the Quadi, the wars that had finally broken the Marcomanni. Each man he spoke to stared back, blankly defiant, no sign of understanding his words. But at last, he found what he sought.

A rough-faced barbarian – a tall man, his hair touched with grey, deep-carved lines of laughter spreading from the corners of his eyes like cracks from ice. The Emperor spoke of his son to this man, and a bare flicker passed across his face.

'You speak our tongue, don't you?' the Emperor said.

No response to this.

'I ask you no betrayal of your people. But you shall speak with me.' The Emperor raised his hand, and one by one he pointed to the boys who stood and trembled in the ranks of the prisoners. 'Or I shall crucify them. You understand this word, crucify?' The barbarian made no answer, but he did not need to. The Emperor could see written upon his face that he understood well enough.

For there had been more than the sign of language on that face – there was also something of the father about him. Most of those people seemed blood-mad enough to forget all bonds, but there were those, it seemed, who yet possessed the weakness of love.

'You shall speak with me?'

The barbarian raised his head, and nodded in defeat.

'Good. We shall talk of many things. But first – tell me this. Tell me your name.'

8

It was no travelling camp that Kai and his companions made that night, but one of war.

In the days before, when they had thought the danger a little way behind, Kai had let something of the nomad's slackness drift into their night camps. What koumiss they had passed freely, the fires burned openly, and when a mounted sentry followed a path that struck his fancy or sounded out a song to keep him company on the watch, no reprimand was offered. And the talk about the fire had been of the past and future, not the bloody matter of the present, the work of sword and spear.

Now, with the smoking ruins of Iolas a day's ride behind them, the sentries moved in silent circles, and the others gathered close around the fire with their cloaks spread wide to hide the sight of the flame. The smoke they could do little about but hope it might not be seen in the night sky, that it would be mistaken for a twisting band of cloud or mist.

The talk around that fire was not wistful tales of the dead, nor the drifting talk of travellers gathered under open skies. The talk was of killing, of one grip of the lance compared to another, and the endless decisions of how the warband should be ordered. Which riders paired well with each other, where each man and woman should be placed in the formation, and, perhaps most important of all, the politics of their horses. For those horses had their own silent friendships, the bloodfeuds that could only be settled in death. Battles had turned in a moment when one horse could not abide the company of another and the line of the charge fell to pieces.

It was to that war fire that a figure came in from the dark. Kai took it for a sentry coming to be relieved, but he soon saw that it was a man from one of the outer fires, where the unproven and the unlucky were made to sleep. Gaevani, those sharp eyes of his glittering in the firelight, one arm restlessly kneading the other that had been wounded in the duel. The wound itself had mostly healed, Kai thought, but still the man picked at it, the ghost of an injury.

A few of the men shuffled reluctantly aside, but Gaevani made no move to sit. 'Oh, don't trouble yourselves,' he said. 'I don't come to share the fire. I come to speak with the captain.'

'Speak then.'

'Alone.'

Tamura stood on the far side of the fire. 'You have no need to speak with him,' she said. 'You take your place, and keep your mouth shut.'

'Oh, the foal grows fast, I see,' Gaevani answered. 'I'd let him decide that. He has reason to let me speak, don't you, captain? Or keep me quiet.'

A sharp moment of silence, the warband waiting, alive as any pack of strays to the slow ebb of authority, the sudden bite of mutiny.

Kai shrugged. 'Any of you may speak with me, while the moon is young and the fire strong.' He paused, and grinned. 'And while there's no man or woman in my blankets to keep me company.'

Laughter then, and while the sound danced in the air he stood and gestured for Gaevani to join him. Another shadow rose from the fire – Laimei, falling into step with them, and neither Kai nor Gaevani spoke a word to make her stay behind. They both knew that there was no denying her will, whether Kai were captain or not.

A difficult thing, to find privacy in the war camp. Always the sentries circling, and they could not go too far beyond the fire. And so they went to where the horses were tethered, keeping their own silent counsel. For Kai remembered an old proverb his father had once told him, that only a horse might be trusted with a secret.

'Speak then,' said Kai, once there were none but the horses who would hear them. 'Though I think I know what you wish to say.'

Gaevani did not hesitate. 'You should not still be captain.'

Kai hooked his thumbs in his sword belt. 'Yes. I *do* know your words already.'

'It was to be to Iolas, and no further.' He looked to Laimei. 'She knows it, too.'

'And there is no village left,' Kai said. 'Or should I hand my captaincy to the ashes?'

'Clever, aren't you? I suppose you speak all your oaths with that fancy tongue of yours. Swearing in riddles that you shall never have to keep.'

'You have an oath of your own to keep. Sworn not on a riddle, but a sword. Keep your silence. On your—'

'Yes, yes. On my oath.' Gaevani kicked at the frozen ground. When he looked up again, in the dark his eyes were two dark hollows, like the gaze of an eyeless corpse. 'I should have spoken the truth around the fire that first night,' he said. 'Before you swore me to silence.'

'Yes, you should have. But you did not.' A softer voice, then, such as Kai might have used to calm his daughter. 'Listen, Gaevani, I do not keep this for my vanity,' he said, as he tapped the captain's mark on his chest, the emblem of sword and circle. 'But so that they may have someone to follow.'

'There are others who can lead.'

'No, there are not. You are a shamed man to them. And the others are lost, no captain there amongst them.'

The other man tried to point, by instinct, with the arm that was wounded. He hissed with pain: 'They would follow her.'

In her silence, Kai had almost forgotten Laimei. She had stood with her arms crossed, almost still. Just a gentle rock back and forth on the heels, such as a confident wrestler will make before a bout begins.

'They would,' he said. And then to his sister: 'The captaincy is yours, if you want it. And if you can speak.'

She looked from one man to the other, gave a little

shrug, a little backhanded cut of one hand through the air. Then she folded her arms once more.

'When she speaks,' said Kai, 'I am your captain no more. When we find the others—'

'If we do.'

'If we do not, it shall not much matter who is captain or not, no?'

A pause. Then Gaevani said: 'Not much choice you give me, is there?'

'No.'

'It shames me to be led by you. The others would be shamed, too. If they knew of your father—'

There was someone else there, close by. All three of them knew it at once, with the touch of cold at the back of the neck, that ghostly feeling of being watched as the horses turned and muttered towards a shadow in the darkness. And when Kai called to that shadow, it was Tamura who stepped forward, the moonlight shining upon her pale face. How long she might have been there, Kai could not say. Nor how much she had heard.

'Forgive me, captain,' she said. 'One of the sentries thought she saw something. Maybe smoke from a fire, to the north and the east.'

'You did well to bring this to me,' said Kai. 'We shall head that way tomorrow. The gods offer us good hunting.' He hesitated. 'Gaevani, go back to the fire. Laimei, Tamura, you stay a moment longer.'

A muttering in the dark, and Gaevani was on his way, short, quick, furious strides that took him close past Laimei.

Too close, for there was a ringing slap as she cuffed the back of his head, hard enough that the horses tossed their manes and snorted at the sound. Gaevani turned, teeth shining and his fingers drifting towards his belt, but he checked himself – Laimei's hand was already on the blade at her side. Gaevani backed up, palms towards her, a sour smile on his face as he walked away.

When Kai looked to Tamura, even in the dark, she could only hold his gaze for a moment before her eyes went to the ground. 'You can move quietly,' said Kai. 'I shall have to remember that when I need a scout.'

'I was always the scout on the cattle raids,' Tamura said. 'Before the war.' She looked at her hands. 'I was never much use with a spear, but they found other uses for me.'

'You did not have the skill for the killing, or the heart for it?'

'Maybe a little of both. I have never been brave.' A head raised, then dropped once more, the slow fall of shame. 'I have never told anyone that before. Please do not tell the others.'

'I will not,' said Kai. For he knew all too well that the Sarmatians were not kind to those whose courage faltered. 'We have both heard secrets tonight,' he said. 'Or I suppose you have heard half of mine.'

'I did not mean to hear what I should not.'

'I know.'

He put his hand to her shoulder. 'I will tell you the other half soon, I promise. But not today. It is no story for the hunt, but for the fire at the end of the journey.'

She nodded and smiled shyly, like a lover trusted with a secret.

'Go back now,' Kai said. 'You ride at my side in the morning.'

And she was gone, hurrying away, leaving Kai alone with his sister.

They shared a silence for a time. Distant, the muttering from the campfire. Closer, the sound of the horses shifting and moving in their own unspoken counsel. And all about them, the calling of the wind rolling across the steppe.

'I was not lying to him,' Kai said at last, 'when I promised you the captaincy. When you can speak—'

A hiss interrupted him, a hand held up, palm towards him. He saw her swallow, her tongue dart out across dry lips. And then, she spoke.

'Can talk.' She winced – the words had forced her wounded mouth a touch too wide. 'Little. Gaevani. Spared him. Why?'

'Something Bahadur always said. That we would be the greatest people in the world, if only the five clans were united. I have seen enough of Sarmatians killing each other.' Kai looked down to his right hand, let the hand clench and relax as though it were winding around the hilt of a sword. 'You can speak. Enough to lead, if you want to. You never needed fine words for others to believe in you.'

'No. Soon. Not yet.'

'Why not?'

She cocked her head to the side, asked a question in silence.

Kai spoke again. 'Why not take this from me?'

She pointed at him. 'Fought. For me.'

'And you did the same for me.'

She rolled her eyes, gave a little hiss of irritation, and Kai had to catch himself before he smiled. He remembered that gesture, too, from a long time ago. An ache, low in his belly. For the feud between them had been so long, that he had almost forgotten how once they had spoken. In word and gesture and look, the private, secret language of brother and sister.

'Owed you,' she said. 'No more.'

He slipped a glove from his hand, tapped a bronze ring with his finger. 'Our father would be proud of you.'

At once, Kai knew he had misspoken. Her foot scraped across the thin snow as she shifted to a swordsman's stance, her head dropping low and her shoulders rolling forward.

'Me,' she said. 'Not you.'

'You are right. He would not be proud of me.'

Her mouth twitched and for a moment he thought that she might speak again. Wounding words, or words meant to kill, for she had that murderous light on her face that always came before rough talk or swordplay. But she did not speak – perhaps to wait for another time when she might wound him more deeply, and have others there to see the wounding.

She was away then, back into the darkness and then to the fire, her silhouette lit by the low flames for a moment before she took her place with the others.

Kai did not follow her, for he knew there would be no sleep for him. He made his way amongst the horses, his hands outstretched as though he were feeling his way through the woods in the dark. A few stamped and snorted when they found him in their midst, but soon they settled, there was the soft touch of a nose against his neck. He inhaled the sweet stink of horse, and felt the warmth they gave together, the strange heat of the herd that was stronger than any fire he had ever known, for it must have been long before men and women had first struck fire that the horses had kept themselves warm through the winter. Kai leaned back and wrapped his arm around the neck of the horse that stood silent behind him.

For a moment, holding that warmth close against him, he might have been holding Tomyris, remembering the way his daughter liked to press close against him, as if she could not believe him there except through touch. And as he looked on the shadows of men and women gathered about fire, a memory came of Arite, the gold and silver of her hair shining as she danced by the fire at a festival long forgotten.

Kai clutched the horse close, so that he could mistake it for itself and nothing else, and let the darkness take the memory from him. He could not let himself hope that Tomyris and Arite still lived.

He looked towards the east. For the sun, and the hunt that it would bring with it.

9

It was on the third day after they fled Iolas that Arite found it – the place where they would fight and die.

The edge of a half-frozen river, thin-sheened with ice, broken through and running sluggishly in places. Yet the ground would be soft enough to break the enemy charge, and drinking the fresh icy water might give them strength and courage. For some reason, in that moment, it seemed a terrible thing to die thirsty.

And so Arite called her ragged column to a halt, those women and children who had made it with her so far. They slid from their horses with exhausted gratitude, assuming that it would be another of the few rests they had made since they fled the village. Only Arite knew, for now, that they would not start again. That it was here that the Romans would catch them at last.

Arite had not even thought to live beyond the battle in the village. But the greyhairs had made their plan without speaking, pushing forward at the charge. Toothless, some weeping and trembling even as they took their place, others roaring with laughter, those that had long since given up any hope of a glorious death in battle and saw the chance

offered at the last. There were few young women who were
not glad to be free of the warband, but as they grew older,
and they saw the deaths that waited for them – the slow,
winding murder of disease, the bloody end many found in
childbirth – they felt something of that youthful longing
once more for the quickness of the spear.

One charge through, and Arite had called the retreat
knowing that not all would answer. That those who chose
would stay to die. She led them away, across the snow
and under the moon, and she looked back only twice. The
first time to see the glint of moonlight on silver hair, as
the women fought and died behind them. And the second
time, to see the fires burning on the horizon, as her home
vanished to the sky.

They had fled for two days, heading north into the
foothills of the Carpathians, hoping to lose their pursuers
there. Snatching sleep in the saddle where they could, resting
only in the deepest darkness when it was too dangerous to
ride, where a horse might lame itself on bad ground. And
always, behind them, the Romans drew closer. They knew
that if they had left the children behind perhaps they might
have outpaced their pursuers, but that was no choice at all.
Running with little hope of escape or rescue, only to buy a
few more days of precious life for those who rode behind
her. For the children to take in a little more life, for the
mothers to make their last whispers of love.

And so, on that third day, without telling any of the
others, she found herself looking for a good place for them
to die. The river seemed a fitting place, for that was where
the others lay, the men and the women of the warband,

upon the Danu. And perhaps a soul might travel the waterways – she had heard tales told of that, had seen herself the way that grieving men and women were always drawn to the edge of the water. When they died there, they would only have to wait for the ice to thaw and their souls would flow towards their loved ones.

And when she called for her company to rest beside the river and did not call for them to ride on again soon after, it did not take the others long to understand. A little weeping, but most were too tired now to care, and there were a few that almost seemed relieved. They kissed their children, tested the balance of what few weapons they carried. They waited for the Romans to come.

It did not take long, for their pursuers had not been far behind. Wearing heavy furs and glittering with iron, grinning at one other to see their prey finally cornered. Many of the Romans were double mounted, for the greyhairs had aimed their spears true back at the village. But there were many Sarmatian horses who bore a second rider, too. Children mounted before their mothers, and in most of their hands there was the glitter of a weapon – a dagger of flint, some wooden toy to act as a club.

It was bad ground for cavalry that lay between them, soft and uneven. It was likely that whoever tried to charge first would be undone by it. And so they stood facing each other, for who knew how long, to see whose nerve might break first.

And the Sarmatians were calling then – every insult and curse they could think of, for perhaps if they could draw an unruly charge there might be a chance against the odds. But just as it seemed that the Romans were about to scatter forward, a voice called them back into line, a captain shouting them into silence.

Arite saw that the captain wore the fine armour of one of their leaders, a crested helm that hid most of his face. At that distance she could see his reddish-gold beard – at least they would not be killed by a beardless man. And then the Roman was looking amongst the Sarmatians, and Arite thought that there was a hesitance there that could not be from the odds of battle. His men were calling for the charge, yet he rode up and down the line, irresolute. His eyes found hers, and something must have given away her leadership. For he offered her the last thing she had expected. A warrior's salute, one captain to another, sword raised high.

It was over, then, the last hope taken. There would be no mistakes from the Romans. And so Arite, her voice cracking, called to the others to make ready. They had no horn to sound the charge – her word alone would call them to fight and die.

No reason to delay, to wait any longer for what little courage the Sarmatians had left to unravel. Let them die cleanly, at least. And yet she found herself hesitating. Some instinct or omen telling her to hold on, to wait.

The wind blew hard, whipping up from the south. It carried something with it – a rattle of armour, the clatter of horses' hooves, the flap of a banner. Sounds from beyond the Romans. And still, Arite could not let herself believe, even when she saw the enemy line shiver and twist, for it seemed that they heard it, too.

She could not believe even when, from behind a hill line, she saw them riding in. Another band of Sarmatians – ghosts, she thought at first, come to salute the battle courage of the women and escort them to the Otherlands.

But a horn was calling, lances rattling, and war cries filled the air. And it was only then that she believed that these were warriors of flesh and blood, come against all odds. That still, there was a chance they would live.

A toss of his horse's head, a cold touch at the heart – that was all the warning Kai had, before they turned about a fold in the land to find the Romans before them at the banks of a frozen river.

Only a moment to see it, to take it all in, but there was no need for any more than that. Two ragged lines, a bowshot apart from each other. The Roman raiders and the Sarmatian women, ready to make their last stand. It must have been a pitiful chase of exhausted, overburdened horses pursuing more of the same. Kai's warband was little better – sleepless, half-starved, men and horses lamed with injury. But they had the killing hunger now, a strength beyond what seems possible.

Kai gave no word of command. His order was of thought, and it was answered in kind. For they were as one mind then, in the way that only those steeped in hunting and killing may know. The horses sprang forward, and their riders sounded the war song one last time, and far beyond them the Sarmatian women were charging and giving their own wordless cry of revenge.

Over the roar of the hooves and the chanting of the riders he could not hear the call of Roman horns, but he could see the man at their centre, their captain like some great god of iron in his cuirass and tall helm. Kai could see the cords on that man's neck standing out as he screamed his orders.

Once more, the sense of falling across the land. Then the rushing crash, the awful screaming that only comes when cavalry charge against cavalry. As if the horses found it a blasphemy to kill their own, and cried out against the crime.

Kai was lost in the press for a moment – a horse rearing before him, an enemy past in the blink of an eye, the sudden pressure and the crack of an unseen blade glancing from his armour. And the hot smell of blood that filled the air, as men and horses began to die around him, the scrabble of hooves sliding upon blood and ice.

Everywhere Kai looked he saw Romans staggering, ripped off their steeds, surrounded. There were men mobbed by three or four riders at a time and hacked from their horses without giving a blow in answer. Kai saw one dragged off his horse, a lasso about his throat, disappearing beneath the kicking feet of the mob. For the Sarmatians had the numbers, the scouts and raiders of Rome were no match for them. Already it was becoming a slaughter.

The Roman captain – Kai could see him, deep within the mob. His helm had been struck off, the pale skin sheened with sweat. Their eyes met through the swirling mob, and in that moment they knew each other.

The duty of the captain to face his counterpart, a hunt

that all on the field conspired towards, a parting of the bloody water to bring the two of them together. Kai knew himself as no fine swordsman and he had an unfamiliar mount beneath him, but he trusted in the weight of the horse, and he trusted in fate. The hungry gods had taken much from the Sarmatians, but they always offered recompense for what they took, a bounty paid in blood.

A space cleared. No time to think, only to strike heels to flanks and send the horse forward. The Roman was half turned away when the passage opened – he turned his horse back with an expert snap of the wrist, but he started too late. Kai had the angle, and he had the weight, a killing solved as purely as a riddle.

But something was wrong. The world was struck grey, bleached of colour like bones washed by the sea. Kai's jaw hung slack, yet there seemed to be no air for him to breathe, a man drowning on dry land. Madness to turn aside, yet still he bore into his horse's flanks with his knees and pulled the reins away, and the horse felt that madness and fear as though it were its own. Even over the din of battle, he could hear it screaming. And he could see the Roman looming large, close enough for Kai to see the surprise on his face. Almost a kind of regret at seeing an opponent throw away his life, even as the Roman stirred the horse forward and raised the long cavalry sword for the killing cut.

All was still. Many had been the times when Kai had felt the closeness of death, that feeling like being submerged in cold deep water. The duel with Gaevani, the battle on the ice, the endless cattle raids and bloodfeuds that had come before. Always, he had met the moment well. Always, he had remembered to be brave, but not now. He could only turn his head away, the way that cattle marked for death seem to know even when their killer stands out of sight, looking away from the blade about to fall.

There was no cold touch to his neck, no sudden numbness of hand and foot, nor the sudden silence or any other feeling that came with a terrible wound. There was only, somewhere close, a scream of man and horse.

The Roman slipping from the saddle, the red blooming from his side like the breaking of ice in a spring thaw. He pitched over the neck of the horse, arms embracing it for a moment before he tumbled to the earth, dragged by his horse until the reins slipped from unfeeling fingers. The horse skipped and turned and danced and kicked, the smell of blood in its nostrils, seeming to feel the wound of the rider itself.

Beyond the frightened horse and dying rider, he saw which of his people had struck. No war cry given, no curse or chant had he heard. For it was Laimei, a broken spear in her hand, who sat astride her horse. Utterly still, as though she could not quite believe herself what she had done.

10

For Arite, once the battle was over, it was as though she had woken from a trance. Her throat hoarse from shouting orders she could not remember giving, her spear marked with the blood of a man she could not remember killing.

Tomyris was still on the saddle in front of her, and she clutched the child to her. For a moment there was nothing but that warmth and closeness, the joy in living that seems to speak only through touch.

Then she remembered the others – a jolt to the heart, as she looked upon the warband who had come to their rescue. On their tamgas and banners they bore the marks of wolves and serpents, but no mark of the dragon, no sign of her people. All about her riders pulling their helms from their heads, wisps of steam rising from skin daubed with sweat, but no familiar faces that she could see.

Then a roar from nearby, and the gallop of hooves, and a terrible hope stirring. For the figure who rode towards them bore the mark of the River Dragon on his helm, and in the aftermath of the battle fever, she could almost believe that it was Bahadur. So many times before, he had ridden home to her like that. And as the rider was pulling the helm from his head, for a single, cruel moment, Arite still saw her husband's face there.

But it was Kai, plucking Tomyris from the saddle as he rode past and holding her to him, burying his face into her neck, seeking the sweet scent that always seemed to hold there. Arite sat tall in the saddle, looking amongst the others for more marks of the dragon, for the two faces she wished to see above all others. But she could not see them.

From close by, Arite heard Tomyris speak. 'Is the Cruel Spear here?'

'She is,' Kai answered. 'But do not trouble her now. She is in a foul mood.'

'You always say that, but she never is. Not with me. Can I go to her?'

Arite looked to Kai, asking a silent question with her eyes. And it seemed he understood, for he wet his lips with his tongue, and said to his daughter: 'Go then, Tomyris. Do not approach her horse on his blind side.' And they were alone together, as alone as they could be. She waited for him to speak.

So many tales that Kai could have told her – that he had been separated from Bahadur, that he did not know her husband's fate. That Bahadur lay wounded but safe nearby, waiting for her to ride to his side. The silence spoke of only one thing.

At last, she said: 'Have you told a story of Bahadur, around the fire?'

He nodded slowly. 'I have.'

She could not have thought that she could feel so calm. 'And have you spoken a story of my son as well?' she said.

A pause – a cruel pause, for it brought hope with it. Then he said: 'I knew no stories to tell of him.'

'No,' Arite answered. 'He had not earned them yet.'

The pain – swift and sharp, the wound bursting open at last. The world swung upwards, her face against the horse's mane, wet hair pressed against her cheeks. Thoughts and sensations flowed through her – her son's little hand encircled by her palm, her husband singing softly beside the embers of a fire, the golden light of the sunset falling upon Bahadur and Chodona as they rode home with the herd. All of the things that could not be and would never be again, like a madness or a fever dream that she could not escape from.

Then a touch at her side, words spoken that she could not hear at first. She opened her eyes and saw Kai there at her side, below her. He had dismounted, clasped one of her hands in both of his.

He said the words once more, and now she could hear them. 'Will you forgive me?' he said.

'For what?'

'He came back to try to save me. Bahadur. In the battle. He came back for me, and they cut him down. He could have got away. Can you forgive me?'

'I forgive you. Of course, I forgive you.' Other words were on her lips as well – *He loved you, Kai.* And they were true words – how many times had Bahadur said that to her, as they watched Kai herd the cattle or practise with the lance upon the plains, whisper it to her when Kai lay asleep by the fire. Bahadur would watch him, the wild smile on his lips, and speak those words over and over again. She should have said them then, but found she could not. For that was the love that had killed her husband.

'Where do we go now?' she said.

His eyes dimmed in pain, and she felt the guilty, quickening touch of revenge. 'The Romans must be raiding all across the border. We shall go east, to the old winter campgrounds. Those of our people who are left will flee there, I am sure of it. And the Red Crests will not follow us that far.' A hand tightening around hers for a moment, and then releasing it. 'I must go and check upon the wounded. Gather your riders at the edge of the river – we cannot stay here for long.'

'My riders?'

He grinned at her, boyish once more. 'You are still their captain, are you not?'

'Yes, I am,' she said, and found there was still a weary pride in that.

As Kai moved across the battlefield, he might have thought it a festival at first. For all about him were open-toothed smiles, the shy and careful meetings of lovers who had not thought to see one another again. It could have been one of the great conferences of the shepherds were it not for the butcher's work going on amidst the fallen – wounded Romans having their throats opened onto the snow, and elsewhere men and women swarming over the fallen horses, cutting strips of meat from them and drinking the quick-cooling blood. For they had no food left save for those horses, and many had not eaten in days.

Elsewhere, Kai could see the children being guided amongst the corpses, for it would never do to pass up a chance to pass on the lessons of war. Most of those children were pale, and he saw one or two pulling up handfuls of snow to wipe the vomit from their lips. But all watched as they were instructed, their lips moving as they repeated back what they were taught.

As he moved through the crowd, he made the captain's count, noting the injured and the dead. There were many wounded, bearing those cuts across arm and cheek that were the mark of a fight between cavalry. Only one of his riders dead that he could see, an unlucky boy with his leg laid open at a gap in the armour, that little place in the thigh that kills a man in moments. His face wearing an expression of utter surprise, as the dead often did. Nearby, his horse circled, one of its flanks painted with blood below the saddle, kicking madly at the air.

The women of the village, unarmoured, had fared worse. Four at least lay dead in the snow, and another lay curled up around some mortal hurt, surrounded by friends who silently watched and waited for her to die. And he could see others gathered around the small still body of a child that seemed to be sleeping on the ice, the face painted red with blood and warped by its wound. Those that watched over her were silent, for now, though he knew the keening would begin soon enough.

Something else he saw there – a gathering circle at the heart of the battlefield, the men and women all unmounted. Only for ritual or duel would such a thing be seen amongst the Sarmatians, and he did not know what he expected to find there, as he pushed forward through the crowd. Two of the hot-headed fighters quarrelling over some fine piece of war gear, or someone struck into a trance by the touch of a god and mouthing prophecies for all to hear. Instead, at the centre of the circle, he saw the Roman captain lying on the ground, his hair and beard a bright reddish gold, his skin grey. And kneeling beside him was Laimei.

He thought at first she meant to take his scalp as a memento of the kill, strip his armour and claim it as her own, though that would not explain why the crowd had gathered so close. But then he saw her hands move, pressing cloth and rag to the wound at his side, or slapping at his face to try to wake him. For he saw now the slightest rise and fall of the chest, the tremor at the lips that spoke of a man still living.

He sidestepped around that circle without breaking it, careful as a duellist, until he stood beside Gaevani. The man stood with his arms folded – his axe daubed in red, but not a fresh mark on him.

'What is this?' said Kai.

'Wish that I could say. The Roman will make a fine kill for her.' Gaevani whistled through his teeth, and threw up his hands. 'Trouble is, she does not seem to want to let him die.'

At this, she raised her head and snarled at them, gasping with pain a moment later. She returned to the dying man, her hands moving uncertainly. They went to the oozing wound, to the man's forehead as though she sought to check for fever, aping the gestures she had seen others make over the sick and wounded many times before. On a horse, with spear or sword in her hand, every motion was precise, considered. It had been a long time since Kai had seen her so utterly at a loss.

Gaevani snorted. 'She never learned the healer's art, did she?'

'No,' Kai answered. 'She never had any use for it.' He risked a few steps forward until he was at her side. Just for a moment, looking on the Roman crest, he felt a ghost of that feeling he had felt before – a flash of white at the edge of his vision, a burning in his throat like swallowed fire.

'Sister,' he said, 'it is no time to be taking prisoners. We cannot feed those we have with us. And this man cannot ride even if he lives. Finish him, and let it be done.'

She inclined her head at him, and levelled a finger at the wounded man on the ground. He remembered the Roman at his side, his horse shying away, the sword rising before him. Her spear snatching the Roman off the horse at the very last moment. He remembered that fear, too, that had come before, and wondered how much she had seen. What she might speak of to the others.

As he knelt beside the Roman, at first he thought it hopeless. A spear to the belly, there could be no answer to that, save for the quick mercy of the knife. But as he knelt down and inhaled deeply, there was not the sharp, acrid smell that usually bloomed from a belly wound like the scent of a rotting flower. He parted the cloth and tested with his fingers – torn flesh and oozing blood, but nothing more than that from the shallow wound. He looked to where the spear lay, daubed with gore. But there was no head upon the spear, just a ragged edge of wood.

'Broken when you struck him?' he asked. She nodded.

Kai put his mouth to the wound – finding the splinters with his tongue, working them loose and pulling them out, spitting them upon the snow. When he had finished, his beard was daubed with blood, as though he had partaken of the old rituals of the Scythians, the eaters of the dead. But perhaps the wound would not fester.

He searched for other wounds, and found only one on the man's forehead, where a black bruise bloomed. Struck on stone or hoof when he fell, no doubt, and Kai did not like the look of it. He had seen men bear such a bruise with laughter, only to be slowly lulled to a sleep from which there was no waking. But he packed snow about the scalp, as his father had taught him long before, and hoped that the man would wake.

'Keep him warm,' said Kai. 'Feed him blood, and milk if there's any left. A little koumiss, but not too much.'

'He shall live?' she asked.

'I do not know. Perhaps.' And at that she waved him away dismissively, for it seemed she had no more use for him.

As Kai walked away, there was a figure strolling at his side – Gaevani again. The man had a careless air about him, as though drunk on the battle gone well.

'How did the Roman taste?' Gaevani asked.

'Of good wine. And good living.'

A laugh. 'Do not tell the others. They shall devour him.' He looked back, cocked his head to the side. 'Think he shall live?'

'If he does not take the wound fever, or the cold does not finish him, he may live. Or he may starve. I do not know that we have the food to feed him.'

'I think she will make sure of that, don't you?'

Kai looked back, and already she was at work. A silent, baleful captain, stalking through the camp and making her wishes known through gesture and wordless snarling.

'Most woman are glad enough to make their third kill,' said Gaevani, 'and find themselves free of the warband.'

'Most women are not my sister.'

'Does she really think that any would take her spear from her at a time such as this? She must have killed many more than three already, no matter what she says.'

'I do not think she wishes to take that chance.'

A pause. Then: 'What happened out there, captain?'

'What do you mean?' said Kai.

'Why did you turn away from the Roman? Thought you had him.'

Kai hesitated. 'You were watching?'

'Always a good thing to keep an eye on the captain in a scrap like that.'

'It was my horse. We do not know each other well enough yet.'

'I see.'

'You do see, don't you? Careful not to see too much, Gaevani.'

The man tapped one finger to the side of his head in

a kind of mocking salute. Then he was gone, back to the looting of the dead, for he had no friends or lovers to greet.

Kai watched him go – the cold feeling of shame winding around his guts, like a snake wrapping about a hare.

11

They rode east across the ice and snow – no longer a pack of strays, the remnants of an army, or an errant warband. They were the beginnings of a clan now, men and women and children riding together, driving a little herd before them. For now, at least, they had more horses than they had riders.

Arite still captained the survivors of Iolas, while Kai's warriors rode in a second column a respectful distance away. Only the children moved between them – Tomyris delighting in the sight of her father as a captain, the other children speaking with a fearless innocence to those warriors from distant clans. But otherwise, they rode apart.

Arite wondered, as they rode, why Kai had insisted it would be so – a strange, shy courtesy, that he would not challenge her leadership. Or perhaps he knew that feeling of madness that dances against the mind like a knife, that only duty to others could keep away. For every warband was filled with the dead eyed, the half mad. Those who had lost too much, who cared nothing for their own lives, would throw themselves upon the spears of the enemy the first chance that they got. But give them the leadership and those to protect, and they would fight for their lives in earnest. A captain's mark could save many lives, when it was well placed – more often than not, it was the captain themselves who was the first to be saved.

They had no map to guide them across the open steppe, and so they pursued the ghosts of those who had come before them, the exiles and nomads who had fled from the frozen Danu and crawled their way to the north and east. They chased those who had come before the way a hunter may follow the deer when all tracks are lost, by thinking as it must think and seeing the land as it must have seen it, removing all possibilities but one.

Some of their choices were guided by necessity. They forded rivers in the only places where it was safe to do so, or camped in the one place on a plain where they might find shelter from a killing wind. Other choices were more artfully made. Given the choice between two ways across the steppe, they chose the one that the winter sun caught best, for they knew that those they followed would be seeking that path themselves, answering the longing that every nomad felt for the beautiful journey.

And as they went, they found clues of others who had passed before them. Black firepits where the children ran to blow in the hope of lighting embers. Circles in snow left by round tents, furrowed tracks left by warhorses. And, from time to time, the pile of snow and stone that might mark a grave. They left some of those markers behind themselves, for the wound fever killed some, and others were taken by hunger, or the cold, or loss of will as they lay down to die.

That was how they made their way to the north and

east. The way rivulets join streams, combine into rivers, and at last flow into the sea. Each day much like another, and Arite found herself riding in a kind of wordless trance, a merciful forgetting. Only one moment that she could remember clearly, afterwards. Their third or fourth day in the saddle, when a rider broke away from Kai's warband and rode towards Arite.

No need to guess at who it was, for there was a second shape on that horse, the Roman slung across the back like a deer from the hunt, and as Laimei rode beside Arite, their horses matched their steps. No words at first, just the wordless commune of the nomad. But at last, Laimei did speak: 'You lead them well.'

'I do. So did Kai, to bring you this far.'

Some kind of growling chuckle made its way from that cracked jaw. 'Perhaps,' Laimei allowed.

'I thought that you could not speak. Kai said so.'

Laimei sniffed, and looked scornfully back on Kai's company. 'None worth speaking to there.'

Arite made a half bow from the saddle in answer. Again, the growling laugh answered her.

'Always wished I got to ride beside you, back when you fought,' Laimei said. 'Heard that you were good with a spear.'

'Yes,' Arite said simply. For though she remembered little of the battles she had fought in or the three men she had killed to free herself from the warband, she remembered that feeling of courage – a kind of stillness, it seemed to her. She bore the scars on her cheeks as marks of bravery, for it was cowards or the careless who were wounded in the back. And she had been told by others that she had killed well.

'You miss the fighting?'

'No,' said Arite, for that had been true for as long as she could remember. Then that pain again, the hot sharp touch at the heart, as she remembered how little was left to her. 'At least, I did not. Now I do not know.'

A pause. Then, hesitantly: 'Good fighter. Bahadur.'

'He was. Not as good as you.'

'No. But who is?'

A point of light at the front of the column drew Arite's eye – the bright winter sun playing off Kai's armour. She had always liked to tease Bahadur, to tell her husband he was a fool for letting a handsome man like Kai into his tent, and there was a shadow lifted from Kai now that he wore the captain's mark. About the fires at night, she had heard the whispers spoken by the men and women that he led. That he was touched by one god or another, a man who had risen from the dead on the battlefield to lead them to safety. That he was a man who could not be killed. She had heard those whispers, and she knew they would not last.

'The others do not know, do they?' she said. 'About Kai, and his father. Your father.'

'No.'

'Will you tell them?'

A pause. 'No.'

'Will you make peace with him?'

Another snort. 'No.' Laimei tossed her head, like a dog seeking to calm itself. She stirred her horse forward, but turned back as she went to speak once more. 'Watch him,' she said.

'I will. I understand.'

'No. You don't. He does not matter.' Laimei looked at her brother, and Arite wished that the Cruel Spear was wearing her helm. Then she would not have to see the way she stared at Kai. 'For Tomyris,' said Laimei. 'Watch him for her sake. She loves him, and so he must live. For now, at least.'

She liked to come at him unexpectedly. From behind a horse, her body hidden by its legs. From the shadows beyond the campfire, always waiting for the time when the wine and koumiss had flowed freely, when his head began to droop with drink and tiredness.

Then Kai's daughter would move from the shadows and pounce on him like a mountain cat, arms wrapping up close about his leg or waist. Or, if she caught him sitting, she would loop her arms about his neck and hook her heels about his body like a wrestler. She was already practising the warrior's art, the way all the children fought and brawled with one another. Or perhaps it was that she had grown tired of seeing him ride away all those years, seeing him choose when he would come back to her. She would fight on her own terms now, it seemed. She was the one to choose.

And always he would roar until she shrieked, stumble and stagger like an ogre lamed by the quick sword of a hero. He would prise her loose and spin her in his arms, but always be sure to carry her away to some quiet corner of a tent, a warm place beside the fire where they might talk softly and freely. For always he knew that she only hunted him when she wished to speak. Often, it was the child's talk – of hunger, of stories, questions of the past. But sometimes they spoke of other things.

Perhaps it was the sixth night they had travelled together, curled up close to the fire and staring at one another in silence. For he felt no need to talk – for him, it was enough to see her, to hold her close, to know that as long as she lived his life held purpose and meaning. But at last, she spoke.

'The other children talk,' she said.

'Of what?'

'Of you.'

'I am sure they do.' He hesitated, feeling once more the catch about the heart that always comes with shame. 'Are they cruel to you, my love?'

'No. Only one or two.' She made to speak again, then turned her head away, scratched restlessly at her scalp.

'Do not pick like that little one, you shall hurt yourself.' His hands fell to her hair, shifting and parting and stroking, as he might have calmed a frightened horse after a storm upon the plains. 'They are cruel to me, though?' he said.

She nodded, but did not answer.

'Why do they not speak more loudly then, and tell the others?'

'They are frightened of *her*.'

'As well they should be.' Kai chuckled to himself. 'But you are not, are you?'

'I am not a fool, like them. She would not hurt me.'

'No, she would not. She loves you, as I do.'

'Would she hurt you?'

He scratched at his beard, and thought it over. 'I do not know. If she thought that I had earned it.' He shrugged. 'She saved my life. So it seems she does not wish me harmed.'

'She will teach me to fight. She promised me that.'

'Not for a long time, child.'

A forbidden and shameful thought came to him then. If it were the end of their people, she would not have to fight. She might remain a true child, untouched by the killing, all the way up to the end. For that was the sweet sadness of the Sarmatian mother and father – to raise every child a killer.

She nestled closer to him, a lazy smile on her face.

'What is it that makes you smile, my love?'

'I like my father being a captain,' she said, as haughty as any princess of the plains.

He laughed then, but there was a catch in his throat as he did.

'When will we find the others?' she asked.

'Soon.'

'What shall we do then?'

'I do not know,' he said, even as his fingers touched the captain's mark on his armour, and felt a piece of it flake away under his nails.

It was on the next day that Kai saw it – once more, the smoke rising into the air. But it was not the black smoke of a burning village that rose on the horizon, nor the sign of some little band of travellers, but many twisting strands of grey smoke all joining together. Soon they could smell the scent of cooking fires, the rich tang of hemp. All the signs of a great gathering ahead of them, such as was rarely seen upon the plains.

The songs were echoing freely amongst his company, then. Not the kind of music that had so often been their trail companion – the sweet soft death songs of those in a battle against hopeless odds, the keening chords of those mourning for the lost. He listened to them sing out the bawdy tunes of drink and lovemaking, the hard proud stories of long-lost heroes. For though they rode in the twilight of their people, they knew too what those fires meant, that the night had not yet fallen fully.

And when the ground turned once more, and they saw what lay before them, a great, ragged cheer broke from both companies of riders. For it was not the ordered camp of the Romans, nor one of the distant townships of which their traders spoke, where the Naristi and the Buri gathered to trade wine and silk for horses. It was a careless and wandering encampment of the Sarmatians, the horses and caravans scattered across the plain and gathered by the banks of a river, the great mountains looming high above them and guarding against the killing wind. The old winter campground of their people – abandoned long before when their grandmothers had sought to build villages and learn the art of the plough, but alive once more, out there upon the horizon. For it seemed that all the tribes had been driven eastwards by the Romans, leaving their burned homes behind them.

An order and discipline was there, but paired with the art of the steppe, like a twisted tree that has curved its shape against the wind. A greater gathering than any that had been seen for generations, for already at a distance they could see the different banners that marked the people of all Five Clans – it seemed that most of their people had fled to this place on the eastern borderlands. Old barrows ringed the camp, burial grounds from the old times, from when their first people had crossed the mountains and come to this place from Scythia and the great Sea of Grass that lay beyond. They would have the counsel of the dead as well as the living, to decide what must be done next, and how their people might survive.

Kai's warband came closer, and there were cries of greeting rising to meet them. Hot words, too, when one rider picked out another with whom they had a quarrel, one whom they thought already dead and the feud dead with them. But Kai thought that it was with a kind of grateful hate that they called their challenges and insults, for even a feud brought a kind of familiar comfort.

Yet there was something else rising, as they rode into the camp, when the Sarmatians saw that it was Kai who was the captain, the one who led them. For there were survivors of his clan there, many who bore the banner and tamga of the River Dragon. Others too, not of his clan, who knew the stories. And all about them, Kai heard them begin to whisper.

He knew his riders were confused. For they rode in

carrying iron and a prisoner, they did not bear the haunted, broken down look of those who have been cut to pieces on the trail, as so many others around them did. Of all the warriors who rode into that camp, they alone rode with a victory to call their own, the fresh scalps on their saddles to show for it. They could not understand the whispers, the mutterings of shame.

He knew they were looking to him for an answer, but he gave them no response, could not bring himself to meet their gaze. He sat low in his saddle, a sour smile upon his face.

They reached the heart of the camp, the great chieftain's fire where the high tents were pitched. Kai flung up his hand, and for the last time there was the pleasure of command, to hear that company, doubting as they were, halt at his signal.

Kai trotted his horse forward, bowed low in the saddle to the five men who sat there. The great leaders of the clans, richly dressed in iron and gold. Zanticus of the Wolves of the Steppe, bearing a cape of scalps of those he had killed. Pidos of the Shining Company, half-handed and part-scalped from a bloody feud many years before. Sason and Aldis, who had led their clans against each other in an endless war dance for the better part of a decade, but who had sought a brotherhood as soon as the Romans came. Banadaspus of the River Dragon, his own chieftain.

Kai dismounted, pulled his sword, plunged it into the ground before them. He took the banner from the side of his saddle, and he cast that down as well.

'I have brought you riders for the warband,' said Kai. 'I have brought you the women and children who will keep the fire. But I am no man to be their captain, and so I gift my company to you.'

The Five Chieftains watched him, and did not speak. Most of them gave no sign of recognition that he had spoken at all. Only Banadaspus gave any more than that, his head dipping a little nod that was like the press of a blade against Kai's heart. A gesture of acknowledgement, not of forgiveness.

Kai mounted once more, and addressed the company that gathered behind him. 'I have delivered you here, as I promised. And now, I am your captain no longer.'

Silence from the company. Until one voice spoke, and simply asked: 'Why?'

He should have told them then. They had earned that right to the truth. But, at the last, he found he did not have the heart for it.

'Take a place at the fire,' he said. 'Speak to the others, and they shall tell you soon enough.' He nodded to Gaevani. 'Or ask him. He shall tell you the tale, I am sure. For I release you from any bond of silence, your oath of service, and you may do what you will.'

Gaevani spat upon the ground. 'They shall hear the story, I am sure. But it will not be from me.'

Kai looked at him for a moment longer, irresolute. Then he turned away, found Tamura amongst the warband. 'Now you shall have the other half of that story,' he said. 'I have kept my promise.'

A kind of bitter lightness then, as he began to ride away

alone, save for the child that clung to the peak of the saddle in front of him. Where there is no prize to claim, where victory, such as it is, brings loss with it, there is only the weary pride of having done what others could not.

Then, from behind a calling of his name.

It was Laimei who spoke – a roll and turn in her voice that had not been there before, for her jaw had healed crooked in a way that marked her speech. But she called out high and clear, and if there was any pain in the speaking she gave no sign of it. She rode forward, the Roman captive riding beside her, for he had been allowed to ride upright as his strength returned.

They looked at each other in silence for a time – her grey eyes that gave nothing away, the hope on his face there for any child to see. For it was the time for forgiveness, if ever it was to come. What dishonour he had earned in her eyes, perhaps having brought them back with iron on their backs would wipe it out. For this time, he had kept his promise.

She waved the Roman captive forward, as she might have invited a horse to drink from a river. When he did not move, she barked a curse and slapped his mount on the flank with a gauntleted hand. The warhorse danced and bucked forward – perhaps it could smell the Roman on its back, and knew he did not belong. But the captive kept his saddle well and brought the horse to Kai's side.

Laimei spoke again. 'Take him,' she said. 'I have no more need of him.'

'Is that your command?'

'I suppose I am your captain now?' A crooked smile upon

her face. 'Then yes. It is my command. A last command, for you have no place in the warband now.'

Kai and Tomyris, their prisoner in tow, made their way to a tented wagon, the nomad's wandering home. Inside to the comforting darkness, all about him the smell of sweat and leather, the hard wood of the base of the wagon beneath, the softness of the felt against his fingers when he reached out to touch the folds of the tent. Some strange family they made – the shamed man, his daughter, their prisoner.

Above all, there was the longing for sleep – Kai could not remember ever having been so tired, not even in the great weariness that comes after hard battle. But he knew that there was something that he must do first.

He shook the armour from his back, a dead and weighted second skin. Little light came through the thick fabric of the tent, and he found what he sought more through touch than sight. Fingers hunting over horn and iron, until he found the captain's mark upon the cuirass.

A scraping, rasping sound filled the air, the soft echo of a battle sound. The familiar scratch of metal against metal, as Kai cut against the mark with his knife – clumsy strokes with no force behind them, for he had no heart for the task. The knife danced and skittered, and at any moment it seemed that it would skip from the metal and plunge into his hand.

A strange voice in the tent, speaking with a heavy accent: 'I will do. Let me.'

Kai started at the sound – it was the Roman who had spoken. The fair-haired man reached forward, a beckoning hand. 'I will do,' he said again, for it seemed he knew a little of their language.

Kai laid the armour gently on the ground, the knife on top. He put his head to his hands so he would need to see no more.

He heard a snapping of fingers, a barked command – Tomyris, ordering the prisoner to work. A moment later, that scrape of metal once more. Firm and steady as the Roman patiently, carefully, began to cut away that hero's mark.

The hour was late in Aquincum. Here and there upon the walls of the fort one could see a sentry half asleep, the head nodding and rising, nodding and rising, as regular as the turning of a water wheel. But though most of the Romans slumbered, the Emperor did not. And neither did the Sarmatian that he spoke with, the one picked out from the prisoners.

The barbarian wore the Roman garb now, at the Emperor's insistence. One might have mistaken him, at a distance, for some friend or consort, if it were not for the glint of iron at his ankles, the long braided hair and the tattoos upon his cheeks.

Slaves entered, bearing wine, and the barbarian held up his cup eagerly, spilling the red liquid with a trembling hand. When first he was brought to these chambers, he had refused to drink. They always did, the Emperor found. They feared poison or some spell cast over the wine. Or they refused from pride, wanting no luxury or charity from their captors. But always, at last, they broke. He could see the sadness come over them – the blankness in the eyes like dusty glass beads. The knowledge that they would never be free again. And so, if that was to be their life, and the only pleasure left to them the call of the wine, then why not drink?

On previous nights, they had spoken of many things.

The Emperor asked no secrets of war of him, no questions of numbers or generals or strategy, for no matter how deep into the cups the barbarian fell, always he remained guarded, and what he thought of as secrets he would not give out (though, as the Emperor well knew, torture made all men speak eventually). But of the world of the plains, the life of horse and spear, the old songs and stories of heroes and gods and monsters – of these things, the barbarian might speak. And as the Sarmatian told of the life that he had lost, he did not seem to notice the Emperor's lips were moving, silently repeating the words to himself. And later, when the barbarian was taken away or had fallen into a deep drunken stupor, the Emperor would scratch the words onto wax. Like a sculptor carving at marble, one patient stroke of the chisel at a time, until at last his vision of the Sarmatians was complete.

On that night, the fires were burning low, the air thick with the stink of wine, when at last the Emperor asked this question: 'What would you have me do with your people?'

The barbarian's head, lolling from the lateness of the hour and the weight of the wine, snapped upwards. For he could feel the danger, the way that the man who is watched by the wolf can feel the animal's eyes upon his neck, even if he cannot see it amidst the trees.

The Emperor put his cup of wine down. He leaned forward, and steepled his hands together. 'Once I have defeated them – and I shall, you must believe that – what is to be the fate of your people?'

The Sarmatian was silent for a time. Then: 'Why ask me?'

'*Why not you? You are as good as any to decide. You are intelligent – for a barbarian at least. Old enough to know your people, and to know yourself.*' A dry chuckle. '*I would not ask a young man such a thing. For they know nothing at all.*'

'*Let them go free,*' the barbarian said at once, though he might as well have asked the Emperor to pluck the moon from the sky.

'*That I cannot allow. They have shamed Rome. I shall have barbarians raiding on every border, and half of my provinces in open rebellion. You have come once too many times over the Danubius. It shall not happen again.*'

'*Then what are the choices?*'

The Emperor thought for a time. Then he spoke, his tone as simple and matter-of-fact as a tutor describing a principle of grammar. '*There are two that I see. One is that I shall put them all in chains, to serve Rome.*'

'*Warriors?*'

'*No. A few shall be gladiators. But I will not have your cavalry left roaming to cause trouble. They shall be field slaves, house slaves. Catamites. Whores.*' The Emperor reached out his cup, and a slave filled it at once. '*Or I shall wipe them out,*' he said, offhand, as he took another sip of wine. '*Every last one.*'

'*You could not do it.*' There was fire now in the way the barbarian spoke, enough to make the guards take half a step forward from where they stood at the entrance, their spears dropping down. The Emperor, with an irritable, fatherly gesture, waved them back.

'*I am an old man now,*' he said. '*I have no wish to spend my last years here, chasing your people across the plains until the last one is piled on a corpse fire. But I shall do it. We have done it before, at Carthage. We shall do it again, if we must.'*

Still, there was defiance etched into the barbarian's face. The Emperor felt a little admiration, and perhaps pity. Like children these people were, they knew so little of the world. 'You doubt me? A shame, that you do not understand what Rome is, even though you have fought us for so long. You have told me that your people value your honour above all else?'

The barbarian nodded slowly.

'My people do as well, in our own way. But for us, honour and power are one and the same thing.'

'You cannot do it.'

A little smile on the lips of the Emperor. 'They have all said that. "We, our people, we are different." But they never are.'

The Emperor stood – a little unsteady, a hand upon the desk to give himself the strength to rise.

'I am going to show you something that none of your people know,' he said. 'A secret, of sorts. It will be only my words and a few scratches on a map, no more proof than that. But I shall speak the words, and you shall know them to be true.'

With the soft clink of chains the barbarian rose, shaking from the wine and with fear. And with slow and trembling steps, he came forward to receive that secret.

From the entrance of the tent, the Praetorian guards watched. Hand-picked veterans, they had long served as the Emperor's bodyguard, and they had seen such scenes many times before. The Emperor was speaking softly now – too soft for the words to travel to where the Praetorians stood at first. The finger pointing again and again to different places on the map, placing a gold coin down as some kind of trophy or token, tracing a grand outline that encircled many nations. One of the guards listened closer, and thought that he could hear the words. And it was not words, but numbers being spoken. The counting of thousands, and thousands, and thousands.

Just numbers, but the guards could see the barbarian shivering at them. Then bowing lower and lower, until at last he sank before that desk, as a fearful, pious man might lay himself before the altar of the god he had angered, to beg forgiveness or await a judgement.

Once again, the Emperor spoke, loud enough for all to hear clearly. A question, but spoken with the tone of a command.

'So, tell me. What shall I do?'

There was no other noise for a long time. The snuffling, weeping of the barbarian, the soft whisper of brazier and torch, the mutter of the wind.

At last, the barbarian raised his head. And he gave his answer.

Part 2

THE TWICE DEAD MAN

12

Once more, the circle and the dream. The smothering darkness, and a nameless terror wrapped about the heart.

The chanting warriors surrounding Kai, the doomed man at his feet. A man condemned by no crime but age – his back bowed with unceasing pain, numb hands that could no longer hold the reins. And so now this, in place of the death in battle. An honourable end of sorts.

The circle fell silent, the sword heavy in Kai's hand. And as always in the dream, Kai swung too slow. As always, the man raised his head. And it was his father's face that he looked upon.

But this time, the dream was longer, worse. Something different, and all too familiar. This time, he saw once more the shame of what he had failed to do.

The sword falling from his hands, and as soon as it touched that dream ground it vanished, the mistake already irreversible. And he was moving back, sliding half-steps, his hands raised in supplication, surrender.

Silence from those who watched, those shifting, changeable faces of the dream. All those that he had ever known, it seemed, were there to bear witness. The only sound came from his father – Kai had heard the screaming of gutted men on the battlefield, the maddening keening of women holding stillborn children to the breast. But he had never heard a worse sound than that low moan of shame.

Then from the circle, a figure walking forward. The light on the blade, the swing and the cut. A scream.

Kai woke to darkness, stillness, the sound still ringing in his ears. An awful longing to return to the dream, to that impossible hope of changing the past.

He felt Tomyris stirring against him – not yet fully awake, still locked in some dream of her own. Carefully, so as not to rouse her, Kai reached out a hand to the flap of the tent and lifted it aside. For a time, he watched the falling of the snow. All about there were the Sarmatian people – emerging from the wagons of tented felt, gathered about fires, bartering and pleading with one another. A world there, but one that he was sealed away from, like those realms of the old stories, cities hidden beneath water that could be seen but never reached. He was alone in his shame.

For he was a captain no longer. Not even a place in the warband, without Bahadur to pledge for him. There were few that the Sarmatians killed or exiled – only the worst of men, the rapists of children, the murderers of kin, blasphemers against the gods. But there were many whom they killed in slower, quieter ways. The outcasts and the shamed, pushed to the fringes of the clan, with whom none would share the gift-friendship that a nomad must have to live, the flask of wine and bowl of stew that is given freely to those who need it. Now perhaps there was only a waiting for sickness or hunger to claim him. Waiting to watch his child die.

A voice close by, the breath against the hollow of his neck. 'What will happen now?' said Tomyris.

'It will be a hungry winter, my child.'

'After, I mean.'

'A spring, like any other. The herd, the raid, the taming of horses. We shall ride together under the sun – you would like that, wouldn't you? Why should it be any different than before?'

'Our home was not burned before. They have never come that far before.'

'Too far, and we darkened our spears to prove it. You do not need to be afraid.'

'I am not afraid. Not for me.' She hesitated, bit at her lip. 'But what will you do?'

'I do not know,' he said. And he did not.

She pressed her face against his chest, and he looped his hand into her hair as though he were stroking a horse's mane. For they both knew the truth she spoke.

Outside in the campground, Kai saw a dark shape moving, a familiar figure stalking through the snowfall like a wolf. As if his hand was burned he let it fall from the edge of the tent, let the light dim once more. Too late, for the footsteps were quickening, and soon the winter sun was upon them once more.

'Are you an old woman or a swaddled infant?' Arite said. 'Do you mean to lie there all day?'

He answered, stung: 'Little work for a shamed man to do.'

'You may put your Roman to work, at least,' she said. 'Or do you let him lie idle and wait upon him as though you are his slave?'

Hot words were there upon his lips, ready to be spoken. But as his vision adjusted to the sharp light he saw her hair was still unspooled in mourning and falling free about her shoulders, a wandering madness in her eyes. And so he turned his reluctant daughter from the blankets, and threw the fur cloak across his shoulders, beckoning the Roman like a dog. Soon enough they were all out in the snow, stamping at the ground to keep warm.

Arite was eyeing the Roman, as she might have judged a doubtful horse from the herd. 'What may he do?'

'I do not know,' Kai answered. 'He is one of their captains. I have heard they cannot even mount a horse without a slave to help them.'

'And what is his name?'

Kai did not answer.

'I would not leave a dog without a name,' Arite said reproachfully.

But at this, the Roman spoke for himself. Gaunt and grey-faced from his wound, he drew himself up tall. 'Tend horses, I can,' he said, the accent thick. Then, tapping at his chest, he gave a name: 'Lucius.'

'Tend horses, he says.' Arite grinned. 'And he speaks a little of our language. Perhaps he will be worth something after all. Tomyris, put him to work amongst the herd. I shall join you soon enough.'

Tomyris set off at once, one arm outstretched and pointing the way, looking for all the world like a miniature cavalry captain signalling the charge. A look of disbelief from the Roman, to be given into the charge of a child half his size, but he followed her nonetheless. When Kai went to follow them, he felt a hand upon his shoulder, bidding him to stay.

'There are others to keep watch over him,' Arite said, 'and besides, she has been tending fiercer beasts than that Roman for a long time now. She does not need you to guard her.'

'Then what would you have me do?'

She did not answer at first. Her eyes were darting about the camp, to where the women were shaving down the horns of the cattle, and where a hunter tossed scraps to his sighthound. Then she said: 'You led those riders off the ice when no other could have done it. I always thought you would make for a fine captain.'

'I did,' he said. 'But little that is beautiful lasts for long.' The words fell from his tongue without thinking, and he felt the twist in the gut, the sharpness at the back of the throat, as he remembered who had taught him that saying.

'Bahadur used to say said that to me, too,' Arite said, her voice soft.

'He always spoke the beautiful words.' Kai hesitated, scratched at the snow with the toe of his boot. 'I wish he were here. He would know what to do.'

'I know what he would say. If it were summer, and we were at peace, he would tell us to feast and dance. Not to think of what had come before, or what would come tomorrow.'

'And what of winter?'

'To do what we must,' she said.

Kai nodded slowly. 'You want me to go to Laimei.'

'I do.'

'You are right, to claim you speak Bahadur's mind. He asked the same of me, before the battle on the ice.'

'It was honest advice, was it not?'

'It was. It did no good then, though. I cannot think that it will now, either.'

'What else will you do?'

'There are other captains I might ask a place of. Perhaps another clan, if I took a wife of their people.'

She shook her head. 'It must be her. None of our clan will have you if she says you nay. And I do not think another clan...'

'... will take a shamed man.' Kai knew the truth of her words. Yet still it seemed impossible to him to do what she asked. 'You know many things, Arite,' he said, 'but I think that this is something you do not understand.'

'Oh, I do know something of shame,' she said quietly.

'What do you mean?' An eagerness then that he was not proud of, to know that there was another who might share that pain.

'No.' She shook her head – sharp, insistent. 'I shall not speak of *that* today. But if you will not fight for your daughter, then all that they say about you will be true. And this is how you fight for her.'

To that, there was no answer. He remembered the duel

with Gaevani – his leg remembered too, the wound aching in the cold. The decision to fight, and die, against the odds.

And so he walked with Arite to the herd, and called his horse. She trotted to him eagerly, for though they were new partnered they were already learning to love one another, that love born of loyalty. For Kai might trade away every scrap of iron he had for food that winter – perhaps his own body, if it came to it, for there was much that was done at night by the desperate in a starving campground. But no Sarmatian would trade away his last horse. Better to choose the quick death of the knife than that.

As he mounted, he saw the eyes of the Roman on him. Unthinking and by instinct, Kai waved to him as he might have waved to any shepherd of the people, and Lucius answered with a solemn nod – a warrior's salute, perhaps. Good fortune to those who go to battle.

Arite watched Kai go. Once more the shadow upon his face, the captain's light gone from him. An ache about the heart to see him so diminished.

A shrill chatter, close by, as Tomyris spoke and set the Roman to work. Arite went with Lucius amongst the horses – an escort to protect him, for she saw the rolling lips, and the ears pressing flat as they marked him as an outsider. Even with her there, it seemed most likely they would kick and stamp him to death before they would submit to his touch.

But the Roman knew his trade. Careful and patient, he worked to earn the trust of the herd. She saw Lucius pick out at once the gentlest horse, a placid roan mare that would never make a warhorse, watched as he circled to her and slowly won her trust with touch and whisper. His hands searching for the rubbed wounds that an ill-fitting saddle might leave behind, peering close at the nodding head and hesitant step that spoke of an injury, the foam upon the lips and panic in the eyes that might mean sickness. Lucius moved amongst the herd carefully, almost shyly, a priest at the ritual, and he did not yet dare try to lift a hoof, not yet. He would have to fight hard for such trust.

Arite could hear him speaking as he worked, soft words cast into the air. The babble and chant of a man soothing restless horses, but they were not in a language of his own. It was the Sarmatian tongue he spoke – she started as she heard echoes of her own conversation with Kai, as the Roman mouthed those words over and over as man might when he is trying to unpick a riddle, feeling the weight of the words on his tongue and seeking an answer.

Interrupting her thoughts, the trot of hooves and jingle of tack. A rider, dark-haired and swarthy, galloping up too fast to the herd, making the horses call and dance and scatter. One of Kai's riders, the man called Gaevani – he offered her a mocking bow from the saddle but gave no word of greeting. He seemed content to watch the Roman work, a sour smile on his lips.

It was only when one of the horses danced up and feinted a kick, forcing Lucius to slip and stumble away on the frozen ground, that Gaevani broke the silence. A barking laugh, and he spoke to Arite: 'The Red Crest knows his horses, I grant you that. But they know him, too. That stink of Rome. They'll kill him one day.'

'Perhaps,' she answered. 'Do you care to wager?'

'I shall lay two flasks of wine against one of yours that he does not last the winter.'

'Bargained and done,' she said. 'Is that why you come here, to gamble over another man's life?'

'Little enough to do in winter. I thought I'd take a look at your captive. I want him to teach me how his people die.' The Roman started at the last word spoken, and Gaevani grinned. 'He knows that word, does he? Die.'

'He has learned a little of our speech,' said Arite.

'Well, he is learning the important words first.' And Gaevani spoke again, but this time to Lucius, and in the hard and musical language of Rome.

'What are you saying to him?' she said.

'I tell him of our wager.'

The Roman spoke now, slow and careful, as though still disbelieving that they might understand him.

'He wants to know why he lives,' said Gaevani.

'Tell him that Laimei did not want to claim her third kill.'

'He will not understand that.'

Arite shook her head. 'He does not know of how a woman may leave the warband?'

'They know nothing of our people. The Romans are fools. Amazing that they have conquered so much when they know so little.'

'Tell him, then.'

And Gaevani spoke once more – stumbling from time

to time over the unfamiliar language, his hands dancing in the air to mime the words he did not know. Arite felt the Roman's eyes upon her, tracing the scars across her skin, the relics of wars long past. She tried to remember the three men she had killed to earn her freedom from the warband twenty years before, but they were faceless shadows now. Two Sarmatians and a Dacian, killed in feud and border raids. She had been free, then, to take a husband, raise children and leave the killing behind. A life that she had fought for and won, and yet now she had nothing left to show for it.

When Gaevani had finished, the Roman spoke again. Slow, halting words, as though dragged up from some place deep within him.

Gaevani smiled sourly. 'Perhaps the Red Crest does have more courage than I thought.'

'Why?'

'He asks to be given a warrior's death, and not live shamed as a captive.'

A heat under her skin, as though she were put to some torture of fire. And she was speaking then, so angry that the Roman, not understanding her words, took two paces back, raised his hands as if to ward away the stroke of a sword. 'Tell him there is no glory in killing one who wishes to die. And that he shames himself, to seek such a death.'

Gaevani spoke – at length, more than seemed necessary to translate her words. The Roman gave her a wary nod, and returned to his careful work amongst the horses.

'What more did you tell him?' Arite said, breathing away her anger.

'That you do not care to kill the helpless.' He gave a shrug, palms turned up to the sky. 'And that no doubt some fever or sickness will take him, and that shall be the end of it. He has no need to hurry towards death. They do not breed Romans strong enough to live on the plains.'

Once more, the sound of a horse approaching, and a half-stifled cry from Tomyris, watching them from the other side of the paddock. For it was Kai coming back, hunched over the saddle like a man wounded in battle, the horse wandering carelessly, barely guided. His daughter calling to him, but he gave no sign of hearing. He slipped from his horse and let it wander back to the herd unguided, and returned to the darkness of the tented wagon.

Gaevani spoke once more, his eyes on Kai's tent. 'We all must live with our shame, no? But they did not breed him strong enough either, I think,' he said. And Arite thought that the other man spoke not in scorn, nor in the bitter tone of revenge, but perhaps with a certain quiet regret.

13

The heavy snows came. Perhaps a blessing from some kindly god, for even the Romans would not march in that weather. Or a curse from some trickster deity, sealing the nomads in place, forcing them to sit and wait. And to starve. For the Sarmatians only knew plenty and famine. Even with so many left dead upon the ice of the Danu, there was not enough for all to eat. Some had come to that great campground with their winter herds, some with only a few sacks of grain. And so it was a time of waiting, of whispering in the dark, of creeping slow death.

In the days that followed, Arite returned again and again to Kai and Tomyris, bringing what food she could. She watched Tomyris's eyes growing large in her head, impossibly large, as she grew thinner and thinner. With Kai, she saw the hollowing of the ribs, and, worse yet, the breaking of the will. Of what had passed between him and Laimei, he would not speak.

Piece by piece, she traded away the iron that Kai had brought back from the river. She unlinked the mail shirt and traded its rings for haunches of meat and bowls of blood, gave away the iron-headed Roman spear for honey and milk when Tomyris took a winter fever. It was dangerous work, for out in the camp there were battles between the half-starved and the starving. Sometimes it would be just a pair of men, sometimes a sudden brawl involving half a hundred. The captains would come to end the squabbles, but sometimes they were too slow – the flicker flash of a knife, a gurgling whisper, and a corpse was left laid upon the ground when the bands of warriors were separated, its fresh wounds steaming into the air. One less warrior to face the Romans, throat slit for coveting a rotten scrap of meat from another man.

When the last of the iron was gone, and the winter season was still but half spent, a clearer day came. Brilliant light in the sky, falling through the scattered clouds like golden arrowheads, and no murderous wind. A day with all the feeling of an omen about it, and so Arite took her horse from the herd, and ventured further than she had before. Out beyond where the tented wagons huddled together, past the chieftain's fire.

All about her, the camp was a place of stillness – the occasional scurrying shadow moving from tent to tent. Figures huddled besides cooking fires, shivering hands outstretched to the flames. It was only at one corner of the campground that one always saw movement. Horses and riders, dressed for war. A great circle scratched into the snow, the ground within it marked and cleared, scored deep with the tracks of horses, the imprints of men thrown down, scattered with flecks of horn and wood from where weapon struck armour. And there the riders moving in the same familiar patterns, over and over and again. The mark of madness, or of desperation.

As Arite drew close, a snap of a lance passed through the air, followed by the wet fall of a body into mud as one rider was knocked from his horse by a blunted spear. Fresh red tassels ran from that weapon, for it was Laimei who turned and circled the horse back to where a boy lay in the mud, struggling to stand in the heavy horseman's armour. With another tap of the lance she put him on his back once more.

'Stay down,' she said. 'You would be dead from that stroke, and dead men do not rise.' She looked at the other riders in the circle, who hooted and laughed at the boy upon the ground. 'Who is next?'

The laughter faded then, for many of those who watched had taken their turn in the dirt, and the rest knew that their time would come soon enough. The riders looked at the ground, and would not meet their captain's eye.

'No one?' Laimei tossed her head. 'There is one braver than all of you.' And she pointed towards Arite, stirred her horse towards her, and said: 'Perhaps one of you will have found your courage when I return.'

'You flatter me,' Arite said, as Laimei rode up beside her. 'I am no captain for you to impress, or a lover to woo. Just one who has come to look on the warriors and remember her youth.'

'You are not so old. More gold than silver in your hair, and you are more of a warrior than any of them,' said Laimei, eyeing the other riders with scorn.

Arite found it impossible not to think of her own memories of the warband. A time in her life that was a rushing, teeming, roiling river – a madness, like the love of youth that one can both long for and never want to feel again. 'They will have to learn fast, then,' she said. 'There are not many left to us.'

'True. And they are shadows of those who came before them.'

'Why train them now?' Arite asked. 'We are a long way from the raiding season.'

'There are rumours that came with the last riders before the snows. That the Romans will come across the water in spring.'

'They say that every winter. Stories to frighten children. But spring always follows winter, and the Romans do not cross the Danu.'

'Perhaps. But this year is different.' And Laimei was smiling, then – the brilliant, terrible smile of the fanatic, or of one in love.

'You think that we could defeat them, if they come?'

'The stories say our forefathers dug their own graves and threw themselves in, at the very end.' She gestured with an open palm towards the warband. 'We shall dig our graves well, at least.' And as Laimei looked her over with a brisk, warrior's gaze, Arite had the sense of being evaluated, like a mare outside a horse trader's tent. 'Why not join us here? You still know how to hold a spear, I have seen that myself.'

'I earned my three kills a long time ago.'

'I do not think it matters anymore.'

'Yet you were careful enough to avoid your third. The Roman.'

'Yes, I was,' Laimei answered. She looked down at the reins in her hands, ran them between her fingers, the way a man may touch his lover's hair. 'I would not have my spear taken from me.'

Arite hesitated. 'Why is it that you stay in the warband?' she said softly.

Laimei's horse shifted beneath her – a restless step and turn, answering some hidden thought of his mistress. 'What other kind of life is there for me?' said Laimei. 'One such as yours?'

'Is that such an ill-seeming thing?'

'Why would I wish to end up like you?' she said. 'Weeping over a dead man, my children butchered. Nothing left to you except tending to broken things like my brother.' Laimei shook her head. 'I have no need of broken things.'

Arite could find no answer. She could not seem to find her breath.

Laimei spoke again. 'I do not say it to wound you. I only answer your question. And you came here with another purpose. To beg Kai's place for him, is this not so?'

'It is so.' Even as Arite said it, the words seemed to come from so far away, as though it were someone else who was speaking.

'Always the maker of peace, aren't you? I like you more at war, I think.' Laimei shook her head, picked restlessly at one of the tassels on her spear. 'Why do you fight for his life? I already told him no. Why should I answer differently to you?'

'Give him back his place in the warband. For Tomyris, if not for him.'

A mocking smile, and Laimei said: 'Bring her to me, if she is the one you care for. I shall care for her as my own. But not him. I have no place for a shamed man.'

Arite spoke once again, and the words came with a cold sensation – a killer's certainty: 'Who are you to deny him his place? You who ran from the battle on the ice, when he did not.'

One could not help but admire it, how little Laimei gave away. A certain stillness, the face like a painted mask, the soft and strained sound of gloves tightening around the leather of the reins. But that was all.

'You must have done,' said Arite, 'to live. You lost your horse, and you ran from the battle on another. For all your death-mad boasting, you ran. And if you still have the right to be in the warband after that, then so does he.'

'You dare say that to me?' Laimei whispered.

'Yes, I will say it, even if no other will. Because I am not afraid of you.'

The soft blowing of the wind across the plain. The rattle of armour and spear. The rest of the warband had fallen silent – at that distance none of them could have heard what was spoken, but they did not need to. Every Sarmatian learned to feel when a battle was close.

'Very well,' Laimei said. 'I shall spare what food I can. I shall send for him, at the end of winter when the time is right. And you may tell him that his champion fought well for him.'

'I will. And I know I will answer for the insult I have given, when the time comes.'

'Yes,' Laimei answered simply, 'you will.'

14

Kai heard it first as music – the chatter of water in high places, atop hill and crag, as the first springs began to thaw. The world growing louder, sound no longer dulled by the heavy weight of snow, the particular silence of winter.

They had survived the darkest months. Some bargain had been struck by Arite that she would not speak of, and warriors from the warband came from time to time, bringing what food they could spare. The charity given to keep a fighting man alive through to the summer, to last until the killing season.

Now it was almost spring, the time when the Sarmatians heard the plains calling to them, as sure as a sailor hears the whisper of the sea no matter how deep into land he goes, no matter how much he tries to forget. A gentle time for Kai's people, when there was no war to be fought. A time for the traders and explorers, those wanderers who longed only to see what lay beyond the next turn of the plains. A time to break wild horses by driving them upstream, until, exhausted at last, they would turn back as a man will return to his lover after a quarrel. But this was no time of peace, for lovers from different tribes to make their way across the plains to meet each other at river and grove. It would be a spring of raid and feud, the settling of blood debts.

It was a crisp clear day as Kai rode his horse about the fringes of the camp. The horse moved well beneath him, for throughout the long winter he had spent much time practising alone with his new horse, teaching it the tricks of horsemanship as he knew them, trying to teach it love as well, that love between rider and mount that can save both in the hard times. And as they turned and circled, he heard the footfalls of another rider approaching, the muffled wet sound of hooves through mud and snow.

No warrior from the warband this time, sullenly bringing meat and milk to a shamed man. It was a child, and at first Kai thought it was his own daughter who had come to find him. The girl was near to the same age, and with her face marked with mud and hollowed by hunger it was a simple mistake to make, for winter starvation made all seem kin to one another. But it was not Tomyris – he knew from the horse first, for it bore no markings that he recognised. As she drew closer, he saw the girl's head marbled with ringworm, the ragged clothes crudely patched and stitched. One of the lost souls of the camp, raised by all mothers and none. And she rode to him and spoke with a foundling's studied bravery: 'I was told to bring you with me.'

There was no need to ask who it was who summoned him, for the girl held a red tassel in her hand, the gift for her service, a treasure beyond compare for a child that age. And there was no question of refusing such a summons, and so he set his horse behind the girl and let her lead him, as a warrior might have ridden before a king or captive.

He thought he might be taken towards the council fire – perhaps it was that Laimei wished to speak with him before the chieftains, for many feuds had been settled by their judgement. But they did not go towards the heart of the encampment, nor did they go to the proving grounds at the outer ring, where the warband sparred and trained. They went instead towards the second ring of the camp, a place between worlds where the sacred things were done.

A part of him knew then, but did not want to believe. Even when they came to those places where the ground was already black with blood, he told himself it was the sign of old sacrifices, that he was being taken to a seer or prophet. For he was a man who had risen from a grave on the ice, and one of the dream speakers might see an omen in that.

In a sense, he was being summoned to a sacrifice. For he saw it then, the sight he had witnessed many times before, the shape of his dreams. A killing circle, the Sarmatians in their war gear, the high chants carried on the wind. A taste of copper on his tongue, the feel of sweat upon his skin, as Kai said to the girl: 'She commands me there?'

'She does.'

'Then you have done your duty,' he said, absent fingers fumbling for some token to offer. He thought to give her some little trinket of war – a splinter of an arrowhead, a lock of hair cut from the head of a foe, but when one hand ran over another he found the ring half slipped from his finger. An omen, no doubt, for his father had worn that band of bronze, long ago.

He offered it to her, just as he had offered it to his sister before the battle on the river. And the girl's eyes were alight but not quite believing, waiting for the trick.

'It is yours,' Kai said. The light caught on the bronze as it spun through the air, and the girl took it like a hawk taking a sparrow.

The ground was soft beneath his feet as he dismounted, the circle of men parting like water before him, accepting him as one of their own. All about him was the stink of sweat, the chants of war, the rattle of arms and armour. And when he made his way to the front rank of the circle, he saw what lay within, the sight from his dreams. A man upon his knees, and a boy standing above him, weapon held high.

The man looked young to be in such a place. His temples touched by silver and his face worn like old stone beneath a river, but he could not have seen fifty summers. Kai wondered what infirmity kept that man from his saddle – fingers too pained and weak to hold the reins or steady a lance, or that splintering pain at the base of the spine like an unseen arrow shot by the gods. It was not that his mind had been broken by curse or fever, for those eyes of his were bright with life and love, as he looked upon his executioner.

The boy was young – perhaps the rest of the doomed man's sons lay dead on the ice of the Danu, and this was the eldest who was left. No colour in his face, but his hands steady on the haft of the axe. Kai watched the boy, and prayed for his courage.

The chanting grew louder and louder, the clash of arms all too real, until Kai could feel that quickness of heart and the heavy sweat on his skin that came before the battle, his body remembering the killing, the closeness of death.

As one, without a sign being given, the circle fell silent. It was time.

But the boy did not swing. His father dropped his gaze – hoping, perhaps, that this would make it easier. Lips moving, some words to encourage his son, but they seemed to do no good.

The boy's eyes were lost, imploring, looking about the circle for help. And when he turned his face to Kai, there was some recognition there. The child's face became that of a man for a moment, for long enough, for he had seen the future that waited for him if he did not act. And so he swung the blade down, and painted the snow red.

For a boy, it was a killing well done. It took him only three strokes of the axe before the man at his feet lay still and silent. The man was brave, too – he only screamed once, right at the end.

All was as it had been before, as though it were a trifling thing that they had witnessed. The circle broke, the air alive with stories of the dead man, men and women making their way from that sacred circle as though they woke from a dream. Some came forward not to embrace the boy, but to clap him on the back and offer him wine for doing a man's work. And there were those few who stood still in the moving crowd, like pillars of stone thrust up from the shifting sea.

Arite and Lucius on the other side of the circle – Kai did not know if it was chance that brought them there, or if they too had been summoned as witnesses. But Arite did not seem to see him, her gaze fixed on the boy beside his bloodied father, her face corpse grey.

He had no sense of moving, but he was at her side then, his hand to the crook of her arm.

'Can you help me away from here?' he said.

She nodded slowly. 'Yes,' she said. 'I can do that.'

To the horses – restless beneath them, as they rode in the close fashion, side by side. The way that a father teaches a son to ride, a daughter guiding her ailing mother on one last journey across the plains towards a burial ground. And lovers too, sometimes.

Soon they were back to the tented wagon, moving inside, the sunlight dimmed by the thick felt that surrounded them. Kai and Arite huddled up together, for comfort as much as warmth, and the Roman sat apart, quite still. Kai could not shake the image of him as a sort of honour guard, a charm or protection of some kind. A man from another world, who might protect them from the cruelty of their own.

'Where is Tomyris?' Kai asked, for he could think of nothing else to say.

'Laimei sent for her,' Arite said, 'to practise with horse and spear.' Her voice lowered. 'I suppose she did not want the child to see it.'

Silence once more. The aching kind of silence, a longing for words that cannot be spoken.

But then there was a voice – the Roman, speaking slowly

and carefully in their tongue, for he had learned much over the winter. 'Who were they?' he said. 'That man and boy.'

'A father,' answered Kai. 'And a son.'

An unspoken question, heavy in the air.

'When a man grows too old to fight,' Arite said, 'what does he do? In Rome?'

'Retires to his farmlands. Plays at politics, or…' Lucius hesitated, and mimed writing in the air, for there was no word for it in the Sarmatian tongue.

'Your chieftains do that, the ones with gold. And what do others do, those who do not have gold?'

'Their families take care of them.'

'Those without families?'

A pause. 'They beg. Or starve.'

Arite nodded slowly. 'The steppe is no place for those who cannot ride. And we can care for the children, but not the old. And we do not care to beg for our lives.'

'A man hopes to die in war,' said Kai, 'or in some chance accident from the gods that might spare him the shame of growing old. If he does not, he is given a different kind of death. At the hands of his eldest son.'

The Roman said nothing at first. Then: 'It is always so?'

'There are stories. Of sons who spare their fathers in the myths, like Badan and Badanaquo. But they are just stories that fathers tell to little boys so that they will not be afraid. It is always so.'

'Why tell me this?'

'I do not know,' said Kai. 'Perhaps I wonder how it seems to a Roman.'

'I see no father of yours here.'

'There is not. And he did not die in battle.'

The Roman nodded, as if he understood. 'That is why she hates you? Because you killed your father?'

A sour twist of the mouth. 'No,' Kai said. 'She hates me because I could not. Because she had to.'

There was silence between them. And in the darkness Kai saw it once more – the armoured figure pushing through the killing circle, his sister taking up the blade that Kai had cast down, the light on the blade, and the blood upon the grass. The first man she had ever killed.

Then the Roman said: 'A terrible thing, for a child to kill their father.'

Beside him, Kai felt Arite shudder. 'And what about those who kill their children?' she said.

It was then, at last, that Kai thought he understood. He turned to the Roman. 'Get out. Now.'

Lucius crawled past them, out towards the light. And he paused at the entrance of the caravan – perhaps there was something that he too longed to speak. But, it seemed, the Roman could not find the words, and then he was gone from them.

Through the walls of the tented wagon, deadened a little by the fabric, Kai listened to the movement of the camp. The barking sounds of an argument, one of those petty quarrels of starving men. The rasp of a weapon being sharpened, over and over again, as though its bearer hoped that a sharper sword would somehow undo the force of the Legion. One of the gentle, looping songs of their people, where rhythm became ritual and the old stories were told over and over and over again.

Somewhere there was weeping – for a moment he thought that it might be Arite, but when he put his hands to her face he found it dry.

'You saw something out there, I think,' said Kai. 'Something worse than I did. A ghost?'

She nodded. 'Two ghosts.'

'You can speak to me of this pain. If you want to.'

'It is shame. Not pain.'

'Then you may tell me of that instead.'

'Did talking of your shame help you?'

A pause. 'Mine was never hidden.'

She spoke then. Not in sadness, but with a kind of still fury. If her words had been the stroke of a sword, it would have been the final, downward cut. 'Do you know why I sent my son with you?' she said. 'He was so young, younger than his years. A gentle boy, who played with those wooden horses you used to carve and shunned the spear. None would have questioned Bahadur if he had kept Chodona behind. And it was I who insisted he must go.'

'Duty,' Kai said at once. 'It was a brave thing, to send him with us. You did your people a great honour.'

'No. It was not for that. I wanted to believe it was so at the time, but it was not for that.'

It took her a long time to say anything more. Kai remained as still as he could, for perhaps it was only in forgetting that he was there that she might let herself speak the truth.

At last, the words did come.

'I wanted him to go with his father,' she said, 'for I thought it might mean Bahadur would keep both of them safe. He would have his son to protect, and would not take a hero's risks. I thought they would both come back. That they would run, if they had the chance.' She reached out her hands to Kai, but closed her eyes as she did so. Perhaps it was to imagine that he was someone else that she could touch.

'I gambled them both,' Arite said, 'and I lost them both.'

Silence, then.

'You have nothing to say to that?' she said.

Kai pulled his hands away from her, for he had the old longing now for sword and spear – that close feeling in the chest and touch of heat at the centre of the back. The warrior's longing to fight, to kill through that pain. To contend with something other than shadows and grief.

The tears did come then, hot and quick as blood from a blade. And they were not her tears, but his.

Afterwards, he would wonder at why it happened. If it was still a ghost she sought in the darkness, or perhaps she simply did not know what else to do. For she took him into her arms then, held him close against her, and she began to kiss those tears away.

15

For a moment, as she woke, Arite could believe it was her husband's arms that she lay in. That touch of flesh, the feel of a body in the darkness almost familiar. But her hands traced across the shoulder and searched for a scar that was not there, and in the hollow of the neck, the smell of sweat and flesh that was not the one that she loved. For not even in the great stories of gods and heroes was there an unravelling of time, any more than water might flow uphill. The dead remained dead, and what had been done could not be undone.

The light was still strong when she left the tented wagon, but not so strong as she thought it would be, the sun falling from the sky. There was another light close by, from the embers of a fire that should have gone out many hours before. And there, tending those embers, was Lucius.

He looked up at her. 'The fire was dying down,' he said simply.

She said nothing for a time. Then: 'Did you think to run?'

'I did. To take a horse and some food. Follow the stars and the rivers to the west.'

'Why didn't you?'

'I do not think the Roman has been born that might outride a Sarmatian.'

'I think that you are brave enough to take the chance and find out.'

'Perhaps that is true.' He stirred the fire once more, and when he spoke again, it was slowly, each word carefully weighted and measured. 'My gods are different to yours. I have my own way of speaking to them. And they did not tell me to run.' He hesitated. 'What would they have done to you, if they found me gone?'

'I cannot say. That would have been up to the chieftains. Nothing, perhaps. They might consider you a stray horse and nothing more. Our own foolish loss.' She sat down, the patterned soles of her boots towards him. 'Or they might have had us flayed alive,' she said, matter-of-factly, 'for letting an enemy escape.'

'I would not wish that for you.'

'Why not? You rode into my village to kill me.'

'I might equally ask why you let me live.'

She inclined her head to him, the way a sparring partner might acknowledge a good touch. 'I do not know what will happen to you,' she said. 'When we leave this place.' She gestured about the camp, that impossible gathering of warring clans. 'This is a place that exists out of time. A stolen season, while we decide what path our people will take. When it is settled, other things may be settled too. Some may look on you as bad luck.'

'That would be reason enough, I suppose. Men have been killed for less than that.' He hesitated. 'Is it true, that you sacrifice people to your gods?'

'I have heard that our grandfathers did. The Scythians, out upon the steppe. But no longer.' She held a hand towards the fire. 'If it is to be death for you, I shall give it to you quickly myself.'

'If it is to be death for me, I shall die by my own hand. My people have never feared to do that.' The sunlight shone on his hair as he looked away from her, watching the motion of the camp. For it was stirring to life, horses and wagons carrying their burdens towards the heart of the encampment. Men stood combing and braiding their long hair, women could be seen gathering in circles and practising the intricate steps of a dance. 'Something happens tonight?' he said.

'There will be a feast.' She smiled then, seeing the doubt on his face. 'Oh, we came close to starving this winter. But you shall see. Our people can find a way to feast and dance, even at the ending of the world. And after the feast, we break camp. The Five Clans will part, and return to their lands. We shall return to the west.'

'And you shall make a home with Kai there?' he said carefully.

She laughed at him. 'It is a wearisome thing, to be in love with young men. I am glad to have left those times behind me. You do not have lovers in Rome?'

'We do.'

'Well, it is just so. A thing of a season. He will find a

young wife, and perhaps I will find an old lover, and that shall be the end of it.'

The Roman hesitated. 'Perhaps it would be better to ride east, rather than west.'

'There are tribes beyond the mountains that would not welcome us. This is a hard land, but it is our home.' She raised her head proudly. 'And your people give us good raiding beyond the Danu. The Red Crests will forget us, and all shall be as it was before.'

He did not answer.

'There is talk,' she said, watching him carefully. 'That the Romans mean to cross the Danu this year. You think it more than talk?'

'There is no knowing the mind of the Emperor. But there is a great anger in my people, when they are roused to it.'

'You speak of them as though they are not your kin.'

'I do forget it, sometimes.' And he looked out across the plains – the low sun dancing across the frosted grass, that beautiful light that makes the earth seem touched with fire. 'This is a place to inspire forgetting.'

There was more to be spoken – she could see the Roman's hunger for it, having spent so long a wordless prisoner. And she could feel that longing too, for here was one to whom she had no ties. It would be like speaking to a spirit glimpsed in a mirror, the way that the seers did. But she could see Tomyris riding back towards them, drooping in the saddle from a hard day upon the practice fields, could hear Kai stirring in the tent nearby. And so she set to tending the cooking fire, and let the moment pass.

★ ★ ★

Late in the day, they huddled under blankets by the embers of the fire, the earthy smell of the meal still thick in the air – grass and bone, and whatever other scraps they could find to make the watery stew. Arite leaned back against Kai, felt the warmth of his neck against her face, and watched the others across the fire.

A mirrored image of a kind – Tomyris and Lucius sat close together, sleeping upright. Something had changed between them. No longer was he a prisoner to be watched, it seemed, and so with the instant and wordless forgiveness of the child she no longer hovered about him when he worked with the herd. She took it upon herself to teach him the ways of the nomads, for while he knew much of horses he knew none of the subtle arts of the steppe. They made a strange pair amidst the camp, her berating him furiously while he patiently nodded and followed the commands of a girl half his height, lighting fires with bone and dung and scavenging together for the little herbs and flowers that lurked beneath the frost.

Kai stirred a little, and against her skin she felt the thrum of his throat as he spoke. 'One might almost think them brother and sister, don't you think?'

'If one were half blind,' she answered. 'But they do have something of that urgent, quarrelling kind of love.'

A pause. 'What do you think Laimei meant, by summoning me to that circle?'

'More than hate, if that is what you are asking.'

'You truly think so?'

'She does hate you, Kai. But there is more to it than that.'

'Yes, there is.' She felt him shift, move, hold her a little tighter. 'I think that she means to teach me something. But I cannot tell what it is.'

Silence, for a time. Somewhere distant, a keening cry of mourning broke out over the camp – another dead from a winter fever, or a wound gone rotten. From another fire close by, the sound of laughter, the smell of hemp smoke twisting into the air. For it was festival and funeral all at once, it seemed, in the campground of the Sarmatians.

She took his hand in hers, turning its palm towards the ground and tracing across the back of it. Her skin rough and calloused, first from the spear, and later from the work of herd and field.

'Some charm you mark there?' he said.

'No. I just enjoy the feel of the skin. I had forgotten what it was, to have a young lover.' She felt him go tense behind her. 'Was it a thing of pity,' she said, 'that passed between us? You may say if it was. I am no heartsick girl.'

'No, it was not a thing of pity. You are beautiful.' Kai hesitated. 'I think of him. That is all.'

'I think of him too. And somewhere in the Otherlands, I can hear him laughing at this. And he will mock you for it, when you go to meet him beyond. And perhaps he'll chide me for it, too, when I see him again.' She turned her head to the side, as though trying to hear some whisper spoken from above. She grinned, and spoke gently to him. 'Can you hear him laughing?'

'I think that I can.'

Suddenly she was serious again. 'It means nothing more, Kai,' she said. 'I do not want you to…'

'Oh, I am not so foolish as you think,' he said. 'I do understand.'

'The feast tonight, for those that go to the west. The fire, and the dance. And after…'

'And after.'

He caught her face and risked a kiss. For a moment, the stillness of the nomad life stole over her, that sense of all things in their right place. A fire and family before her, a man at her side, the enemy far distant and a journey ahead.

Then, beyond, she saw something that brought her back to the world, that set the river of time flowing once more. Laimei.

She was on her horse, that great one-eyed beast, the two of them circling the edge of the camp. It looked as though she had been riding towards them, but now she stopped short. Her mouth a little parted, as though in surprise. She nodded once, and Arite felt herself marked in some way she could not understand. Witnessed in something forbidden.

But then Laimei turned away – the moment passed. They huddled close for warmth, and together, in silence, they watched the sky, wishing for the sun to fall from the sky, and for the night to begin.

16

At the heart of the campground, the fire rose in the night.

It was not the kind that had marked the passage of winter, those little smoking fires made just strong enough to warm a foul stew, to stave off the cold biting death that rotted fingers and toes black. All winter the Sarmatians had eked out their fuel as misers, every bone and twist of peat counted, the dung from the horses collected and dried.

This fire was a wild and roaring thing, a pillar of flame reaching up to the sky. No longer had they any need to count and hoard, for soon they would be gone. Nothing would remain of the Sarmatians in that place but ashes, footprints, the furrows of wheel and hoof marked in the ground like sword cuts upon a shield.

They burned it all to give a lightness to the journey ahead, and more than that, there was a defiance in their greed. Reckless strength, the battle joy, the smile before the execution – all came from the same place. For what better way was there to show the gods that one stood unafraid than by excess and plenty? Burn every scrap of fuel and drink every drop of wine. Find more tomorrow, or die.

The air was thick with the smell of cooking meat, the tang of sweat, the babble and chatter and song of a free people. And everywhere, they fought and played. The wrestlers who contended with the art of weight and balance, hacking at heels and twisting arms. Drunken archers loosing at the mark, betting every scrap of iron and gold they had on a single shot of the bow. For everywhere around the fire, little fortunes would be won, lost, traded, and spent before the dawning of the new sun, and the warrior who had begun the night a rich man and left it without a scrap of metal to his name would still be laughing. For still the wheel turned.

The crowds gathered about great bowls of watered wine, as big as tables. Every so often a great cry would go up, as some young rider would step up on the edge of the bowl, seeking to dance about the rim without spilling a drop of it as the old heroes were said to have done. Most barely made half a dozen steps before they were toppling off and tumbling with hoots of laughter, howling like wolves at the half-moon above them. Further back, shifting about the fire were those who danced in shifting circles, those arcing loops that the Sarmatians so loved, twisting and turning and never-ending.

Into the crowd Kai went, a swimmer into the water. No longer the marked man, the outsider, the shamed. In the darkness, his face lit by only the occasional flash of firelight, he was but another one of the people, and even those that knew him still smiled and greeted him as a brother. All was forgiven for one night alone.

They had gathered at the edge of the world and made

ready to enter a new one. No longer an army or a nation, but something still remaining. A fragment of a people, a last ember of a fire. They had all been killers, out to the west. But now they gathered as children, as playful and fickle as the young. And in many of them – those who were new newly blooded in the warband, those who had lost their families to war and fever, the brilliant, the lonely – there was something else. A kind of pleading in their eyes, as they waited for the moment of the choosing.

For Kai knew that was the edge of the blade that glittered amidst that reckless joy, the unseen spear point that pricked at each of those who drank and danced around the fire. The question that remained unanswered – who was to be honoured, and who would not. And he knew that pleading look was in his eyes, too, the longing in the heart.

The time came when the songs fell silent and the games of hand and foot ceased. For they were coming through the crowds, silent as ghosts – even the great chieftains gave way before them, all their gold and their rank counting as nothing before those who walked.

They were the ones honoured already, their faces daubed with white paint. The light of the fire glittered across the scales of the armour – the dull sheen of fire across horn for the most part, but here and there the sharp light of fire upon polished iron. For while the rest of the revellers wore the belted jackets and leather trousers of the traveller, they alone came dressed for war. The champions, those who had killed bravely.

This was their moment. Not the ugly death that might await them in the west, impaled on the tip of a Roman spear, pulled to the ground and hacked apart, or festering from a rotten wound. Here, in this place, witnessed before the people – this was the feeling that they were willing to trade their lives for. And so there were others crying out, pleading to be chosen. Men and women both, calling for their place, shouting the great deeds that they had done, the courage they had shown.

Kai saw Laimei walking through the crowd with the careless ease of a queen from the old stories. All about her there were hands darting out, withdrawn just as fast, as though they feared to touch her. One by one, she made her choices. Seemed at a whim, cast to chance, though no doubt there was a reason behind every choice that she made. Some particular light in the eye of the young man from their clan that she picked out. The man from the Wolves of the Steppe, perhaps it was the scars on his face and his hands and the steady way that he returned her gaze that made her select him. Laimei had little time for beggars, but there was something in the imploring cry from a young woman (her wrists marked with the blue ink, her hair unspooled in mourning) that made her daub that face with white, tears carving runnels through the fresh paint.

A few places left to choose, and Laimei seemed to slow, turning one way and another through the crowd, one finger tapping against her lip. Her eyes flitted across, met Kai's for a moment, and just as quickly passed him by.

But there were others then, gathering around the fire, gathering around him. At first he did not recognise them in the darkness, their faces pits of shadow. It was not until the first one spoke that he knew them for who they were.

'Choose Kai,' she said.

It was Tamura – thin from the winter, painfully thin, her head seeming too heavy for her body now, overripe fruit on the bough. But she stood tall and proud, and the light of the fire made something more of her.

Another stepped forward – Saratos, another of the riders whom Kai had led, the light of the fire upon his silver hair. 'He brought back iron, and led us from the ice. Choose him. It is right.'

And they were all speaking then – the riders he had led from the river. Those that had lived through the winter, scattered amongst the crowd and come together once more. Only one remained at the fringes, and even in the darkness Kai knew Gaevani by the proud tilt of his head.

A moment's stillness, Laimei staring at him in the light of the fire, her face unreadable. Then soft footfalls, drawing close, and she was amongst them, her hands reaching for him, the heavy coldness of the paint running on his face, the fingers roughly pushing his head down and to the side like one disciplining a wilful hound before she let him go.

Kai reached out, a took a cup of wine from a still hand nearby. 'I follow my captain to the death.' He lifted the horn cup to toast her and drank deep, the wine running down his face like blood from a fresh cut.

With a careless toss of the wrist, like one casting aside an empty skin of wine, she threw the horn bowl of paint into the fire. And with that gesture, a shivering madness swept over the crowd. No longer were they still and silent, for they swarmed forward, screaming and laughing and weeping, hands reaching out for one another as though they had almost all their senses stolen and only touch remained.

Kai could feel open palms falling against his back, fingers plucking at his arms, trying to draw him and those he stood with into the shifting crowd. But Kai and his riders stood firm as spearmen in formation, turned in amongst themselves to block out the rest of the world. A circle within a circle, a band of their own. The hands clasping and unclasping at the centre of the circle, their heads bowed low so that their foreheads rested against each other. Some were laughing like children, others bared their teeth in wolfish grins, and there were some, like Tamura, who were as still and attentive as those in prayer. And it was only when they were ready, when each one's hand felt the touch of all the others and they had felt that bond renewed between them, that they broke away and let themselves be taken by the crowd. Yet still Kai fought for one path in particular, against the movement of the people. For Arite was there, on the other side of the mob.

Like the battle on the ice, it was a sightless battle fought by inches. Twisting and prising, feeling for a gap and turning into it, judging the passage of the crowd and swimming through it like white water. But the memory held no fear for him, for he knew that he was safe. He knew what waited for him on the other side.

He was through then – her hands strong about him, her breath hot against his face. For that was the only way that they could speak in that press of the crowd, lips to ears, held close against one another.

'It is a thing of a season – of winter, yes?' he said.

'Yes,' she answered. 'But it is still winter tonight.'

A madness at those words, a fire in the blood, and his arm was about her waist as he made to lift her up and carry her away. But at that moment the pace of the festival began to slow, the dancers fell to stillness, lovers looked on one another with open hunger, the drummers paused to shake the life back into their hands. And in that silence, another sound from the western edge of the camp.

The beating of hooves. A single rider, coming from the darkness.

Everywhere there were people making signs against evil and misfortune, for only the lost and the mad travelled alone on the steppe. There was no war gear upon that newcomer, no lance in hand or armour on his back, no banner that might mark his clan. Wrapped in fur and cloth, his clothes too ragged to tell what people he came from. Hunched over the saddle, the mark of a sleepless hard ride, and beneath him his horse a thing of bone, and it made a sound almost like weeping as it stumbled towards the fire.

As the newcomer came closer, they soon saw why he remained on horseback as he moved amongst them, for this was a man who could not walk unaided. A corpse it seemed at first, so hollow were the cheeks, the skin stretched tight across the skull, the legs withered to almost nothing. They thought he might be one of those war trophies, a dead man tied to a saddle and sent home as a curse and warning. But the head moved from side to side, and the lips moved. He searched and spoke, though so soft that none might hear him.

Still they did not believe him to be living – some rider

from the Otherlands, come to take a tribute in blood. A few, half-hearted, reached for their knives and called at him to stop, but the rider did not slow. And though he wore no weapon there was something that made them fear to touch him.

He reached the edge of the fire, and bowed all the way forward in his saddle, his forehead touching the mane of his horse. Prayer, or relief. Then he half fell from the saddle, both hands clasped to its horn to hold himself upright.

He was looking about then, absent and muttering, like those old men who have lost their wits and are being led to the mercy of a killing circle. Speaking too soft to be heard, but there were none who dared to come close, it seemed. Until a child came forward, some young girl of the people who slipped from her mother's hands and went to him, leaned close and heard what was whispered. She did not seem afraid until she turned back to see all eyes upon her – she blushed, and looked at the ground, and spoke.

'He asks for Kai of the Dragon, if he lives.'

For a moment, Kai thought that the first thought must have been true – that this was a visitor from beyond. That the gods were angered enough by the honour he had been marked with, that this was his punishment.

From close by, he felt Arite plucking at his arm, and he heard her cry out a name. For she knew it before he did, but only by a moment.

Kai was running then, putting his arms about that man, more to hold him up than an embrace. The words spilling from his lips, formless and meaningless, for there was everything to say and yet no way to say it. And that man buried his head against Kai's shoulder and wept like a child – the same way that Kai had wept against him, so many times before.

For it was Bahadur who stood there, against all the odds.

17

There are some men who wear the favour of the gods as surely and lightly as a wolf wears its fur. The lost sheep from their herd wander back of their own accord, the dice fall their way on every bet that truly matters, the charging bull checks at the very last moment as though commanded by a god. Life and luck follow them as spring follows winter, and none of their kin or companions resent them for it. For the lost sheep that finds its way home is slaughtered and given to a neighbour, the winnings from the lucky dice are gifted amongst the players, and their survival against the odds has the makings of a story to be shared. They return the love that the world has shown to them and give it to their people, and all are richer for it.

Such a man was Bahadur. Of all the men to see so broken, Kai could not have foreseen it would be him. For those god-touched souls meet the quick death when their time comes. A few brilliant summers, before the death by blade or swift sickness. They are spared the slow rot, the breaking of defeat. That is the greatest sign of their blessing.

But he was there, hollowed by starvation and sickness. And they were speaking together then, lips to each other's ears, even as the crowd roared and screamed about them.

'I thought I saw you killed upon the ice,' said Kai.

'Worse than that. A prisoner of Rome. So I am as shamed a man as you are, Kai.'

'Never will you be a shamed man to me.'

'Nor you to me.' And Kai felt the other man hold him closer, until the bones were pressing against Kai's skin like knives. 'Why did I say such a thing? I am so sorry, Kai. I cannot think.'

'You must never apologise to me. Never.'

The madness was close, like a living thing in the shadows around them. But then Kai could feel Arite's hands upon him – almost a lover's touch, as she unwound the men's embrace and took her husband into her own arms.

All around them, panic and madness breaking through the crowd. Kai could feel it more than he could see it, the same way one could sense the fear of a herd, the rout of a warband on the battlefield. Figures coming forward like wolves in the night, hands reaching and clawing, the dream readers and the seers crying foul omens for anyone to hear. But close by, the white-painted faces, the chosen warriors looking back upon him, awaiting a command.

'Keep them back!' Kai said, and once more he was obeyed. No weapons in hand, but no need for them either – they looked foreboding enough, almost a circle of the dead as they surrounded him, their palms open towards the surging mob. And the crowd beyond seemed to withdraw, the madness passing.

They were moving then, carrying Bahadur away as they might have taken a slain king from the battle, wishing to deny an enemy the prize of the body. Past the emptied bowls of wine and meat, the marked ground of the wrestlers and the feathered targets of the archers, until they came to the tented wagons. Bahadur screamed at the sight of them – some memory, perhaps, of confinement and darkness, that sent him twisting and clawing away. But Arite was the stronger, and she forced him within.

Those white-marked riders there once more at his side, waiting for their orders. And Kai felt for the very first time the weariness of command, when one had no good order to give. When one longed to be told what to do oneself.

'This man must rest,' he said. 'If any of you have wine or honey to give, spare it if you can. Otherwise, go and rest yourselves. Whatever omen he brings, you shall need your sleep to answer it.'

They were gone, and under the light of the moon Kai could see the unpainted faces of those who remained. Then there were shadows moving in the darkness, a pack of men pushing through the crowd. At their head Kai could see Gaevani, the white of the scar across his scalp like a victor's crown. Beyond him, a figure towered above the rest, the moonlight glittering upon iron and gold, and upon something else, too – a great cape of hair and skin. Zanticus, chieftain of the Wolves of the Steppe, bearing his cloak of scalps.

'I will speak with this man Bahadur,' the chieftain said shortly.

'He speaks to no one tonight,' said Kai. 'He may still die before the morning. A chance in a thousand, for him to ride through the land alone so early in the season.'

'I have always heard him to be a fortunate man.'

'Does he look lucky to you now?' Kai snapped.

'No, he does not.' The clink of iron, as Zanticus put one hand under his cloak. 'He has come from the Romans. His words will not wait.'

'How do you know of that?'

'You have just told me, of course.' Zanticus shrugged. 'But surely it can be guessed. Where else would he have been all winter? Living in a cave like a bear?'

Another scream broke out from the tented wagon behind them, and Gaevani stepped to his chieftain's side. 'We shall get no sense from him tonight. I shall ensure we hear his words tomorrow.'

Zanticus grunted. 'See that you do.' And he strode away, his bodyguards flocking behind him.

Gaevani lingered behind a moment longer, and for a moment the mocking smile seemed to slip from his lips. 'You had best get him speaking tomorrow,' he said. 'Zanticus will not be patient.'

'Perhaps,' said Kai. 'I will think on it. Now get out of here.' And one by one, they all wandered away, until Kai was alone.

Everywhere, the fires flickered out, the great bonfire at the heart of the camp gone to embers entirely, the seething pile like a sleeping dragon. And at every shadow that passed the fire, every set of footfalls, his eyes danced up to see who it was that approached. He saw lovers wandering back towards their tents, their arms draped about one another. A weeping mother passed by, a trace of white paint on her cheek, marked there by a last embrace.

He thought to remain there all night, a watchful sentry. But again a keening rose from the tented wagon – not the sound of mourning, the greeting to the dead, but a cry of loss, of the broken. He could not tell if it was Bahadur or his wife, or both. Even when he was kneeling upon the ground, hands to his ears like a child, the sound would not stop.

Running once more, his bowed horseman's knees aching in pain, tripping and stumbling in the darkness until he found the place where the children slept. They were gathered together around their own little fire, nothing but embers now, wrapped in each other's arms. All asleep it seemed, save for one – the Roman, bound to the wheels of the cart, once more guarded by children, shivering away from the embers.

The knife was in Kai's hand before he knew it, as he walked towards the bound man. And the words seemed to fall from his lips of their own accord – softly spoken, for he did not wish to wake the children. 'I have heard it said that you Romans think of yourselves as one people. That an insult to one is an insult to all. An injury to one is an injury to all. Is it so?'

Lucius nodded. 'It is so.'

'If I were to hurt you, it would be to hurt Rome?'

'It would.'

'I would like that very much.'

The Roman did not speak – no scratching at the

ground with his feet, no worrying at the knotted leather thongs with his teeth, no screaming for help that would not come. He remained quite still, and his eyes alone made a proud answer.

'You shall not beg?' said Kai.

'No.'

'Never?'

A pause. 'Never for myself.'

'Yes. That is as it should be.'

Kai leaned down – even then, when he had almost decided, he was still testing with the quickness of the blade. Perhaps he would have cut that throat if the Roman had flinched or screamed. But instead, the only sound the sharp parting of leather as the bindings fell away.

'Come closer to the fire,' he said. 'Warm enough there, but cold back here.'

Kai did not wait to see what the Roman would do. He picked his way through that rough carpet of sleeping children, until he found a place beside his daughter. He sat down then, one hand upon his sleeping child. He placed the other across his knees and leaned against it, and let the tears come at last.

A moment later, a touch and a weight. A hand upon his shoulder, and with his head down, Kai could pretend it was one of the children who held him close in the darkness.

It was worse to see Bahadur in the daylight.

In the darkness, Kai's mind had played tricks, shown him what he wanted to see, like a child painting from memory. But there was no hiding the truth of things under the spring light.

The marks of the body were bad enough – the dry, sallow skin, the birdlike bones almost exposed beneath the flesh. Worse was the blankness of the eyes, the way Bahadur would keep pausing during a simple movement. The hand that wandered to a wine cup would stop part of the way there as though he had forgotten what it was he was supposed to be doing, or a hand would scratch ceaselessly at the scalp until it drew blood.

They sat together cross-legged upon the ground, a woven rug laid beneath them – the charred and half-burned one that Kai had taken from their village. And on it were placed the gifts that Kai's warband had brought like offerings to a king. Clay jars of honey and bowls of blood, scraps of meat and skins of wine. Bahadur ate and drank like one discovering food for the first time, while Kai, Arite, and Lucius waited in silence for him to speak. For that was all Bahadur had said that morning, once he had learned they had a prisoner amongst them. That he wanted the Roman there.

At last, it seemed, Bahadur could eat no more. He closed his eyes, and let the spring sun wash over him. And with his eyes still shut, he said: 'Those white-faced riders. The ones from many different clans, who brought these gifts. Why do they answer to you?'

'I led them here. After the battle on the ice.'

'You were a captain?'

'Of sorts, for a time. No longer. They honour me still, though I have not earned the right.'

'For that I am glad. That I lived to know that you earned a captain's mark.'

Bahadur fell silent, and did not speak for a long time. Once more the forgetful motions, his finger tracing the rich patterns of the rug beneath them, the drawings of monsters killing horses, men killing monsters. Hunters and hunted, the path of life and death and rebirth. The story of their people, told over and over again.

And when he spoke again, it was not to his wife, nor to Kai. It was to the Roman.

'Have you ever been close to your Emperor?' said Bahadur. 'Talked to him, as we are talking now?'

'No,' Lucius answered. 'I saw him, once. But I never had the honour of speaking to him.'

'Honour, is it?' Bahadur shivered once. 'Perhaps for you. I wish that I had died, rather than be honoured in that way. To know what I know now.'

'You spoke with him?' said Kai.

'Yes. Many times. Though not as men speak with men. It was as if... as if I were some dog of his.'

Arite said: 'It is a message that you bring from him?'

'It is,' said Bahadur. 'I thought of all the ways that I might say it, when I came here. I thought that I knew, but now...' The words trailed away.

'They mean to make the peace cost us,' said Kai. 'We all know that. You—'

'You do not know what Rome is!' And Bahadur was shouting then, the words ringing like the sound of sword against shield. 'You think he is some angry chieftain come to make war with you,' he said, 'from some border tribe stirred up by a bloodfeud? You think to give them tribute and offer an honourable peace between worthy warriors?'

Arite reached out to him, a tentative hand on his, and he snatched it away as though he had been burned. 'Do not touch me,' he said. 'Do not paw at me as though I am a sick child.'

'Tell us, then,' said Kai. 'What message do you bring?'

'There are no terms but these. That we submit to him and make ourselves his slaves, give them rulership over our lands and our people. Or they will destroy us all.'

Silence, then. Only the sounds of the camp – from somewhere close, the laughter of a playing child, the hiss of a cooking fire, the sharp whispers of an argument between lovers. What a thing it was, to know the ending of the world before any others. To see the rest of one's people go about the day unknowing, when nothing that they did mattered any more.

'You might as well have said that they meant to reach out and stop the sun in the sky,' said Kai. 'They cannot do it.'

'They can. They think us wild children, playing with sticks. Or starving wolves that harass their sheep. You would kill those wolves any way that you could, would you not? Track them to their caves and strangle the puppies, and you would think it a good day's work. And so it is with them, and us.'

'Then how do we defeat them?'

'You cannot. I think that only Rome could defeat Rome.'

'What would you have us do?'

'Lie down and die. Or beg for their mercy. It is all the

same to them. It is all the same to me.' And Bahadur
covered his face – not to weep, but to pull and claw at it, as
though it were a mask he sought to lift away. Arite began
to reach towards him once more, but, this time, checked
her hand halfway.

'You must rest,' she said. 'The chieftains will speak of
it, and decide what to do. In the spring, we shall send our
messengers—'

'No. I have but a few days here.'

'What do you mean?'

'I have to return. That was what he told me. And if I
do not go back, then that shall be his answer. That he will
have to destroy us all.'

Kai understood then, every little pause that Bahadur
made, how hesitant and forgetful he seemed. It was not
the mark of a man who had lost his wits, but of one trying
to fix the memories in his mind. To not let any gesture
or moment pass by unobserved and unnoted. To do the
impossible, to take his home back with him to the west.

'He will not do such a thing for a single prisoner,' said
Kai.

'He will do it. He can do it. I tell you again, you do not
know what Rome is. Who this man is. They have their
own honour of a sort. No, not honour. But revenge. They
know much of that.' He choked then, hacked and coughed
and spat upon the ground, reached a trembling hand back
to the skin of wine. After he had drunk, he wiped the wine
from his lips with the back of his hand, and licked that dry.
Then he spoke again: 'They would burn a whole nation
to nothing. Salt their fields and destroy their treasures.

Melt gold away as though it were dung upon a fire. For no profit, nor to protect themselves. Not to honour the gods. But simply because they said that they would.'

Kai let his gaze drift to the Roman, for the man had gone quite still. 'Could this be true?

'If he says that he will do it,' said Lucius, 'then he will. The Emperor does not lie. The soldiers love him for that. Always, they are lied to by their masters. But he does not lie, even if he means to send men to their deaths.'

'And do you have an oath that you can swear, that I might believe what you say?'

'I swear it upon the names of my ancestors,' said Lucius, 'and the gods of my people.'

'Something other than that. Strong oaths, but...' Kai hesitated, licked his lips. 'Do you have a daughter? For I would swear by my daughter. By Bahadur, or Arite. Can you swear in the same way?'

Nothing, for a time. Then: 'A wife and a son, both long dead. A sister – taken in a raid across the water. Dead now, I think, or a prize for some chieftain's bed. But I shall swear by them all if that will make you believe me.' The Roman went to place a hand over his heart, and then, leaned forward to touch the sword at Kai's hip, placing one finger upon the point and swearing in the way of the Sarmatians.

'I accept the oath,' Kai said. 'And now I ask you this – can they do it?'

'It would be a great risk to them. But they can. The other border tribes are beaten. There is no trouble at home that might draw the Legions back. If it remains quiet elsewhere… then yes, they can do it.' The Roman hesitated. 'Will your people surrender?'

'To be slaves? No. They shall die,' Kai said simply.

'And what if they could remain warriors?'

Bahadur snarled at this. 'To fight beside our conquerors?'

'You have fought beside the Romans in the past.'

'As equals, not slaves. And this Emperor would not allow it. He said so, and he does not lie.'

'He may not have a choice.' And Lucius was carving in the dirt with his fingers then, marking another map into the ground. 'We are surrounded by enemies on every side. Now there is peace, but it is never long before another war upon the border. Always, some senator at home wishes to take his chance at the purple and make himself Emperor. And when that time comes, the Emperor shall not let eight thousand heavy cavalry rot by serving wine and ploughing fields.'

Silence between them for a time. Then Kai said: 'Always the hunt, always the war. I do not trust to much, but I trust to that. There may be a chance.'

Arite spoke then, to her husband. 'How much time do you have?'

'I was delayed in the swamplands,' said Bahadur, 'lost the spare horse they gave me to a broken leg. The Roman horses are so weak… I have a day or two, perhaps. I have so little time left. I must have an answer by then.'

On his feet once more, Kai felt his head swim with the motion – the feeling of nausea, like one deep into the wine, or upon the eve of a battle.

'Rest now,' he said. 'I will tell the chieftains what you have said. What we have said. Perhaps they shall listen.'

'Tell only them, Kai,' said Arite. 'The camp will tear itself to pieces if they hear that spoken.'

He nodded, and swallowed. 'Bahadur...' And the words were there upon his lips, the confession that would release him. But once more Arite's eyes were on his – already they had that intimacy of lovers, that she could command him to silence without a word being spoken. Bahadur looking at him too, dull eyed and not watchful for a lie.

'If you go back, you shall not go alone,' said Kai. 'And that, *I* swear.'

No knocking of distant thunder, nor eagle's call, nor any of the signs that might mark an omen. Yet Kai felt it sure enough, the whisper-soft feeling of a god acknowledging the oath. For he knew that they bound men most surely to those kinds of oaths – those given in haste, and to cover a lie.

Away then, the soft grass falling away beneath his feet, hurrying towards the heart of the campground, towards the chieftain's fire. Hurrying, to try to seal away the secret in his heart, before his traitor lips might speak it aloud.

There was a river that cut through the campground the way lightning cleaves the night sky – shallow, quick-running, one of the nameless waterways of the steppe. Gift to the living, passageway to the souls of the dead, and at different times one would see it running black with dirt or red with blood, a story told in water.

When at first Arite tried to take Bahadur to that place, he would not go. His clothes were stinking rags, his skin marked with the traveller's grime, yet still he resisted. But at last he let her lead him there like a stubborn horse, head down and back bowed.

There were many bathing naked there – not lingering long, for the water still ran sharp and cold as whetted iron, but crouching in the free-running water and scrubbing themselves with grit before they leapt out once more, whooping and whistling at the cold air on wet skin. But they fell quiet when they saw Arite and Bahadur come to the side of the bank, moved away and made signs against ill omen.

She cut the clothes from his body, piled them carefully to the side so that not a scrap would be wasted, for it would all be kept for patching and kindling. At last, he was bare-skinned and filthy – shy as well, rolled half to the side and covering his nakedness. She remembered when they had been wed, twenty years before, the longing to see his skin like a kind of madness in the blood. Now she searched for the marks of torture, a wound that she could bind. She found nothing but a few red-raw sores from the journey, and all the signs of a half-starved man.

She did not coax him fully into the water. She filled a wineskin up and poured it over him a handful at a time, watching the water cut runnels through the dirt as he sat and blinked and shivered before her, rubbed at the skin with cloth and a scraper of horn, until he was clean and winter-pale under the midday sun. She took a comb and teased out his matted hair, cut away what seemed irreparably tangled, and, at the last, she marked him with a little oil – another gift from one of Kai's riders, a shy young woman who had parted with her own private treasure.

All throughout it, she waited for him to speak – a word of kindness, some question of how she had survived the winter. Some fragment of a song that she loved. But he wrapped himself in blankets, watched her with pebble-black eyes, and remained silent.

'The Roman lands must truly be as beautiful as they say,' she said. 'Fields of crops taller than a man on horseback, gold upon every woman's neck, iron in each man's hand.'

At this he stirred, and spoke. 'Why would you think such a thing?'

'For otherwise, why would you so regret returning here?'

He flinched at that, caught, and for a moment there was something of the man she had known. That fear he had of hurting another.

'There was nothing beautiful about what I saw there,' he said. 'Oh, the sweetest wine I have ever tasted, wonderful foods that I could not name – that is right, your eyes see it well enough, there was no torture for me.' He looked down at his hands. 'He did not need that to break me.'

'How then?'

'He showed me the end of the world,' Bahadur said simply, as he might have remarked on a change of the wind, or the look of rain on the horizon. 'All men must die. Women too. And... and our children. But I saw the end of our people there.'

'Not yet.'

'A scattering of years. No more than that.'

'Always you were a man of the day. Feast or famine, love or grief.'

'I had lost less, then. And who can throw their life away for nothing? When our people have no future?'

Together, they listened to the river for a time.

'I hoped,' he said, 'that perhaps you would not be here. That you would be at some other sanctuary on the plains. That you would not have to see me, and...' He hesitated, then spoke again. 'That I would not have to see you.'

'That is why you asked for Kai? And not for me?'

He nodded.

'Perhaps they shall not send you back,' said Arite. 'Perhaps they will choose to fight.'

'Then we shall have to watch each other die.'

'That was always to be the way of it, we knew that when we made our promises, long ago. There is something more that you do not wish to say.'

His hands drifted to the pile of fresh clothes she had brought – picking at them absently, but he did not seem to know what to do with them. She took them up, and began to dress him as she might have dressed an invalid. But as she tied his jacket around him, for a moment, she let her hand drift to a different kind of touch. Then he took her hand in his, and there was a moment where he held it hard enough to hurt her.

'I did think of you,' he said, 'when I was a prisoner. I thought of why it was that you sent our son to fight with me. Why you insisted he must go.'

She said: 'There was never anything that I could conceal from you.'

'Our son should have stayed behind. He should be with us, now. You sent him to be a hostage to my heart. I should not have had to watch him die.'

And he rolled up in the blankets they had brought, and turned to face the water.

She found herself on her feet – no decision to rise, yet there she was. She could not leave him alone there at the water's edge, and yet she did. Striding away, hands balled into fists, longing for something to fight. A hunger for touch, an ache beneath the skin.

Always before, the crowds of a winter camp had brought her comfort, a great embrace into the people that held her close. But now it was choking, suffocating, the stink of horses like black smoke, every accidental touch of a body against hers as fearful as the touch of a sword.

There were those she knew in the crowd, voices calling and hands reaching. But she kept her head down, leaving them to shout and curse behind her, until she was back at the campfire where Kai and Lucius and Tomyris sat together. A treacherous relief, to see them, and to be free of her husband.

Kai was rising then. She saw his eyes hunting about, in search of Bahadur, and anger there too, at first, when he saw that she was alone. In that moment she hated him, fell upon him with fist and foot, tearing at him with her nails. His hands were about her wrists and he pulled her close, leaned against her like a wrestler trying to recover his strength. She let her weight fall upon him until they were in an embrace – a wonderful, terrible kind of embrace, and she did not know what it would mean.

18

The rumours spread through the camp, as wildfire passes across the steppe in a dry summer. Everywhere he went, Kai heard the people speaking to one another of what the rider from the west might mean. They came to him with wine and iron, smiling like children, expecting him to tell them everything he knew of what Bahadur had said. For his people were not keepers of secrets – one must share everything to live upon the plains, and the silence and the lies sat uneasy upon his lips.

He had spoken of the Emperor's message only to the chieftains of the Five Clans, and each day he returned to the centre of the camp to await their answer. Always before the chieftains had spoken on the open plain, and any man or woman might witness what was said and speak to it if they had the courage. But in a tall white tent the chieftains gathered now, and their sworn bodyguards chased back any who drew close. For there were many others who now gathered in that place with Kai, kneeling in circles and waiting, and though they knew not how, they knew that their fate was being decided. Supplicants before an altar, awaiting a sign of the gods.

And the gods themselves were asked to speak, for again and again the seers and diviners would come before the great tent, casting stones or scoring lines and dots into the ground with a branch of sacred wood. Perhaps it was that even the gods could not see a path for the people of the plains, for every oracle was inconclusive. The gods remained silent.

Others came and went, summoned to the tent and sent away once more. Some were champions of war, others the far travellers who had ventured beyond the boundaries of their lands, others still the old women who had lived longer than any others. And when each one emerged, stony faced, the crowd begged them to tell what was spoken. But their lips were bound by the strongest of oaths, and they would not break their silence.

Kai went there day after day, waiting for the chieftains to make their choice. Yet when finally the decision was made, it came at night. The time amongst his people when only the secret, shameful things were done.

He was woken by a scraping at the felt of his tent – the sign a shy lover might give, but for Kai it had another meaning. When he was a child he had heard that same pawing sound, just like that, when his sister had some risk for them to run or a childish wager to win.

When he emerged from the tent, he could sense others in the darkness, close by, and he reached out to know them by touch. A gloved hand that batted his reaching arm away – Laimei. The warm rounded cheek of Tomyris. Bahadur's shoulder, sharp and hard like a bone picked clean of meat. And Arite, a calloused hand that found his for a moment before she drew it away.

'I come with word from the chieftains,' Laimei said. 'Bahadur, you are to go at first light. We shall...' She paused, and even in the darkness Kai could see her mouth twisting. Then she said: 'The chieftains will surrender to Rome. Cowards that they are.'

A shivering cold twisting up the spine – the feeling of the gods setting their plans in motion, and Kai saw Bahadur stand taller, lighter. Released from some great weight.

'There are those that watch us,' said Kai. 'That watch him. That shall know it when he leaves.'

'They are going to break up the clans tomorrow. Each people back to their territory. Who will notice a rider slipping away in such chaos? Bahadur shall go west, and bring our message back to the Romans.'

'There will be more than one rider slipping away, I think.'

'Yes,' she said, 'more than one. They thought to send him alone, but I made them think better of it. I shall keep him company on the path to the west.' She hesitated. Then she said: 'I told them that you would go, Kai. That you *should* go.'

'Why would you ask such a thing of me?'

'That is not for you to know,' she said. Then, with a bite to the words: 'Perhaps because you know better how to surrender than most.' But when he offered her his arm, she took it – a warrior's clasp of one sword arm to another, the other hand upon the heart.

'I thank you,' said Kai. And then he knelt down, beckoned the others to join him.

No words for a time. They spoke only in little touches, a choking sob, a shaking of the head, a brave smile half glimpsed in the moonlight.

'I go west again, little one,' Kai said to Tomyris. 'Do you understand?'

She nodded, solemn as any warrior.

'You must stay here,' he said, 'and watch the herd. But you can help me find my friends. The white-painted riders, you remember them? They came here with gifts. For Bahadur.'

'I remember.'

'Find as many as you can, and say as little as possible. Just enough to bring them here.'

'What shall I tell them?'

'To bring their war gear and best horses. To say their farewells.' Kai hesitated. 'And that it matters. That what we will do shall matter more than anything.'

'What will you do?'

'I will search too, for one in particular. Let us go, now.'

Others were trying to speak then – Bahadur, and Arite, talking over one another, clutching at his arm. But Kai cut them off. 'We do not have long, and it will be a hard search in the darkness.' He hesitated. 'And you must say your farewells, too.'

Before they could say any more, he was away – hands outstretched to guide himself in the darkness, tracing his passage along the side of wagon and tent. He looked back only once, as he hurried through the labyrinth of the camp.

He saw Laimei speaking with Arite, leaning close and whispering, and in the light of the stars, he thought he saw Arite's face turn pale as milk. As though she were one of the chosen, marked with the white of killing. Then the two women faded away from him, like a memory or a dream.

No barriers or signal fires, totems or cairns to mark the divide. But Kai knew at once, when he crossed the invisible boundaries between one clan and another, and he trod carefully once he was amongst the people of the Wolves of the Steppe. There was little love lost between their people, and though there was peace that winter, it was a fragile one. Much was done in the night that was forbidden in the day, loving and killing.

As he moved through the shadows, he could hear them trading rumours around the fires – that their chieftain Zanticus had come back furious from the council tent, that there would soon be war between the clans. Kai even thought that he saw the chieftain himself, a towering figure that strode amongst the tents, speaking in clipped whispers to the bodyguards.

Kai had to get close to the fires to look on the faces, to search for one in particular, risk a whispered conversation with a child and lone woman he met between one wagon and another. Soon there were shadows behind him, breeding and gathering in number. Silent at first, but soon they found voice – calling insults, drinking in a murderer's bravery from their wineskins, and the light of the stars upon a knife brandished towards him.

He was just deciding whether to stand and fight or run for his life when he heard a voice calling from the darkness. Even in the dim light, Kai knew Gaevani at once from the dark hair, broken by the ugly flap of scarred skin across the scalp, as he came forward and ordered the others away.

'Some lover of yours?' one of the shadows called out.

'No,' Gaevani answered. 'I have better taste than that.'

The others slunk off, and Gaevani held a careful distance. As though they were messengers meeting before a battle, offering a parley that they knew would be refused.

'So,' said Gaevani. 'Bahadur rides to the west.'

'You know of this?'

'It is the rumour that sounds the most truthful. Obvious enough, to any man with wits to think. And I have never seen Zanticus so angry as he is tonight.' He sniffed. 'A fool's errand.'

'You believe so?'

'I do. These people will never surrender.' But there was no pride in Gaevani's voice as he spoke.

'You think that they should?'

'Of course. You remember, I knew we were beaten long ago. Before you rode to the fire, and that horse won your duel for you.'

'You rode with me then,' said Kai, 'because you had to. Will you do so again, because I ask you to?'

The other man went quite still. 'You go to the west? To the Romans?'

'We do.'

'I did not think the chieftains would send *you*.'

'Laimei convinced them.'

'She really must hate you,' said Gaevani. 'To have chosen you to go and die.'

'Perhaps it is a kind of love, from her. I shall find out on the way. Why not find out with me?'

Gaevani cocked his head. 'The others too?' he said. 'And Laimei?'

'As many as will come, from those I led back from the ice.'

'The company that should have been mine.'

A silence for a long time. Gaevani with his hand across his mouth, staring into nothing. 'You think yourself in one of the old songs, don't you?' he said at last. 'No. I will not go. Perhaps I wish I were fool enough for that. But I am not.'

'You think as Romans do,' said Kai. 'Always to have the odds in your favour.'

'Yes, perhaps. That pet Roman of yours wishes himself a Sarmatian, I think. Perhaps we were both born to the wrong bodies.' Gaevani hesitated once more. Then he said: 'Come back, if you can.'

'Why?'

'Unsettled business, between us. It is my spear that should kill you. Out here, on the steppe. Not some Roman in the west. What would that death mean? So come back. And we shall finish things.'

'I do not think that I shall return. But I will, if I can. And if that is still what you want, it shall be so.'

With that, Gaevani was away – muttering to himself as madmen do. And as he watched him go, another omen came to Kai with a quiet certainty. He knew that he was not meant to die on Gaevani's spear.

'So I do die in the west, then,' he said to himself. And he felt a lightness settling upon him, beautiful and barely felt, like a scattering of snow, light and gentle and cold. The gods whispering to him, whispering *yes*.

One by one, Arite watched as they came in from the darkness.

Tomyris first, bone tired, mumbling a report like a weary sentry before she stumbled to the tent to collapse and sleep. Then Phoros and Goar – a near wordless pair of young men with the hungry, lean look of hunting dogs as they knelt before Laimei to honour their captain. Kai soon after, an absent look to his eyes as he paced about the fire. A sound from the darkness, the moonlight on silver hair, and Saratos walked in, grinning and cackling like a man half his age.

'Should have known that you would come,' said Goar. 'I suppose an old man like you gets lonely on the cold nights.'

'Oh, I'd wager I keep more company in my tent than you do,' Saratos replied. 'But I am growing old. I'd not have my son kill me.' But he clasped Kai's arm after he said it, and there was kindness in his words.

A lull, then. A nervous quiet, as they looked at one another, and wondered if they were all that would come. And Arite, sitting upon the ground with her husband, put her hand to Bahadur's shoulder, hoping for something she could not describe.

No words had passed between them, in that time the others had been gone. She had called the Roman out of the tent, set him to readying the horses and gathering supplies. But she had found not a thing to say to her husband. He sat upon the earth, pulling up handfuls of grass and letting them slip through his fingers like grains of sand, a weary relief written upon his face. That they were soon to depart had lifted some weight from him. Yet still, he would not speak with her.

Arite thought again of what Laimei had said. And there must have been some invisible message that spoke through her skin, some way that her pain passed through her touch, sharp enough for Bahadur to know it in the way he always seemed to. For his hand was upon hers, and he looked at her like one waking from a fever.

'Forgive me,' he said. 'I was not myself, before.'

Behind Bahadur, she saw Kai cease his pacing back and forth, his gaze upon hers. She let her head fall forward, until her forehead rested against her husband's and he could take, in her silence, the answer that he needed. She closed her eyes and welcomed the darkness, the still quiet, until a dancing step of hooves gave her something else to look towards.

For another shape came from the shadows – a horse without a rider it seemed at first, as though it had heard the call go out and answered it alone. But there was a small shape moving beside it, almost seeming to hide in its shadow. Tamura, prayer-solemn as she took her place amongst them, eyes wide as a man's who is drowning.

More came then, men and women that Arite did not know, the hungry and the proud and the lost, until more than a dozen were together in the darkness, clasping hands and embracing, just as their horses were mingling and rubbing up against one another, remembering old feuds and friendships of their own. Until the first touch of light was in the sky to the east, and they knew they could wait no longer.

'I did not think Gaevani would come,' said Tamura.

'I hoped otherwise,' said Kai. 'But it is done now.'

'And what of the Roman?' This from Saratos, and they were all looking on Lucius then, as they might have looked on a horse of dubious heritage.

One of them, a man that Arite did not know, said: 'Could buy some goodwill, returning a captive such as him.'

'No harm in having a hostage,' said another.

'Can't trust him with us, or to stay behind,' said Phoros. 'Who knows what he shall do or say? Better to slit his throat and be done with it.'

They were looking to Laimei then, awaiting her decision. But she gave a restless shrug. 'He does not belong to me.'

'Kai?' This from Saratos, and Kai was smiling then, teeth shining in the dawn light, to be asked to command once again.

'We shall ask him,' said Kai. He spoke towards the Roman, who stood still, almost at attention. A man awaiting sentence or reprieve. 'What should we do with you?'

'Do you mock me,' Lucius said slowly, 'or do you ask honestly?'

'No mockery. You are an enemy, and a slave. But you have earned the right to speak, and we shall listen.'

The Roman passed a thumb across his lip, lost in thought for a time. Looking upon them both standing there, the Roman dressed as one of them and with his beard untamed and hair thick, one would not have thought them enemies or of a different people. And it was another world Arite saw for a moment there, one free from the endless patterns of raid and war she had known all her life. An impossible fantasy, but beautiful for all that.

'You should keep me here,' the Roman said at last. 'Others of your people will miss me if I am gone, will they not?'

A murmur then, from the Sarmatians. No longer were they smiling as those carving meat for the feast.

One spoke from the back: 'A brave thing, to pass upon the chance to go home.'

'If it is to be peace, then I shall be home soon enough,' said Lucius. 'And I am no prize amongst my people. I shall bring you no favour.'

Saratos hissed through his teeth. 'And now he speaks thus, and I *want* to take him.'

Laughter then, as the breaking of soft thunder in the distance.

'It shall be so, then,' said Kai. 'We have lingered long enough. Let us be gone.'

All was motion then – riders making their last preparations, tying and retying the knots on saddle and pack that might save a life, the horses tossing their heads and stamping at the ground, winter-mad and hungry to feel the steppe rolling away beneath them. Always, in such chaos, the time for the secret farewells.

A hand found hers, in the shifting crowd. Kai, his face solemn – nothing of the lover there now, only the captain.

'I will keep him safe,' he said, speaking so softly that she could barely hear him. 'I swear—'

She cut him off. 'There have been enough oaths sworn in haste, I think.'

'Perhaps so.' He hesitated, as another man jostled close. 'I think that I must tell him what has passed between us.'

'I ask that you do not.'

'A hard secret to keep.'

'I ask no oath of you,' she said. 'Just to keep it, if you can.'

'I shall keep it.'

'If you can,' she said again.

His head nodded slowly – more in weariness than in accord, she thought, but perhaps it would be enough. And for a moment she had the hope that he would ask no more of her, that she would not have to lie to him. Then he spoke again.

'What was it that she said to you? Laimei, when I went to search for the others.'

'I asked her why she chose you,' Arite said. 'To go to the west with her.'

'And what was it that she said?'

This was the time – these were the words that she had practised, over and over again while she waited in the dark, and when it was needed the lie came easily. 'That you had earned your place.' And Kai was grinning again, the shy smile of a child, and so Arite tipped her head forward and let the hair fall about her face so that she no longer had to see that smile.

'Go say goodbye to your daughter,' she said.

One more touch of his hand against hers, and he was gone. She looked about her, suddenly fearful, for when one lies in such a way it seems the whole world must know. That the wind whispers into every ear, that the chattering streams spill the secrets to all who walk beside them. And there was one who watched her, who had been close enough to hear them speak.

Not Bahadur, for he spoke closely with Saratos, those silver-marked veterans sharing an understanding of their own. Lucius watched her, solemn faced. Perhaps there was something of pity there, and she felt the old killing rage rise within her, to be looked upon in that way.

'And what is it you think of,' she said, 'to stare so at me?'

'I do not think that I have seen you lie before,' he said.

She had been ready to speak hot words, to beat him as she might have beaten a stubborn horse. It was her right, when faced with a slave who spoke in such a way. But there was something in the way that he spoke that stole the fight from her.

She turned from him then – one more time, to embrace Bahadur, to feel him close against her. Over his shoulder then, through eyes filmed with tears, she saw the rising of a traitor sun, lighting the path towards death.

19

From the western edge of the camp, Arite watched the riders break away. A fragment of the people, a scattering of men and women and horses cast across the steppe. And as Kai and his company began their journey, they had an escort to see them out of the camp. Not of other warriors, or friends, or lovers. It was the children who followed them, the children of those who rode to the west. Sworn to secrecy, to tell nothing of why their mothers and fathers rode away, but they would not be denied their farewell.

She watched them riding side by side, at a meandering walk. One might have thought it an idle wandering, a clan carelessly drifting from one grazing ground to another, were it not for the war gear the men and women wore, the scales of metal and horse hoof rattling and shining under the sun, the long spears tipped up towards the sky.

Occasionally a pair of riders would break away at a charge – little brief races, fathers letting their sons win one more time. Others rode slow and close, heads bowed together, and Arite could imagine the words spoken, the last pieces of advice to the daughters who rode beside them. They all rode so naturally together that there was a sense that the parting might never happen, that they would ride together to the west.

But then another signal passed through them, a wordless command. A restless horse tossed its head, one warrior tapped the spear of the rider beside him in challenge. And then they were away, the hooves beating against the sodden ground, and even at a distance Arite could hear the old songs of death singing from the lips as they put their horses to the gallop.

The children gave chase, trying to stay with the warband just a little longer, to steal one more word or moment from those about to be lost. But the foals and yearlings they rode were no match for the warhorses, and soon they were left behind. Then they were still, drawn up in a watchful, ragged formation. Eyes deadened and lips moving, making vows and promises of their own. Of memory, and of revenge.

Arite looked about, to see if there were any who noted the warband passing. A few shaded their eyes and looked towards where dawnlight glittered on spears, but they seemed to give it little regard. The word had gone out that the clans were moving, that each was to return to its lands. The truce between the peoples to be marked for one more day, but after that the old feuds would break open and run with blood once more. And there were sheep to herd, mounts to ready, offerings to give to the gods of horse and sky. They would all have far to travel before the sun rested once more, and it was only her, and Lucius beside her, who were still and watchful of those departing figures.

Arite heard Lucius whisper in his own language, some

prayer or curse or wish of good fortune. Words of her own burned on her lips unspoken, as she waited until Kai and the others were far outside the camp, a scattering of shadows on the horizon. For she did not trust herself to speak until then, so certain she was that she would call them back, or cry out a warning. For Kai and Bahadur had seemed so young again – men always did, on the day they rode away.

She saw Tomyris and the other children turning back, racing towards those who stayed, to be with what kin remained to them. For a moment it had seemed that the children would not come back, that they would be a second warband following behind the first, to fight and die with their fathers and mothers. But now they returned, and she would have to speak, if she was going to speak at all.

'I will tell you why I lied to Kai,' she said to Lucius. 'I will tell you what Laimei said.'

'Why would you speak of this to me?'

'You chose to stay.' A catch in her voice, and she spoke again, softer than before. 'And I must tell it to someone, or I think I shall go mad. And I cannot speak of this to another Sarmatian. It must be a secret that dies with me.'

'I will keep your secret. You have my word.'

She shaded her eyes against the hard sun, seeing if she could pick out Kai or Bahadur, but they were all mingled together and almost beyond the horizon.

'She said that she would not see him happy. With me. That she wanted him dead before she would see him content. That she would take my lover away from me, my husband too, and leave me alone.' A closing sensation around the throat, a choking grasp of fear and shame that she swallowed away, to speak again. 'I told her that it was not such a thing as that between us, that she misunderstood. But she would not believe me.'

'An evil thing,' said Lucius, 'a feud between brother and sister.'

'Yes, it is,' she said. 'I thought that my killing days were over. But I have killed him, sure enough. I did not know that she could hate him so much.' She stared out towards the riders once more, and watched the line of the earth swallow them up. 'I am glad, for he does not know it either.'

'And what do we do now?'

'We go south and west with our clan, back to our old lands. To wait for the peace or the war.' She turned her horse to face that way, paused for a moment. 'Others can remember them, if they wish to. Tomyris, she shall remember them. But I shall forget them, if I can. Kai, and Laimei. Do not speak of them to me again.'

She set her heels to her horse, in search of the place that every Sarmatian knew. A place where the rushing air quieted all voices, where the earth lay suspended between every hard stroke of the hooves. For at the gallop, one could, for a moment, be taken to another world.

But, like one of the cursed and fated women from the old stories, she found herself looking back one last time. And there, on the horizon, a point of light answered her gaze, the glimmer of sun against metal, a figure that seemed to stand still for a moment even as the others moved on. The sun on the tip of a spear, perhaps. Or a gauntleted hand, waving goodbye.

* * *

Kai's warband rode lightly at first, back across the plains
and towards the river, the foothills to the north of them.
The touch of warmth from the spring sun upon their faces,
the long grass dancing in the wind and no longer stilled by
frost. They rode back towards the Romans, and perhaps
to death as well, but the company travelled with song and
laughter. Later, Kai knew, would come the fear – sharp
and quick like the cut of the knife. Shame as well, for they
were a people who did not know how to surrender, did not
know how it was to be done. But at first there was only a
pleasing sense of symmetry, a closing of the circle, as they
returned to the west once again and chased the setting sun
each day.

It was the horses that seemed to know before the riders.
For by the second day they tossed their heads, were dull
against the pull of the reins, kicked and bit restlessly even
at those who were their close companions. The next day,
Kai felt it too – the cold touch that pulled one's head
around, like a hand of ice splayed against the cheek and
wrenching at the jaw. The prickle of the skin, a maddening
itch that could not be scratched.

The day after that, it had gone beyond an unplaceable
feeling. From time to time Kai would shade his eyes and
look to the horizon, suddenly cock his head to one side
as he heard the distant whicker of a horse. All about him,
he could see the others do the same, yet none spoke of it
during the day – to speak of it would make it all too real.
The formation closed up, from the nomad's wandering

herd to the cavalry wedge, and scouts drifted out to roam the flanks without a command being uttered.

It was only in the evening, when they gathered around for their cold meal of cured meat (for by unspoken agreement they chose not to risk a fire), that they spoke of what they had first felt, and then seen. And it fell to a captain to speak first. Laimei leaned forward, and stared about the riders, and asked the question that they were waiting for.

'Who amongst you have seen them?'

No answer at first. Then, Tamura spoke, glancing uncertainly to Kai as she did so. 'I did. Just for a moment. They were trailing us well, staying out of sight. But one of them was over the rise of the hills to the north. Just for a moment, and with the sun at their back, but I saw them.'

Laimei's mouth twisted, as though she had bitten into something rotten. 'You are certain?'

'I wanted not to see them, but I did. So I am certain.'

Others spoke then. A flank scout who had seen a shadow skate across a cliff face, another rider who had dismounted to check the hoof of his limping horse and caught sight of a figure in the distance. Saratos, letting his horse lap at a pool of water, who had heard some fragment of speech carried on the wind from far away.

There was no doubting it any longer. They were being watched, and followed.

Kai looked to their captain for her command, but she slumped down where she sat, her crooked jaw working as she muttered curses under her breath. He felt the fear spread through the circle, for they saw that their captain did not know what to do.

In open battle, there would be none quicker to lead the way. Hers was no death-mad courage, for her killer's eyes saw further than just the tip of her spear. She could lead a warband in a breaking charge, or turn and flank and strike an exposed position, or lead a cattle raid that brought back a full herd and no empty saddles amongst the raiders. But the dancing shadow at the edge of her vision, the unknown figures on the horizon, the whispers of curse and ill fortune – these, it seemed, she did not know how to fight. And in her silence, others began to speak.

'The Romans could not have moved so quickly.'

'No telling what they can and cannot do. They were not supposed to know how to fight upon the ice, and yet…'

'Do not speak of that!'

'What if it is not the Romans at all? How could they come so far?

'Dacians, perhaps, from the south. Vultures that they are, come to pick at our lands.'

'They have no need to follow us. They would strike, or run. What do we have that would be worth the taking?'

'Enough.' And they did fall quiet, for it was Laimei who spoke now. 'If they were greater in number than us, they would have struck already. If they are fewer, what does it matter? Watch for them. A scout at each side, and we keep to the open ground even if it slows us. But we continue on. They matter not, for now. We ride in our war gear tomorrow, but that is all.'

Again, the muttering that skirted at the edge of dissent.

For they would ride tired and slow, weighted down with the heavy armour. They would be neither running nor fighting – that was how cavalry were destroyed. The meeting of eyes in the darkness, doubt passed silent about the circle like a flask of wine.

'They may be few,' Kai said slowly, 'but if they—'

'Quiet! I have spoken.'

Kai bowed his head, placed his hand over his heart. 'You have spoken.'

She looked about the circle. 'To your places. You know what to do. Sentries, helms off and hoods down – I don't care about the cold, I need your ears more than your eyes, even if you freeze them off. The rest of you sleep light, weapons in hand. But sleep. Trust in your companions, and trust in the gods.'

They broke from the circle, and Kai saw that the others seemed content, given purpose. For even if they thought their orders wrong, they were a captain's commands, a captain favoured by the divine. If they were commands that would kill them, they came from the gods. Only he remained behind, for his sister's gaze held him in place, a silent command. And when they were alone, she said, in words more measured than he had expected: 'I did not bring you to cause trouble.'

'I did not come to be ambushed before we are in sight of the Danu.'

'Nor did I,' she said simply.

He paused for a moment. Then he said: 'Found us quickly, didn't they?'

She tilted her head to the side, eyed him with what he

thought might be a grudging respect. 'Aye. They did. I forget that you are not always a fool. Romans or Dacians, it does not matter who they are. But how they found us…'

'You think they were watching the camp?'

'Perhaps,' she said carefully. 'A hard thing to do through winter. Perhaps they have a good magician in their service, to mask them so cleverly. But I do not think it so.'

'You cannot mean to let them stay behind us.'

'No. We shall catch them. But I do not share my plans with all the warband.' She drew her knife, and picked restlessly at the ground. 'I do not trust you for much, Kai,' she said. 'But I trust that you would not betray our people. You are weak, but no traitor.'

Kai's breath stilled in his throat for a moment. 'You think—'

'Perhaps.' And her eyes flittered about the camp from one man to another, the way a falcon will choose its mark from a flock beneath it. 'I wish it were only those of the River Dragon here. The winter truce is finished now, and the other clans cannot be trusted.'

'What do you want me to do?'

'Take six riders that you know to be loyal.' A pause. Then, grudgingly: 'There are many that seem to look to you. I cannot think why. But do not take it as a mark of honour. I can spare you, that is all.'

'When?'

'Tomorrow. There is a forest, a river cutting through it. Further than we should go tomorrow, but we shall press on late, into twilight. They will have to follow us or lose us.'

'And I stay behind.'

'Just so.'

Kai nodded slowly. 'There may be many of them.'

'You fear to fight against the odds?'

'Just do not think poorly of me if we do not come back.'

A shadow of a smile. 'No worse than I do already,' she said. 'Ride through once, then break away. Do not stand and fight, not even with that pretty Roman sword of yours.' She rose and walked past him, and as she did so, he felt a touch on his shoulder. 'Try to come back,' she said. And then she was gone into the night, and he could hear the foul curses echoing out as she berated one of the sentries.

He sat there for a time, his hand upon the shoulder where she had touched him.

'Perhaps she has forgiven me,' he said out loud, testing the weight of the words to see if they felt as though they might be true.

20

It was when they passed the ford close to dusk that Kai knew the time was near.

They had passed many a good spot to make camp, open ground that could be watched and defended. For most of the company there seemed no need to press on into the forest during darkness. To take the cavalry through the trees that stole every advantage they had and risked laming their horses, yet their captain pressed on. But there were those amongst the riders who had another purpose, and as they rode over the ford they were glancing back, mapping the paths between the trees, noting where the thick roots lay like snares, where a branch looped low to hook a horseman from the saddle. They might not get another chance to see it in good light.

Six, there were – Kai and his companions. And as they passed the ford they drifted towards the back of the warband. Some dismounted, feigning to adjust a saddle or retie a leather thong on their gear. Others turned and looped along the side of the line, as though scouting at something half-seen behind them. One by one they fell back, all of them looking to Kai, waiting for the signal.

He had spoken to them throughout the day – Tamura, Saratos, Phoros, Goar, and Erakas, those ones whom he thought might be most trusted. He had told them little enough, to be at the back and follow his lead after they passed the ford. None had questioned him.

And as it turned to dusk and the sun drew close to the horizon, he tapped his spear against Tamura's, a soft ring of metal against wood. And they turned their horses, formed into a loose skirmish line, and began to trot back towards the ford.

There was no concealing it from the others. But even as Kai's riders turned away there came the quick-barked orders from his sister, the command to keep silent and keep riding. And yet even so there was a voice from behind, a voice calling his name.

'Kai!'

It was Bahadur – pale-faced, clutching at his saddle like an old man, panic in his voice. He made to stir his horse towards them, but Laimei was beside him, her hand tangled in his reins to hold him in place. Her head bowed close to his, lips moving, and though Kai was too far away to know what was spoken he could see they were quick sharp words, like the work of a knife in the darkness. And, before they drew deeper into the trees and lost sight of his companions, Kai saw Bahadur bare his teeth and look away.

A pain about Kai's heart, to think that would be their last parting, as he and his companions rode on in silence, guiding their horses to the softer ground, ducking away from low branches. Now it was that the sounds of the forest came back stronger than those of the men and horses – the low hum of the insects, the sentry calls of the birds against intruders, the creak and groan of the trees as they shifted in the wind. The darkness settled deep. Kai let the reins go slack, trusting more to the horse's memory than to his own eyes to guide them. And then, soft as the whisper of a lover, he heard the calling of the water in his ears. The river and the ford were but a little way ahead.

He looped his hand in a circle in the air, and the riders drew in close. Hands to one another's shoulders, as they had gathered by the festival and the fire, the horses touching their noses together in their own silent communion.

'Those who follow us shall have to cross the water here,' he said, 'if they are to come tonight. Wait for my signal. Charge through once, then back through the trees. Keep the Wolf Star at your right hand, until you find the others at the edge of the forest. And stay on this side of the water, by the gods. There shall be no way back for you if you cross to the other side.'

'They shall be watching for us,' said Tamura.

'They shall be watching for more than six. They shall not see us.'

He looked around the faces gathered there, for the moon was out strong enough for him to see them. Most had that strange look of calm that comes before the battle, where the dice are cast in the air and the only thing left to do is see where they fall. Saratos was grinning, the joy of the chosen upon him. Phoros and Goar had the sour look of men tricked at the market, but resigned to the poor trade they had made – he would have to watch them. Only Tamura would not meet his eye.

Each of them found their place. The point where a tall bush met a tree, providing a shape that matched a horse and rider, the fallen log that one might place themselves behind, the low branch that was thick with leaves to screen the rider, and at a soft command their horses drew still as carved sculptures. For they too had hunted in the night before, and knew their lives depended upon the stillness. They waited.

The darkness was complete, save for the light of the moon low in the sky behind them. Soon came the frightening kind of boredom of the soldier lying in ambush, where time seems to still itself entirely. Kai watched the slow passage of a beetle crawling over a leaf, and it seemed to take an hour to cross half a hand's distance. With the boredom was the sleep that seemed to steal up like a witch's curse, to be blinked away at the very last moment with a sharp jolt of the heart.

Words came to him from the past, the way they do for those at the borderlands of waking and dreaming – a voice speaking sharp in his ear, Bahadur's voice.

'Bad ground for a horseman, a ford. Only a beach would be worse. That is why the heroes in the old stories are always fighting there.' He remembered the older man's smile, the eyes narrow and bright like little gemstones. 'They like to show off.'

He remembered too, then, asking Bahadur how to stay awake on watch, when his back was still raw from a whipping he'd taken. 'Think about women, lad,' Bahadur had said.

Kai watched the others as a good captain should, looking for the dull eyes of one frightened to utter stillness, the nervous hands twitching on the reins of one ready to bolt at the least excuse. And perhaps it was that he was so intent on watching the others, that he did not notice what was happening to him.

There was something winding and curling about his neck, like the hard cord of a garrotte. He put his hand to his throat and felt nothing but flesh, and yet still each breath came shorter than the last. His fingers numb, his other hand growing slack upon the spear, and his head bowing down, bowing low.

It was there upon him once more, that feeling he had known only once before. When he had fought against the Roman cavalry, against Lucius. Not that familiar fear that all know before battle, that comes as strong and passes as swift as a thunderstorm on the plain, but the hollow madness that struck him to stillness and cowardice. He took up the reins with an unfeeling hand, his horse stirring beneath him as it felt his urge to run.

And it was then that the other warband came to the ford.

He heard them before he saw them – the crunch of a branch underneath heavy hooves, the clatter and rattle of arms. Men and horses trying to move softly, but there were many of them, and in the still of the night they could not hide themselves. In the darkness, as the undergrowth shifted and tore forward, it almost seemed that the forest was advancing towards them.

Kai's eyes played the trickster as he tried to count them – one rider suddenly parted and split into two, or a trio of horse were revealed as the shadow of one. He heard the soft inhale beside him and looked to his companions, their eyes shining in the darkness as they silently asked for a command that he knew he could not give.

The soft splash of water, for they were fording the river – an advance guard that might have been a dozen riders on horseback. Shadows in the darkness, no way to see what arms they carried or what banners they rode under, and still Kai could not speak, could not move.

The moonlight broke through, and shone upon the rider in the lead. And from his side, Kai heard one horse try to call to another. It was Saratos's horse, giving a snorted greeting that echoed out above the chatter of the stream, and one of the horses across the water called back.

A stillness, then, just for a moment. As though the whole world held its breath. And Kai called to his riders, and he called for them to charge.

No time to run, for they would be scattered and lost, hunted and cut down. The only hope the darkness that might turn his six men into sixty, or a hundred, for the half-moon was at their back, the shadows dancing and lengthening about them.

He put his nose to the horse's mane, the branches cutting at his face like sword blades. He had to trust to his horse to find its way through, and at every fall of its feet he expected to feel the world lurch and turn about him, to taste earth and blood in his mouth and be buried beneath his mount. For already, close by, there was the high-pitched scream of a downed horse.

He could feel the earth through the pace of the horse, and it changed beneath them, soft and heavy as they charged onto the bank. And there was a shape before him, the shadow of man on horseback looming large and lifting a spear. But that other man had misjudged in the darkness, and Kai's lance was in him with the sharp snap of blade and bone. The shadow screamed and twisted away, and Kai lurched in the saddle, his horse scrabbling and kicking the soft earth at the edge of the bank. He could feel the cool air rising from the river, see the moonlight silvering the spray from man and horse fighting through the water. And about him, he could hear men gathering to kill him.

He fought like a blind man, more through sound and feel than sight. The rank stink of a frightened horse close by, and he turned in the saddle and swung his broken spear like a sword, backhand across the nose of the horse, and it reared and dumped its rider in the water. He felt a pair of hands close about his wrist, trying to prise the weapon from his grip. But the fingers were gone a moment later, and all about him he could hear the war cries of his own riders. Erakas the closest, the rest nearby, and he could hear them all calling his name.

The water was alive with horses; the other side of the river swarmed with shadows of others pressing forward, but Kai's riders held the bank – he had five beats of the heart, perhaps, before those panicking men realised how few faced them.

'With me! With me!' he called, pulling his sword and
rapping it against his armour, as they formed a ragged line
at the edge of the water, formed as though for another
charge, and he could see. The whistle of arrows then, but
shot blind and fast, rattling from the trees, none falling
amongst his riders.

'Back now!'

Back through the labyrinth of the trees, his head
wrenched as a branch struck him, his weight tipping back
and hands grasping at the air. But his horse felt it, slowed
for a moment, and Kai found his balance again.

On the ground, he could see a rider who had fallen –
Goar, pushing the writhing horse off himself, reaching up a
hand like a drowning man. And behind, he could hear the
sound of cavalry crossing the river, so many that it was as
though the river had come alive behind them.

And so Kai put his heels to his horse, the cry of the
fallen rider sounding in his ears as he moved through the
trees, his horse gasping and sweating beneath him, cutting
to the north and the west, the blood pounding in his ears,
until at last the horse could go no further and he knew that
it must rest or die.

Kai swung down from the saddle to ease the weight,
cradled the horse's head against his own and whispered
the words of gratitude that every rider owes his mount. He
breathed and breathed until his lungs were cool and the
roar in his ears fell silent.

He listened to the sounds, and heard nothing at all. He
looked about the woods, and no shadows moved. He was
alone.

21

At the edge of the woods, a single rider waited beside her horse. The horse was still and calm, for when he found himself out of battle unbloodied, the fury and fear passed as quickly as water flowing from a shattered cup. The rider moved her hands restlessly over the horse, circling the neck and the mane, and every so often she looked towards the weapon that lay on the ground beside her. For the tip of the spear shone when the light of the moon fell upon it, bright and undimmed by blood.

They were deep into the night now, the memory of the battle fading already, quick and sharp as a nightmare receding. Still the quickened heart, the stink of fear sweat upon the skin. Once more that maddening fear of waiting – not the fear of lying in an ambush, but of waiting for friends who would not come.

Once she made as if to rise back into the saddle, to set her path to the west to find the warband, or perhaps to go back into the woods in search of the others, for even that seemed better than to stay alone in that place any longer. But her trembling hands went still on the saddle, and she returned to her waiting.

In time, there was sound from the forest. The soft parting of leaves, the turn of mulch beneath a hoof. A shadow breaking from the tree line.

She was in the saddle in a moment – the spear forgotten on the ground in her haste, but too late now to pick it up. Her horse called its greeting, but that held no meaning now, not after what had happened at the ford. She waited until she heard a voice call out.

'Though our lives be short…'

Tamura shivered with relief, and finished the old proverb: '… let our fame be great.'

'A good thing we both remember our stories,' Kai said, as he rode next to her. 'I am glad you made it away safe. The others?' he said.

She shook her head. 'No sign of them yet.'

He dismounted, pulled a glove from his hand and ran it across the body of his horse, feeling for the hot blood of a wound. For the horses often bore their wounds more bravely than men, giving no sign of complaint and going to death silently. He found grazes here and there, places where the hair had been rubbed down to stubble by the scraping of armour against the skin, but no more than that.

'I did not charge with you,' Tamura said.

Kai lifted his head and looked towards her, but found her staring at the ground, wide-eyed, and she would not meet his gaze.

'I am sorry,' she continued. 'I wanted to. But was afraid.'

'You ran?'

'No. But I did not follow you, not until we held the bank.'

'Did any of the others see?'

'I do not think so.'

'Do not let it happen again.'

He heard a soft intake of breath, the choke of tears. 'I thought that perhaps you might...'

'What did you think?' Kai said, sharper than he had meant to. He waited for a moment, to see if his voice would bring death riding from the tree line. But there was nothing but the dark and the wind.

'The horse called out,' she said.

'Yes,' he said. 'I know.'

Another question, hanging heavy in the air. A truth that was not quite ready to be spoken. Perhaps it might have been, if they had been given a moment longer. But another shadow came from the woods – Saratos, trotting up to them with a smile upon his face.

'A good night for a ride. A lover's moon they call this, and here I find you both.'

'Yet always you seem to ride alone,' Tamura shot back.

'Quiet, both of you!' Kai said.' Or would you bring the others down on us?'

'No, captain. Forgive me,' Saratos said. They were close enough now that Kai could see the white skin marked with black across the cheek, dried blood from some near miss. The trembling across the skin that Saratos had tried to still with his jest. They clasped their hands together, and they waited.

As the moon turned through the sky, they stayed in place hoping for others to emerge from the woods. Slowly, achingly slowly, as if entire nights passed between every beating of the heart.

They waited together, silent, for as long as they could.

'Well,' said Kai at last, 'that is it.'

Again, the hand looping in the air to draw them close, and again they formed their circle, clasped their arms around each other.

'I saw Goar on the ground,' said Kai. He remembered once more the sight of that man's face, hands reaching up like one swept into the white water of a river – a man so close to safety, who already knows that he is dead. 'Did either of you see others fall for certain?'

'I think that I saw Erakas die,' said Saratos. 'Speared from his horse. I killed the man that did it, but he was in the water then. I saw no more than that.'

A hard touch in the heart, to know Erakas dead, for he had been the first beside Kai on the riverbank. A memory swam up from the winter – laughter around a fire, the wine running freely, Erakas's arm about his shoulders, a mad and merry smile upon his lips. Then the memory was gone, and the man with it.

'I think that Phoros stayed, that he tried to get Goar from the ground,' said Tamura. And they would not look at each other then. For they had all ridden past, and none of them had found the courage to stop.

'If they are not here now,' said Kai, 'then they never will be. They go to the gods, and bravely, as friends. We shall see them soon enough.'

'Ware, behind!'

At once the three of them were in a line, ready for the

charge, as the undergrowth tore open and a shadow came from the trees.

A single rider – no, a single horse, its saddle bloody and empty, the horse itself snorting and dancing about. But seeing its companions there, it gave nearly a human cry of relief. For it was only in the worst of times that the horses almost seemed to find a human voice. It came close – still wary of them, but close enough for them to see the pattern of its coat and the markings on the war gear.

'It is Phoros's horse,' Saratos said. 'They are all gone, then.'

'A good death,' Tamura said, a hollowness to her voice.

'Come,' Kai answered, 'we have waited here too long. They might be after us soon.'

They made their way towards the west, just as the first signs of dawn began to touch the sky. The dead man's horse trailed a little behind them – and, perhaps, the dead followed them too.

When Kai led them back into the camp at first light, silent and war weary, Laimei was there to greet them. She did not speak. Kai saw how she looked amongst them, silently noting the missing and the horse that bore an empty saddle, the darkened weapons and hacked armour. But she looked too on the pride they carried in their silence – the arrogant tilt of the head, the gaze sharp and clear, answering her with no shame. This, it seemed, was report enough. A little nod was all the praise she offered in return, a sweeping gesture with an open hand, ordering them to take their place in the line.

It was the others who questioned them – leaning across to whisper in the saddle, three of them clustering around Tamura when they first stopped to water the horses. Kai heard the others speak of the charge by the river, and they spoke more freely when they saw that he would not tell the story, for they would not see the captain – *their* captain – sell himself short. But Tamura and Saratos would not say whom they had fought. No matter who asked him, Kai kept his silence. There was only one that he wished to speak to, but Bahadur rode at the head of the column, head hung low. He alone showed no interest in the return of Kai and the others – lost, it seemed, in some other journey of his own.

It was late in the day, when Kai's riders could be seen swaying like drunkards in the saddle, the battle weariness lying upon them as sure as a curse, that Laimei took him aside. When they stopped to rest the horses, she looped an arm about his shoulder, a pretence of a sister's love for the others to see. For though there was a smile upon her face, her eyes were dull as she led him to the edge of the line, out of earshot of the others. Still smiling, she said: 'Now, tell me what you would not tell the others.'

'Some day,' Kai answered, 'I shall find out how it is you know such things.'

'Your face is like the painting of a child. I do not know how the others cannot see it themselves.'

He looked about, for riders in a warband were as

curious as children, gossiped like old men. But there were none, he thought, who rode close enough to hear.

'I could not tell the numbers exactly,' he said. 'But it was a well-chosen size. Small enough to move quickly, to track us and catch us. And—'

'Great enough for the advantage if they fought us.' He saw the killing madness in the smile then. 'They know our number. Well then.'

Kai hesitated then, at the look on her face. 'There is more,' he said. 'Our horses knew each other. And I saw one of them clear in the moonlight. They were—'

'Enough.'

'You do not believe me?'

'I believe the horses,' she said. 'That is enough. What do I need to know of what you thought you saw, or thought you heard.'

'You do not seem surprised,' said Kai.

'Why should I be? What else would make sense? I thought they would be Sarmatians.'

He felt his skin cool at that, at the naming of their people. For though a part of him had known when he saw the armour of horn scales in the moonlight, since one horse had called to another, to have it spoken aloud was something else entirely. That they were hunted by their own people.

He watched her think for a time. Her eyes shifting about the camp, making the captain's endless judgements. Numbers and spirit, speed and weight. And time, always time above all.

'We shall press forward, lose them in the next few days,'

she said. 'You did well to bloody them. It was bravely done.'

A surge in the heart then, to hear her praise him, and he hated himself for it. 'You mean to go on?' he said.

'Of course. The Romans shall not wait for us. We have our command, and must take Bahadur over the water.'

'Laimei, we must go back. Some of us, at least.'

She stared at him then, and made no answer.

'I do not know what it means to have our own people trailing us,' he continued. 'But it counts for nothing good.'

'It does not matter.'

'You do not wish to know what it means? Why we have been betrayed?'

'If the message does not make it to the Romans, then nothing matters.'

'At least let a single rider go back.'

She smiled again, her ghastly, murderous smile. 'Oh, you look to escape at the last? I thought better of you.'

'Send someone else. Go yourself, none doubt your courage. A word of warning to our clan, that is all.'

'Brother.' How long it had been since she had called him that, he thought, as she gestured to the riders scattered about them. 'They ride towards death gladly,' she said, 'for they feel there is no choice. Give it to them, and they will desert in but a few days. We have both seen warbands break that way. The courage of men is such a fragile thing. All must go, or none.'

She looked at him, and for a moment there was nothing of their feud etched upon her face. Only something imploring in the softness of the eyes, a hand half reaching towards him. A sister wishing for her brother to make the right choice.

'You are the captain,' Kai said at last. 'And I ride at your command.'

'That I am. You have done well. Go and take your place in the line.'

He turned back towards his horse – he would have to lose himself, then, in the rhythm of the horse beneath him, the feel of spear in hand and the taste of the spring air upon his lips. But before that, he asked one more question. A question that he knew the answer to already.

'What did you say to Bahadur?' he said.

'The truth, of course,' she answered. 'As I always do.'

22

Those days that followed all passed like one another. Hard riding, seeking to outpace those who followed, and more besides. A moment of shame or cowardice, a broken heart or a lost fellowship – all could be forgotten in the movement of a horse across the plains. To forget what lay behind them, to believe it an impossibility to turn back as though the ground fell away into some black abyss behind the horses' hooves at every step. That only the world ahead mattered.

The riders drew close on the ride, close enough to be able to reach out and touch another with a crooked arm and an open palm. Closer still at night, huddled together in the blankets, rushing to help each other with the thousand little chores of a warband on the march, careful to do nothing alone. Speaking of many things, but more often holding the silence together. That comfort of the pack, when one man often found his thoughts spoken by another, an action begun that was completed by a companion. And Kai let himself be swallowed up by them, for it seemed that the past no longer mattered. He had his place amongst his people once more.

And so, one night by the fire, when Kai felt an arm
wrap about his shoulder, it was no surprise – every day
found a different companion settling beside him. Yet the
sharpness of the embrace was unexpected, the arm bones
hard across his shoulders. The grey eyes he saw that had
once been sharp and full of life were watery now, the
eyes of a drunkard or an old man. But there was comfort
to be found there still, as Bahadur took the place by
his side.

They leaned against each other for a long time, and they
did not speak.

At last, Bahadur said: 'I was told a story, of our ancestors.
How each man hung a quiver on his tent, and at the end of
each day, he dropped in a white stone or a black, to mark a
good or evil day. And at the end of a man's life they would
turn out the quiver, and so judge it.'

Kai made no answer at first. Then: 'Where did they find
so many stones upon the steppe?'

A hiss from Bahadur. 'Quiet, idiot. Must you spoil the
story?' A pause, and then he continued. 'I think that, were
I to count them for my own life, I would have more white
stones than black,' he said. 'But some of those black stones,
they weigh very heavy.'

'It would be the same for me,' said Kai. 'And that day
upon the ice when I thought I saw you dead, that would be
the worst of them all.'

Bahadur nodded. 'Arite is a beautiful woman, is she
not?'

'She is.' Kai hesitated. 'You must know, I thought—'

'I know, I know.' A hand taking his, holding it in the

darkness. 'No harm in lying with a dead man's wife. I was dead, then.' Bahadur chuckled. 'Just do not lie with a living man's wife. At least, not mine. Though I am still not quite living now.'

'You do live, Bahadur. And I am glad of it.'

'I am a little mad now, Kai. I can feel it there always. As though there is some fragment of a blade in my heart. Every so often, it cuts something, and I lose myself again. I will try not to.' A heavy breath that Kai felt as much as heard. 'She sought to drive us apart. Your sister, I mean, when she spoke to me. We must not let that happen.'

'It shall not.'

Bahadur looked towards the rest of the company – Saratos teasing a thorn from his horse's hoof, Laimei kneeling in prayer to a god of love or war, the others snatching what fragment of sleep they could before the order came to move once more. Kai wondered if the other man was trying to remember his courage by looking on them, to find that bravery they shared as freely as wine and song. But when he spoke again, Kai understood why Bahadur's eyes seemed to linger on the markings on their armour and their banners, the silhouettes of the horses against the low sun.

'Will you tell me what happened at the ford?' he said. 'The truth of it, I mean.'

'If you are asking, then I think you know already.'

'I suppose that I do. They were our people that you fought?'

'Yes. I could not tell which of the clans they came from. But they are Sarmatians that hunt us now.'

Bahadur looked back to Kai then, and there was something of his old self in his eyes. 'What are you going to do?' he said.

Kai started at that – for all that he had thought that Bahadur might say, he had not expected those words. Perhaps it had been that he had forgotten that he still had a choice. Perhaps it was that he had wanted to forget. 'It is her command to continue,' he said.

'But what will *you* do?'

Another man would have given an order, but that was not Bahadur's way. Always the choice, always the trust that the right choice would be made, and Kai felt a bitter little smile force its way onto his face, for what else was there to do when one could hear the gods laughing?

To the west, he felt a longing stronger than love. It might be death waiting for them there, but a death like a sacred river, a place where all shame might be washed away. He had lived so long in shame that he had forgotten what it was to be free of it. He could almost taste that freedom in his mouth, feel its lightness upon his skin. And to be part of a company once more, to bear that mark of honour, to feel those riders at his back and trust them completely, to have that trust returned. He did not know if he could give that up again.

And to the east, the dark stain of desertion, like wine upon fine silk. For what forgiveness would there be from one who ran from the warband? Whatever shame he had worn, it was nothing compared to that. And if he were caught, the death given only to deserters, the slow death by knife and fire.

He searched the air for an omen – an eagle turning one way or another, a pattern of light upon the grass that might speak of something godly. But there was none that he might see.

'I will go back,' he said.

'Tell me why,' Bahadur asked, his voice gentle.

'If I were to stay, I would stay for myself. My precious honour. Not for our people.' He looked to his hands. 'I do not know why they hunt us. I do not know what I may do against that, on my own. But I must try. Laimei—'

'Shall never forgive you? It may be so. But she shall see me to the west first. Nothing matters more than that. Perhaps nothing shall matter after that. I shall try to make the peace with the Romans, and you must see to it that it is kept amongst our people.'

Word passed about the riders then – the command to mount and make ready. Those who dozed about the fire were being kicked awake, the horses stirring and pulling at their tied reins. Bahadur and Kai rose like drunken men, heavy legged and leaning on one another, and made their way to their mounts. And when Kai laid a hand against its neck the horse stirred, fixed one wise eye upon him and turned its head back towards the east. For they always seemed to know before a new journey, to know the mind and heart of their rider.

Bahadur tilted his head to the side – a gesture Kai had seen too many times before, when his friend was trying to piece together a story, or unpick a riddle. 'There are men and women on the plains,' he said, 'who share their lovers as if they are passing wine about the fire. I wish I were one of those men. And if I were, I would want to share my wife with you. But I am not. I cannot.'

Once more, they embraced like brothers. As they parted, Kai felt the sensation of eyes upon his skin, yet when he looked about the company all were busy mounting and arming.

A thought born of darkness and fear, and no more.

A palm laid against the shoulder, light as a lover's touch. A whisper in the ear, close enough to feel the warmth of the breath. And Kai awoke, his half-dream twisting into the world so that for a moment he thought it was Arite beside him, and he whispered her name.

Laughter in the darkness – the low chuckle of Saratos. 'Afraid not, lad,' the old warrior said. 'It is your watch. You can dream of another man's wife at a different time.'

Fully awake now, Kai took the man's proffered hand and stumbled to his feet. They were in the deepest part of the night now, the narrowing moon half hidden by the clouds, and once more, he went to take his place as a sentry.

But something was different this time – the rich scent of pine trees filled the air as they stirred and danced with the wind above him, for they had stopped beside a copse of trees, made a brief camp up against them. And so rather than four other sentries, there was only one that he could see, a young lad half asleep in his saddle, his head lolling and swaying. And without even thinking, Kai gave his horse a gentle touch of the heels, set it forward three paces, waited.

No call came from behind, and so the horse continued, hesitating as it crossed some unseen boundary twenty paces from the camp. Kai felt it too – almost a physical pain, to part himself from the warband, from the thing they were becoming. The weak and foolish found comfort there, and those who were brave found that bravery shared and strengthened amongst the rest until it was a godly power. How hard it was to become but a man once again, when one had tasted such strength. To be just a man and a horse, alone in the night.

A parting of the clouds would undo him, a rotten branch underfoot would be traitor enough, and he waited for the snorted challenge of the horse, the call of the sentry, the questions asked to which there would be no answer. But it did not come.

It seemed that the gods favoured him, as he guided his horse around the copse, and found open ground before him. He had almost made it away when he felt that sensation once more, that feeling of eyes upon his skin.

Behind him, a shadow – a ghost, he might have thought at first, one of the dark riders that haunt the plains, hunting those foolish enough to travel alone. For those without companions were often found dead without a mark upon them, speared from their horses by some unseen lance from another world. But the clouds parted a little from the moon, and he felt a shiver of fate, and love, as he looked upon his sister's face.

'You had to run, didn't you?' said Laimei. 'You could not, even once, do as you are commanded.'

'You saw me go?'

'I knew you would go. It has always been my fate, to know all the foolish and cowardly things that you will do, even before you do them.' The horse stirred beneath her, restless. 'I knew you would not kill our father. That you would shame us all, and I would have to take your place. To do what you could not.'

'And I am sorry for it.'

'That is not enough,' she said, her eyes never leaving his. 'Was it Bahadur who told you to do this? Some deal that you struck? Did he agree to let you share Arite in the bargain, as men might share a horse or a bowl of stew?'

'No. I chose myself. And we share much, but not her.'

Laimei's spear swung down in the darkness, laid across the neck of her horse – not levelled at him, not yet. 'Come back with me,' she said. 'There is still time. If the others ask, we shall—'

'I cannot do it,' said Kai. 'It is as it has always been. You cannot forgive me, and I cannot do as you command.'

'And I cannot let you go.'

'Call the others, then. You have your deserter. Call them and kill me.'

Silence answered him.

'Is this not what you want?' he said.

'I do not need them. And I cannot trust them.' Motion from the spear – a tremor passing down it, from the hands that held it. And when she spoke, it was as though she dragged up the words from some deeper part of herself, as if the words themselves came out bloody. 'They love you more than me,' she said. 'Perhaps that is the worst of it. But I suppose the weak are always loved more than the strong.

272

The way men love mewling infants, and blind puppies, and fools.'

'They do. But that is not the only reason that they love me more than you.' Kai reached forward, stroked the neck of his horse. To calm her, and reassure her, so that she would not blame herself for what was to come. 'How shall we settle this?' he said.

'Wait for the wind to blow,' she answered. 'There is no need for the others to hear this.'

A touch of the reins, a shift of weight, and his horse was moving backwards, one careful duellist's step after another, until they were far enough apart for the charge. He took the spear in both hands, looped the leather thong about his wrist. He waited.

The wind had been strong that night, great cutting gusts rolling across the long grass and through the trees. Yet now the air fell to perfect stillness, and it seemed some god held his breath, giving them a chance to change their minds.

Kai breathed in deeply, took in that beautifully sharp scent of horse sweat. It must have been one of the first things he had smelled – first the gore of birth, and then the smell of a horse. Fitting that it should be reversed now, for there would be blood in the air soon enough. Another circle closed.

A little stirring of wind. His horse's ears flicking against it. Then a great roaring in his ears as the air tore sideways, and the horses were surging forward, the spears tilting low. No time to blink, weeping eyes held open against the wind, the movement of the horse seeming impossibly fast in the darkness.

And, just as they drew close, Kai cast his spear to the ground, and closed his eyes.

A slap of air struck his side, the clatter of armour and hard fall of the hooves passing close. But no sudden force of a blade into his chest, no unseen hand lifting him from the saddle, no hot taste of blood in his mouth. His sister riding past, her spear high in the air. Had she raised it before he cast his down, or after? Impossible to tell in the darkness.

He watched her then, to see if she would come around for another pass. But the horse was turning and wheeling, and she was stabbing at the air all about her as though surrounded in the press of battle, lunging at phantoms that only she could see, roaring and weeping as she gave one killing stroke after another into the empty air.

No time to wait out the frenzy, for the others would surely note their absence by now. No words that he could risk that might stir her from the madness, for he could only think she would seek to kill away the shame if he gave her the chance. And so he struck out into the darkness, taking his mark by moon and star.

He should have kept to a light pace, spared the horse for as long as he could. He might be pursued, and there was that other warband somewhere in front of them, hunting in the dark. But his horse was flying through the night, towards the point where the sun would rise, for Kai already had the feeling, as sure as curse or omen, that he would be too late.

23

The hard wind called from the west, and blew upon on the camp of the River Dragon. The spirit wind, their people called it, for there were unseen messengers abroad in the dark, bringing word from the living and the dead. And so it was that when the hard west wind blew, there were many who did not sleep. They huddled on the steps of their wagons and at the entrances of their tents – wrapped up thick in felt and fur, but with their heads uncovered, ears white with the cold and teeth gritted against the pain, for they would not pass the chance to hear some whisper on that wind. And so it was with Arite.

For days their people had wandered slowly from the winter campground, parting once more into the five clans, a nation divided and on the move once more. The dream of a nation, like all dreams, that dissolved under the light of a spring sun. And Arite's people, the clan of the River Dragon, had moved to the south and the west, back towards the boundaries of their lands. A moving city upon the plain, resting here for only a single night.

Lucius and Kai's daughter lay asleep in the caravan behind her, but the wind called to her as surely as a lover in the night, some turning passage of the wind that seemed to sound her name. She found herself walking far from the embers of the fire, to the northern borders of the camp. The sentries were lost in the darkness, the clouds thick and stars unseen. It was as though she stood at the edge of some great black sea, those waters that had swallowed her husband and children and her lover. And she listened for them, and waited for them to speak.

No words came to her on the wind, from the living or the dead. Perhaps it was that Kai and Bahadur were already slain, that their spirits wandered back slow across the plain and forest, sparing her the knowledge of their deaths for as long as they could. But she chose to believe that they lived. She waited there to see if the wind might change, so she might send a message of her own back with it.

A twist of the air rolled across her skin then, and somehow it carried a warning with it. Not one of sound or even smell – it was as though something invisible were carried to her from someone hidden in the night, some part of their spirit laid across her skin by the wind. For there were moving shadows out there, swimmers in that black sea beyond the camp.

And so it was that she saw them as they came, the line of riders from the darkness. Silent, faces soot-blackened, and even the horses were voiceless, their mouths bound with leather thongs. They were Sarmatians, bearing the long spears and scale armour of their people, and they could have been mistaken for ghosts, her clan's dead riders returning from the Otherlands, until the first spear struck home and pinned a man to the ground at the edge of the camp. His screams drowned out by the war cry of the raiders, a song of the Wolves of the Steppe.

An old pain in Arite's knee shooting fire as she ran, her legs as dull and heavy as though she were running in a nightmare. At any moment she expected to feel the sharp touch from behind and see the spearhead burst from her chest like a living thing, to see the world rolling into darkness and dust. But though they seemed all about her, hooves beating the ground so that she felt it shake and the war cries roaring in her ears, it seemed that none of them thought her worth the killing.

At the wagon, Lucius and Tomyris already there, weapons in hand – the child's face painted with an eerie calm, and Lucius with his eyes rolling in his head, muttering prayers or curses to himself in his own language. For like all Romans he feared the ambush, to be caught in open ground.

In moments she had cut the horses loose and mounted, the horse trembling beneath her, the spear cool and steady in Arite's hand.

'A raid,' she said. 'Our people. The Wolves have betrayed us.'

'What do we do?' said Lucius.

She saw it all in a moment. The raiders passing through like a great wave from the black sea beyond, leaving the dead behind them, drowned on dry land. The light already rising from where the wagons had been fired – so soon, impossibly soon. The war cries that sang out unanswered.

'We must run,' she said.

There should have been no path for escape. Everywhere she looked were the raiders of the Wolf noosing the camp, every way closed by horse and spear. Yet fluttering in the air somewhere close, a Dragon banner rose, some captain of her people leading a doomed charge. She heard the war cries of the Wolves closing about that banner, and through the burning tents, she saw a gap open up, a path to the black open steppe.

Arite charged towards that gap, Lucius and Tomyris close behind. They were through it, past it, the dark plain open before them. And they almost made it away. Almost, they were allowed to live.

For she heard a hunting cry sound high and close. For a moment, Arite could not find the courage to look back – in nightmares, a stalking monster may remain fleshless until it is looked upon, and she had the mad dreamer's hope that if she did not look they could not harm her. Then she heard Tomyris crying out, and she could wait no longer. She looked back upon her death, five riders peeling towards them, pursuing them into the darkness.

The lightest tug of the reins, and her horse fell to a grateful stillness. A little pressure of the right knee, and they were wheeling around. For the horses they rode were old warriors, robbed of the speed of their youth, pursued by eager young killers. She knew that there would be no outrunning those who followed them. She could only hope to wear her wounds upon her front, and before her, she saw their pursuers slow to a walk, too. No need for them to waste the breath of their horses, or trust to uncertain footing in the dark.

Arite leaned over in her saddle, passed Lucius a sword. He gave an experimental swing, testing the weight and the balance.

'It is old,' she warned. 'Not as strong as the ones you are used to. Be sure of your stroke.'

'It does not matter. Thank you,' he said, his voice just as calm as hers.

'Tomyris...' But Arite fell silent as she turned to the girl. She meant to tell her to ride away, flee into the night and follow the river to the east. But what a death that would be to gift the child, alone and starving on the steppe. And so instead, she said: 'Ride close behind, and stay low in the saddle. Use your dagger – at that place on the thigh, or across the eye of the horse.' The child shuddered at that, though more for the thought of the horse than the man. Perhaps she was still young enough, mercifully young, that she could not think of her own death.

Both sides still walking, that maddening slow pace of cavalry conserving their horses. The moon was out once more, and she could see the markings of their gear, the scalps tied to the saddlehead. Trophies that they would join soon enough.

She tried to think that it was well to end this way – a death from the old stories. But there, at the last, she found that she did not believe in the glorious death. There was only a desperate hunger to live. She could feel dewed grass against her fingers, a lover's weight above her, the taste of wine around a fire with close companions.

'One last time,' she said. And then, once again, she spoke

a name, only one this time. 'Kai,' she said. And she stirred the horse to a charge.

One rider of the five before them, standing tall in his seat, checked his horse. He seemed to turn away, and Arite thought at first that he meant to flee – perhaps it was that he had no heart to kill a woman and her child. But then the shadow of a blade rising high, and the rider beside him was tumbling from the saddle with a wet, bubbling scream.

No time to think of what had happened, for all she knew now was that they were three against four. Lucius was ahead of her, cutting to the side to draw a rider away from the pack. A sword against a lance seemed a hopeless challenge, but as he drew close Lucius gave his war cry in the tongue of Rome. The rider he faced shied away – either the horse or the man remembered the battle on the ice, and flinched in fear to hear the voice of the Emperor. And Lucius had twisted past the questing spear, and answered with a reverse cut that painted the horse with blood.

Another of the riders turned his horse to face her – that wondrous lightness, then, of those who know they are soon to die, but know that they may accomplish something with the dying. She knew that nothing mattered but the killing of this man.

She twisted in the saddle at the last moment, seeking just a little more reach. She felt a spearhead rip through the fabric of her dress, a line of white fire drawn across her ribs. Her own spear was wrenched from her hands as though by the force of a god, and when she looked back she saw the other man clutching at his thigh, his life pouring from his leg, hands scooping at the blood as though to gather it back into himself, even as he slid from the gore-slicked saddle.

Her horse was gasping, blown, and she had no weapon in her hand. She saw the last two Wolf clansmen fighting each other, trading strokes of sword and axe – one man screaming and sobbing, the other calm, parrying with the head of the axe and an armoured gauntlet and waiting for his chance.

'Bastard! Traitor!' yelled the first man, even as his silent companion struck and blinded his horse. It screamed and bucked, threw its rider flat across its neck, a victim on the altar. The axe swung and bit, and the screams fell to silence.

A sudden stillness came over them all. There seemed to be no rush, no hurry to do anything. Arite should have turned and fled, or cut this last man from the saddle. But they were held there, waiting in the darkness.

The rider who had turned on his companions reached up and pushed his helm up onto his forehead. And she knew then, even before she saw the scar. She knew from the smile on his face, the sour, proud smile of Gaevani.

He looked upon the dead around him, clansmen and kinsmen, his cheeks still holding their colour despite the butcher's work that he had done. After a moment he said: 'Never much liked them, anyway.' And then he gave a kingly wave of the hand, directing them away.

'Get out of here. Ride back east, and stay off the rivers if you can, they shall be hunting along the banks.'

'Why let us go?'

'A favour that I owed,' he said. 'And you won your

wager, that the Roman would last the winter. You have no wine to give me, but you may call it settled, now.' He grinned at her, his teeth pale and sharp in the moonlight. 'And now I must get back to killing your clansmen.'

'Bastard!'

He shrugged. 'I have no love for it. But my chieftain calls, and I obey.'

'Why have you done this?'

'Zanticus shall not crawl to the Romans and beg for the lives of his people.' He looked back to the camp, and the killing. 'This is a punishment for cowardice, for the thought of surrender your people gave us. We shall take your clan as slaves, and carry the fight to Rome.'

She looked towards the west – the shadow of the mountains, the imagined land beyond. And Gaevani answered her unspoken thought.

'It was a fool's plan,' he said. 'Something from another time, a better time.' Another war cry, loud and close. 'Go now, or we shall be seen together. They will be firing the rest of the wagons, soon.'

'There will be a reckoning for this,' she said.

'No,' he said simply. 'There will not.'

There was no more time then. Away in the darkness, the ground rolling away beneath them, and behind her the fire rising high, the screams settling into silence.

Before the Emperor, the barbarian was kneeling. Shins pressed to the stone, palms towards the sky, eyes averted from the god before him.

'I did not think that you would return,' said the Emperor. 'Perhaps it is true what you have said, and you do have an honour of sorts. You came alone?'

'My companions brought me to the edge of the river, Emperor. I am alone now.'

'And you say that your people will surrender?'

'They shall,' Bahadur answered.

'They shall give themselves up to slavery, without raising their spears against us?'

'Their lives are yours.'

Murmuring about the room then. For there were many gathered in the Emperor's chambers, the Tribunes and the Legate, and they spoke almost with a single voice. That there was to be no trusting a barbarian's promises. That now was the time to destroy them once and for all.

The Emperor let them speak, let the ritual praise of his wisdom wind down to silence. And he said: 'Yes, you are quite right. This barbarian lies to me.'

The Emperor knew what the response to this would be, that there was no insult greater amongst the Sarmatians than to be called a liar or a breaker of oaths. And so it was that Bahadur forgot himself, raised his head, and looked upon a god.

A judgement at once, the blows raining down upon him from the hafts of spears and the centurions' cudgels, the Praetorians offering their rough justice for the affront to their master. A hand thrown up from the Emperor, and the beatings ceased.

'Word already came,' the Emperor said, 'from our scouts across the water. The Sarmatians gather for war, and march to the west, towards the Danubius. But I wanted to see how well he would lie to me.' A tight little smile – the expression of a man used to being disappointed. 'He did it well. His promises of honour were empty things, of course.'

A gurgling whisper from the floor, as the broken man tried to speak.

'Put him with the prisoners,' the Emperor said. 'Call the army out.'

Soon, upon the parade ground before the fortress, the Legion gathered in line and column, marked and precise, golden eagles fixed in flight above them. They stood and waited for the words of the Emperor, like children before a patriarch, waiting for judgement and command. And they were sons of a kind to him – for many, he was a better father than those who had raised them.

On the dais, clad in fur and Imperial purple, the Emperor spoke. In simple and plain words he praised the Legion, commended those men who had earned particular honour in battle, gave thanks to the gods. Dry words, but in the space between them each man there could hear what he wanted to hear, listen to the praise most longed for.

Then, he spoke of what was come. It was then that he told them what he wanted them to do. And these words were simple, too, the command one of the oldest that generals had ever given to soldiers, chieftains to tribesmen, in the countless generations that men had fought with one another. With iron sword, and flint arrowheads. With wooden spears, a rock curled into a hand, the bare hand itself. The command to exterminate, to destroy, to leave none alive.

There was a moment's silence, after the words he had spoken. And then they answered him – no wild cheer or animal cry, for even in fervour they kept their discipline. A single roar, a single word sounded out together.

The sound carried deep into the fort. Cutting over the pounding of the blacksmith's hammer, past the broiling cookfires, passing deep down stairwell and wooden door, to the place where the prisoners were kept. Bound in chains of iron that would have been a fortune out upon the plains, there were fewer now than had been paraded before the Emperor. They had died the way a wild animal will when it is confined. Fed and watered, wanting for nothing, and still they will lie down to die.

A few lifted their heads – there were many who had not the strength or the will to even manage that – but most of those that did gave no sign of understanding the significance of that sound. There was only one amongst them, his body marked with bruises and thin trails of blood, who seemed to understand. For even though they were too far to hear what was chanted, though the distance had rendered it a wordless sound like the calving of ice or the roar of a rockfall on a mountain, it seemed that he knew what it meant.

And Bahadur put his head in his hands, and he wept.

Part 3

AN OATH UPON
A SWORD

24

Twilight on the steppe, as Kai returned to the remnants of the winter campground, the place the Five Clans had made their home and their peace for a single season. The earth marked and scored by wheel ruts and footfalls, scratched and scarred like the etchings of a giant upon the ground. Or a city of ghosts, for it was said that there were places in the world where one could see the workings of invisible cities – the grass parting beneath unseen footfalls, squares of scored earth that sprang up overnight, marking some new building of light and air that housed another ghost.

He had pushed harder than he should have that day, leaving his horse filmed with grey sweat and a rattling breathing that he did not like the sound of. But he was too afraid to spend another night alone upon the plains. There was a madness in solitude that every Sarmatian knew of – the herdsman who wandered too far in search of a lost foal, the scout separated from his companions before the cattle raid, the exiled man riding alone across the plain to beg a place from another clan. Whispers in the darkness that could break a mind.

And so he took his place amongst the traces of his people: the footprint of a child in soft ground, the mottled earth where a herd had moved together, the old firepits and the marks of the wagons. In the morning he would follow those trails, try to pick out his clan from the five that drifted back across the steppe. He would have to remember everything he knew of his people, to read the patterns in the earth that only he might know. The wagons driven a careful distance apart between two brothers who had feuded over a woman for three winters past. That cluster of young companions who always travelled together, a sworn brotherhood of seven children who had not yet had their fellowship broken by age. The way Arite always drove her wagon hard and a little apart from the rest of the clan, taking her place on the sunward edge. It would be a hard enough task for a good tracker, and he had never had that gift. Fortune had carried him so far – it would have to carry him a little further now.

He tried to sing to keep himself company, and the wind caught and turned his voice as though in mockery. He fell quiet once more, and in that silence, he felt the dead gather about him.

They had been there after the battle on the ice, watching him as he alone rose from the piles of the fallen. And they were around the campfire that night. Unseen, giving ghostly touches to neck and shoulder – the ancient dead from the barrow mounds and old pyres, and the freshly killed. Always before the presence of such ghosts had been a comfort to him, to be watched over by ancestors and guided by lost heroes. No longer, not when it seemed that the dead so outnumbered the living.

The spring air was warm enough to pass the night without a fire, and he could not be certain that there would not be men following his own trail, the warband that hunted him in the darkness. But with the spirits clustered thick about him, he scavenged the few remnants of wood from the old firepits, pulled what fuel he had from sack and saddlebag, and put a flame upon the plain. Soon he was guarding it against the wind with hands and cloak, the horse lying close beside him, and when the fire had caught fully he looped his arms about her long neck and held her close. A hard night lay ahead.

The horse shook and trembled, for she too was haunted by ghosts of her own kind. Kai looked upon the fire, and tried to remember – Bahadur's laughter, the pride of seeing how well Tomyris handled a horse, the feel of Arite's body against his. The taste of wine, the pattern of a braided gold necklace between his fingers, the light of the sunset seeming to set the plains afire. Only fragments remained.

Then a sound from the darkness. He did not trust it at first, for on those nights alone he had heard many things – unseen horses whickering and stamping at the ground, the soft murmur of voices, mocking laughter. They had grown louder each night, until he heard whole conservations between people who were not there, the repeated sounding of his name.

But the sound came again, the rattle of tack and uneven fall of hooves of riders moving in the night. There were shadows at the edge of the plain, coming towards the fire.

Kai should have been on his feet at once, mounted and made ready to fight. More likely foe than friend in such a place at such a time – hunters from the warband that had shadowed Kai's riders across the plain, or bandits of the Lacringi raiding from the east. Yet Kai kept his place by the fire – he had no will left to fight or to run.

The shadows seemed to hesitate. Three riders that he could see, weighing up the ill omen of greeting a lone traveller upon the plains. He saw them motion to each other, some debate carried out that he could not hear, only see through mime and gesture. They slowly came forward, for it seemed they too were frightened to pass the night without a fire and company.

Not the hunters who had followed him to the west, then. He tried to guess at who they might be – lovers seeking to flee from one tribe to another, deserters from the warband who had not the courage to go back towards the Danu and the Romans beyond it. They would spend a night together at the fire, Kai would help them nurse their shame, and tomorrow they would be gone. He smiled a little at that thought. Once more he would collect the lost and broken and try to make them whole again.

The shadows closer now, the cold feeling of fate sliding across his skin. Kai's eyes were poor in the darkness, the shapes too indistinct to determine, no sound from them that the air and wind did not swallow. But all at once he was yelling and weeping, calling their names out and running across the plain, bow-legged from a life in the saddle and stumbling like a child, arms outstretched. And the riders came forward to answer him.

Tomyris first, and she was laughing, as though delighted with a trick that he had played upon her. She slid from her saddle and rushed to him, and he took her from her feet, was throwing and catching her as though she were a child half her size, for he would not believe it to be her except by touch and weight. The Roman he took into his arms like a brother, a wrestler's grip locked about his body that the other man answered in kind. And Arite, her eyes shining in the darkness – a hand reached, clasped, then withdrawn, but no more than that.

He led them all to the fire, fearful somehow of losing them in the darkness. And he saw them better there, blood-marked and war-scarred, those who had come from the killing. Fear on their faces more than love now, to find him in that place. For they were all ill omens for each other, their presence speaking only of disaster.

Perhaps there was something written upon his face that Arite did not like to see. She drew close once more and put her arms about him, almost shyly, laid her head against his neck. Only for a moment at first, but as she began to pull away he tightened his grip on her shoulders. Not enough to hold her in place, but enough to ask her to stay. She leaned back close against him, her breath heavy against his neck. A betrayal every moment he held her close, until she drew away from him, her eyes low and heavy and defeated as she took her place by the fire.

As they sat together in silence, Arite waited for the dancing light of the fire to fall on Kai's face, so she might see what had changed in him. Older now perhaps, aged by the few days that they had been apart – a careful weight to the way he moved, the way an old warrior may favour a wound earned many seasons past. And a stillness, too, almost a peace to him, though whether it was that of the defeated or the contented man, she could not say.

They each spoke in turn, the way the storytellers will at a feast. Of the warband that had followed Kai to the east. The duel with Laimei, a battle fought without a single stroke of the sword. Of the raid on the camp, the butchering of the clan, all their hope unravelling with every word.

'There must be revenge for what has been done to our people,' said Kai.

'Why did they do it?' Tomyris asked, her voice breaking as she spoke.

'They think to unite the clans,' Arite said. 'Take the war to Rome once more. They thought it the cowardice of our clan that held them back.'

'It cannot be done,' said Lucius. 'They will be destroyed.'

'They will not let themselves believe it,' she answered. 'And Bahadur's message means nothing now. We have killed him again, for nothing.'

Tomyris crawled over into Kai's arms. He held her close and kissed her hair, and said: 'Laimei will see him safe across the water. There are none who can move and hunt upon the steppe as she can.'

'And the Romans shall kill him when they hear that we go to war against them.'

The wind across the plain, the dance of shadow and fire. The horses watching silently, waiting.

'The dead watch us here,' said Kai. 'They have brought us here for a reason, and I do not think it is to wait to join them.' His hand resting on his daughter's shoulder, tapping a soft, gentle rhythm. 'Lucius, when will the Romans cross the water?'

'Soon, but not yet. They will need to wait for good weather, if they are to bring the weapons and provisions from the west. They shall need to pay the men, too. Always late wages, at the end of winter. They won't march until the silver arrives.'

'And the Sarmatians will not march until the end of spring,' Kai answered. 'They will gather the host, and wait for the hard ground. We have a little time left.'

'What can we do?' Lucius said.

Kai stared into the fire. 'It was a good plan that you had. Submit, wait, trust in the coming of a war to fight.'

'Yet you think it flawed now?'

'You said that we must wait, but the Sarmatians do not wait. Each day is the last day, for us, and we leave nothing for tomorrow. It is how we live, fight, love. Rome must give us a war to fight now, and perhaps we may win over our people. Not sit and rot in chains until they call for us. Give us a war at once, and they will fight it.'

Lucius did not speak for a time. Then he said: 'You think I may do this? I have told you before, I am no great man of my people. A soldier only, not a prince.'

'They might listen to one come back from the dead. Do your people not think that a fortunate thing?'

The Roman shook his head, skin pale in the soft light of the fire. 'You do not know what you ask of me. It is as

Bahadur said. You do not know what Rome is. You might as well ask me to debate with a god and bend him to my will.'

'Our stories are full of such things. I am sure that yours are too.' Kai leaned forward then, put his hand to Lucius's arm. A gentle touch. 'I ask you to try,' he said. 'Will you?'

An ache around Arite's heart, then, as she remembered Bahadur. For it was Bahadur who had taught him that art, to ask a man to be brave and see him do it. She saw the Roman's gaze drift towards the circle of horses close by, his eyes growing soft as he looked upon them. As though he hoped to hear them speak, and offer their counsel.

'Do horses give omens, amongst your people?' Arite said.

'No. But I like to watch them, nonetheless. I have never seen horses such as the ones your people raise.'

'You would like to be one of them, I think.'

He seemed almost surprised. 'Of course. Wouldn't you?'

'Yes. But I did not think to hear a Roman speak so.'

'Most would not.'

'Perhaps you are not a very good Roman.'

He laughed. 'You would not be the first to say so.' The smile fell away from his lips then. 'I do not wish to see your people destroyed,' Lucius said softly, 'and so I shall try. There is little enough to lose.' He tried to speak lightly, yet his voice broke as he spoke, a child caught in a lie.

'I think that you are many things, Lucius,' said Arite, 'but a liar is not one of them.'

A flush at his cheeks, a rueful grin once more upon his lips. 'Yes. There is much to lose. My life, and yours. But get me back across the river, and I shall try.' The Roman stood, suddenly restless. 'We should let the fire die down. I will stand first watch, take a horse and make sure we are alone out here.'

'You are certain?' said Kai.

'I do not think I can sleep. And, besides, I have some words to practise, haven't I? I have never had to bargain with a god before.'

'Tomyris?' Kai said, and a soft, whistling snore answered him. He stifled his laughter with his hand, squeezed his daughter close, then laid her down beside the dying fire.

It should have been the simplest thing, to turn from him and lie down alone in the darkness. Always before she had found courage. Taking the front rank in a charge with the odds against them, the taste of bile hot in her mouth. Burying one child after another as the winter fever cut her family to pieces in a handful of days. Losing Bahadur, and then finding him again, only to lose him once more. Always, there had been courage.

He looked at her. Reached out a single open hand. It still seemed so innocent a thing, that longing for touch, to be held, and she took his hand in hers without thinking.

She closed her eyes, and felt his lips upon her palm, and felt her courage fade away.

25

On the sixth day riding back towards the Danu, Kai saw the shadows in the sky. Distant shapes, arcing and wheeling, the lazy, looping circles of crows who know there is no rush to feed, no contest for the food. Ripe plenty for all.

They had ridden past the ford in the forest, only a few marks remaining of the battle Kai had fought there. A little blood still painted upon the leaves, fragments of sword and spear on the bank, the marks upon the ground of horse and man. They were back into the open country, the great Danu a few days' ride to their west, when they saw the carrion signal up in the air, black birds above a copse of trees. An ill omen, that in other times they would have ridden around. But an answer, too, to a question that Kai could not ignore.

Across the fields of wildflowers and tall grass, into the copse itself, until, through the thinning trees, Kai caught some glimpse of what waited for them – ropes and stakes, the wet and shining sight of bodies stripped of skin. He told Tomyris to wait at the edge of the trees. She was a war child of the steppe and no stranger to killing, but even so, he knew that there was something out there that she must not see.

He thought to ask Arite to stay away, too, but before he could speak she shook her head. 'I have to know if he is there,' she said, her face like a gravemask of wax and clay. For that was the fear that remained unspoken, that they would find Laimei and Bahadur dead, carved into gifts for the gods.

And when they came through the trees and into a clearing, at first Kai did believe it to be his sister and her warband who lay dead there. The corpses scalped and mutilated, pinned out and opened up for the birds to feast upon. Eyeless, skin lifted from the faces, the mouths black with blood where the tongues had been bitten through. And Kai's eyes were hunting around the dead like the carrion crows that danced and pecked from corpse to corpse, looking for some mark of the people he might recognise, the intimate secrets written on the flesh that he knew. The scar on his sister's hip from where a horse had once thrown her, the finger Saratos had lost to frostbite many winters before, the tattoo of a bear and a deer that looped around Bahadur's shoulder.

No sign that he could see on the ruined bodies. Too many to be his sister and her warriors. Looking closer still he saw the trophies of fur each man wore on his hip, the mark of the howling wolf stamped into their war gear.

'The warband who hunted you?' Lucius asked. For he had seen the signs too.

'Never saw them clear enough to say for certain. But

they bear the markings of the Wolves, and they are about the right number. It must be them.'

'Who has killed them?' said Lucius.

Kai pointed to the edge of the clearing where a barrow rose, branded with the remnants of a fire, what seemed at first a blackened sword thrust into it. A branch whittled into the shape of a sword, for those who left it there would not have been able to spare the iron, not in the way their ancestors had once marked their graves.

'Dig into that,' said Kai, 'and you will find friends of mine. Or those who used to be my friends.' He looked once more around the dead. 'This is my sister's work.'

Arite's eyes had not left the barrow. 'You think Bahadur...'

'No. This was after they came back from the river. She would not go hunting until she had seen him to the water.'

Lucius paced about the clearing. 'This is a good campground. A little cover from the trees at their back, a river not far off. Hard to ambush, if Laimei was coming from the Danubius.'

'*If* she came from there. She must have cut wide, scouted them at night.' Kai knelt down, traced the imprint of a hoof marked in the ground beneath a tree at the edge of the clearing. 'Rode in through the trees, the same way we came. And with the numbers this warband had, they would not have thought she would dare hunt them.'

Lucius looked once more upon the ruined dead. 'Is this the custom of your people?' He hesitated. 'Or of your sister?'

'Sometimes, when vengeance demands it. And no. The Cruel Spear they may call her, but she never killed in this way before.' Kai kept his eyes to the dead, and not the living. He could feel Arite and Lucius looking at him, waiting. 'I was not here, so she did it to them instead.' The bile rose in his throat, hot and sharp, before he swallowed it away. 'I always wondered before, with each man she killed or maimed, if she thought of me as she did it. Bahadur always said I was being foolish.'

A hand upon his shoulder – Lucius, not Arite. For he saw that she had turned away already, back towards where Tomyris waited, kicking a crow from a corpse as she went.

'At least she still lives,' said Lucius.

'Yes,' Kai answered. 'And now there is but one warband out there that wishes me dead, rather than two.'

For the rest of the day they rode faster than they should have, pushing on into twilight and leaving their horses weary and gasping before they fell from the saddle, hoping to be tired enough to fall into a dreamless sleep. But it was no use. In the darkness before sleep and in the shifting landscape of his dreams, like one in a fever, he saw the same visions over and over again.

It would have meant nothing to Laimei – she had that warrior's gift granted to one in a hundred, where killing brought only stillness, and peace. It was the others he saw in his dreams. Tamura, hands shaking as she lowered the knife to the scalp of a man pleading for his life, making the clumsy torturer's cuts. Saratos, his careless smile washed from his face by blood, turning his deaf ear towards the screaming captive on the ground. All of the riders he had led from the river and across the plain, the lost, the faithful, and the innocent, being fashioned into murderers.

In the following days, as they travelled back towards the river, they could feel that the Sarmatians were close. Everywhere, there were signs of the great army that was gathering once more. Fires on the horizon, shadows moving across the plain, the great furrows of herd and warband carved across the earth.

A single patrol would have been enough to undo them, for them to be hunted as deserters, remnants of a broken clan. But always the shadows moved on, the fires remained distant. Whether it was luck or fate, they could not say. Perhaps a dark blessing granted by the butchered warband, for the slow death was said to give a message to the gods – perhaps Laimei had wished for that, as she put those men to knife and fire.

Soon enough, they heard the whisper of water calling to them – the great wide water of the Danu, the river at the edge of the world. Kai and the others tied their horses at the last patch of cover, crawled to the river edge like supplicants before an altar. Passing through the reeds until they reached the bank, to look upon the death of their people.

Great machines of war lined up along the banks, the ballistae and catapults that could rain fire and tear a warband to pieces from a thousand feet away. The countless warriors of the Legion, armoured in iron and bearing their great red shields, the eagles high above them all, their watchful golden gods of war. And in the water, the host of narrow, flat-hulled ships that would bring that death across the water.

Kai looked on it for as long as he could, the old fear biting at his throat, until he pressed his face into the mud, so he would not have to see it any more.

They beat up and down the riverbank for half a day, until they found a trader – a little hawk-faced man, his boat loaded down with trinkets of east and west. Half mad at least: when he saw them he snatched up some charm from his wares and cursed them in a mix of half a dozen languages. Lucius spoke to him in the Roman tongue, the words of a conqueror, and he grew calm at once. And after a little bargaining (the trader looking on Tomyris with hungry eyes, but settling for a silver-patterned scabbard), they were upon the water.

When it had been stilled by ice in the winter, it had been a battleground, a place for heroes to do the work of horse and spear. Now it was a border between worlds, a burial ground. The water flowed dark beneath them, yet within it Kai almost thought he could see the hands of the vengeful dead reaching up, fleshless lips calling him a traitor and a coward. For he had lived when they had died, his cowardice proved in every breath that he took, each beating of his heart.

Close to the other bank, and the alarm calls were sounding, archers and spearmen gathering at the bank, calling for watch words and pass signs that none of them knew. There was almost nothing of Rome left in Lucius after the long winter, for he was heavy-bearded and clad in the furs and leathers of the Sarmatians. The trader cursed and shrieked for mercy. The arrowheads glinted in the low light of the sun.

Words in the air, not arrows – the words of Rome, spoken by Lucius. Not the pass words that the Legion called for, but the brawling, quarrelling, loving words of a brother in arms, until one of the Legionaries, a dark-skinned, heavy-set man, seemed to recognise him. Lucius's name was spoken, hesitantly at first, then like a chant or a prayer, taken up by one man after another. For they too must have left their dead in the river, lost friends beyond it, hoped for an impossible moment such as this, to see their dead live once more.

Swept into the arms of his people, saluted by some, clasped close by others. Those warriors of Rome, the blank-faced killers, seeming as men for a moment. Until they had finished greeting their lost companion, and looked upon the prize Lucius had brought with him. Kai, Tomyris, and Arite.

A quiet, then, as the Romans came forward. Slow steps, their hands slack at their sides, moving like sleepwalkers. Kai thought to see their faces marked with greed or envy, for he had heard it was the making of a soldier's fortune to sell such a bounty in flesh. Or for them to be swearing bloody vengeance, come to revenge themselves upon the barbarians from over the water. He had been prepared for anything but this still, dull quiet.

Lucius was speaking – hesitant and stammering, calling them back, trying to remember what it was to command. But the Romans did not listen.

And Kai felt the fear rising further and further into madness, for this was a face of Rome he had not seen before. Not the watchers of the border, those who killed with weary, empty efficiency. This was the Rome that Bahadur had spoken of, the Rome without mercy.

The red crests and cloaks, the short, murderous swords, the gold eagles high above them. That maddening terror swept over him once more, every mark of Rome like a cut into his mind. Voices calling to him, but he could not hear them. The world tipping up, turning to grey, and then to black.

26

'Lucius Artorius Castus.' A smile across the Legate's face as he spoke, as though he looked upon a prize bull, a horse of his that had raced well in the games. 'Welcome back.'

Half a beat of the heart for Lucius to remember that it was *his* name being spoken. To hear his full name, spoken by a Roman, was to hear the words of a dream, a voice from another world. It was only when the Legate's smile twitched impatiently that he remembered to answer.

'Thank you, sir. I serve the Emperor.'

The Legate, Caius Cassius Volesenus, inclined his head in response – perhaps a silent reminder of who else Lucius was sworn to serve. For all about them in the Legate's tent were the trappings of glory and power. The red-trimmed senator's toga, folded neatly but placed openly on top of a locked chest. A Crown of Valour prominently displayed, earned many decades past for storming a barbarian palisade on the banks of the Rhenus. A new slave, a Sarmatian child trembling as he held the wine and waited for commands in a language he could not understand. For Lucius – standing at attention in borrowed armour, his hair quickly and roughly cropped back – it was difficult not to feel more a beggar than a returning hero.

The last time they had spoken was when Lucius had volunteered to lead the raid across the river. A brief audience, where Caius had sat and fidgeted, ill at ease with the paternal duty demanded of him. For that was what was expected, when you sent a soldier to die. And now once more, Caius greeted him with a smile and the offer of wine. A greyhaired man growing a little stout about the waist, his beard cut in mimicry of the Emperor. Not the worst of commanders – one of those idiot sons of a senator who would throw away a Legion on a whim, or a bitter drunkard who, considering himself underpromoted and overlooked, would soak himself in wine while his Legion rotted beneath him. But even so, he was a man who was seeking to forget what it was to be a soldier.

'Well,' said Caius, 'it seems it is the season for dead men to rise from their graves.'

'Sir?'

'Of course, you have not heard.' Caius drained his wine, and held it out for the slave to refill. 'The Emperor came close to death. An old sickness returning, his doctors said. Some fool even sent the messengers out when they thought his breathing ceased. But he yet lives, thank the gods, and so now we are sending riders all across the Empire, trying to convince them of that. A fine mess. There will be trouble from it, mark my words. Someone in the provinces will make a fool of himself, trying for the purple.'

No answer to be made to that, and so Lucius kept his silence.

'But you,' Caius said, 'bring good fortune. A fine omen. The men will be pleased.'

'Thank you, sir. I did not think that I was so well regarded, sir.'

'You are not,' the Legate said flatly. 'One would think you had gone out of your way not to befriend the other officers. Or earn the fear of your men. But a man come back from across the water is a fortunate thing.'

'Thank you, sir.'

'We thought you lost long ago,' said Caius. 'Few of the cavalry we sent over the river came back to us. Those damn Sarmatian horses...' He shook his head. 'How did you get away, and with prisoners in your company?'

'The Sarmatians fell to fighting one another, sir. The ones I brought in thought their chances better on this side of the water, and came to trade me for their lives.'

'Naive creatures, aren't they? And the Sarmatian you brought with you, I hear he is sick? I'll have his throat cut and body burned if he carries the plague.'

'No plague, sir. The fear of Rome. You know how it is with these barbarians.'

'Well, you seem well enough.' The Legate tried another smile that did not seem to fit his face. 'They didn't cut anything off, did they?'

'No, sir.' Lucius hesitated. 'They thought me of too much value to harm.'

'Be glad you are on the Danubius and not the Rhenus. The Germanic tribes do terrible things to their prisoners.

But you have returned just in time to go to war again. The way of the Legion, eh?'

'It is to be war then, sir?'

Caius waved a meaty hand in the air. 'A prisoner came back over the river, gave some story that their people would surrender. But our scouts tell another story. They're gathering again, and so we go to destroy them, once and for all. The Legion needs a war, it shall do them good.'

'Yes, sir. For the glory of Rome.'

'For the glory of Rome,' Caius said, nodding absently. 'I am sure that a few days of light duties will be sufficient for your recovery. There might be a little trouble with your replacement stepping down. Flavius, you know him? Ambitious man, and he shall hold your return against you. But nothing that you cannot contend with, I am certain.' He looked down to the wax tablets on the table beside him – messages, reports, all the business of the Legion about to go to war. 'Is there anything else you wish to say?'

'Yes, sir. I was hoping to speak with the Emperor, sir.'

Stillness in the tent. The wind against the calfskin, the soft scratch of the slave shifting uncertainly from one foot to another. And on the Legate's face, that particular, doubtful expression of a man who has grown unused to surprise.

'The other centurions were lying, it seems,' he said at last. 'You *do* have a sense of humour.'

'I am afraid not, sir. What I have seen amongst the barbarians, the Emperor will want to hear it. Sir.'

The smile fell away then. 'You can give your message to

me, centurion,' said Caius. 'I will relay it, if it is worthy of his attention.'

'I would prefer—'

The ringing slap, a crack of clay – the jug of wine was broken and bleeding its contents upon the ground, and Caius was shaking the pain from the palm that had struck it. The slave, untrained as he was, fell to his knees, dabbing at the wine with his tunic and offering it up to his master, as though expecting the Legate to suck it from the sodden cloth – the child could not conceive of such bounty going to waste.

But the Legate ignored the boy, standing face to face with Lucius and eyeing him like an optio on the parade ground. 'What does that matter?' said Caius. 'What *is* it you want? And do not give me fanciful tales. What you know of the barbarians does not matter.'

Lucius said nothing at first. There was only the searching for the right kind of lie, the art he had never mastered.

'Speak,' said the Legate, 'or I'll have you beaten. I shall not be spoken to so by a centurion.'

At last, Lucius said: 'I have spent a winter amongst the barbarians. Tortured and starved. I dreamed only of this moment. I know that he is in this camp, so close to us now. I saw him once before, when I was sent to die. Let me speak to him, now that I live. I have earned it, sir.'

'Earned it, have you?'

'If I have done good service to Rome, I beg that you let me have this honour, sir.'

Another moment of silence. Then a barking laugh, and a hand clapping Lucius upon the shoulder, the anger gone just as quick as it had come. 'You are all the same,' said Caius. 'Soldiers dreaming of their Emperor. Beautiful, in its own way, I suppose.' He returned to the stool, brushing the slave aside. 'I will ask, but do not hope for much. He has little use for men such as you.'

'Thank you, sir.'

A pause. 'You do know what you are, don't you, centurion?'

'A soldier of Rome, sir.'

'No, that is just the mask you wear,' Caius said. 'Perhaps you even believe it yourself. But I see it in you. There are plenty of dreamers across the water, no doubt, amongst the barbarians. Plenty more buried back in the cemeteries in Rome, poets and philosophers of the old Republic.' He sat back heavily. 'But we have no use for such things here.'

A salute, answered in kind. And as he turned on his heel to depart, Lucius heard the Legate say, half to himself: 'There are no dreams upon the border.'

Through the camp they were taken, Arite and Tomyris, until they reached the place where the prisoners were kept.

An open space within the palisade, with row upon row of barred wagons – mocking reflections of the tented caravans in which the Sarmatians had made their homes for centuries. The cages filled with Arite's people, bound in iron that would have made a chieftain's ransom out upon the steppe, waiting to be sent west to slave markets and salt mines.

Here and there she could see the corpse-grey flesh of one who had died in the night, still shackled to his companions, to be turned out only at the next changing of the guard. Yet even the living were near silent, barely moving. Occasionally a snarling brawl, as between dogs in a pack, as some scrap of food emerged to be fought over, or some old feud broke open again. But they did not have the strength to fight for long – fingers closing for a moment about a throat, a single strike from an open hand, before they collapsed once more.

Then the prisoners saw her being brought to them, and they came once more roaring to life. Keening songs of mourning, curses, promises of revenge, all chanted over and over again until the guards beat at the cages with clubs and the hafts of their spears, screaming curses of their own, and the prisoners returned to silence.

Some bribe had passed between Lucius and the soldier who escorted them, for he did not take them to the first of the barred wagons. He led them back and forth through the rows and columns as a horse trader might show his wares, waiting for Arite to choose her own place. And so she passed by the lost and the hopeless and the dead, until she found the cage where Bahadur was kept.

He was half turned away from her, but she knew him at once. Emaciated legs thrust through the bars and dangling towards the ground as though yearning for the earth they could not touch. His hands working over the links of the chains that bound his hands – not in the way of one searching for a weakness, but the way a child may

TIM LEACH

handle a toy, or a seer a charm of good omen. But his eyes alive with light and life, unlike those of so many of the listless figures about him. Arite had seen enough men taken captive to know it, to tell when one had decided to fight, to live.

He was so lost in that struggle that he did not seem to see her at first. Even when he lifted his head and looked straight at her, he did not seem to see her. Perhaps he took her for one of those tricks of the mind seen by the dying, the starving, the fever-struck. For how many times must he have conjured her in his mind in the time he had spent in that cage?

It was only when she stretched a shaking hand towards him that he saw she was no phantom or memory. And he was smiling then – madly, bravely – at this victory, to see her again.

How easy it was to forget the betrayal with Kai, she thought. To wish only for a new beginning, for he was there once more, the hero she had fallen in love with long before. She reached out to him, and took his hand.

A moment where they held each other, and all was as it should have been. But something passed to him with that touch – a message carried in the quickening of the blood, a treachery spoken through skin.

Better if he had shouted and raged and wept. But his eyes drifted away, a hollowing to the shape of his body, a little nod of acceptance, as his fingers fell away from hers. Age and weariness settling upon him once more like snow upon the steppe.

314

The creak of the cage door, the tap of a club against the small of her back. Inside the cage then, stepping over the living and the dead, feeling the chains close about her wrists as she and Bahadur were bound to each other once again.

27

Lucius waited, as he imagined a condemned man might wait for his execution. Hunched forward on the camp stool in a centurion's tent, thinking only of what must be done, as the rain fell upon the calfskin tent like a hand upon a drum.

When he had been taken as captive by the Sarmatians, Lucius had not expected to live long. For he had been told by his commanders in the Legion that the barbarians rarely took prisoners. On those nights about the campfires, he had waited for the cut of the knife against the soles of his feet, the point of an arrowhead driven up under his fingernails, the knocking of a sword's pommel against his teeth. He waited for the questions to be asked, of Rome and the Legion, or for there to be no questions, for the torture to be for amusement alone. But it had not come, not even when they came to that great encampment, the thousand fires of the last Sarmatians gathered together. Lucius had been certain then that it would be the time to die, that he had been kept for some special torture. To be raised up above a slow fire, to have his guts unspooled and gifted to the gods, his skin ripped from his body and raised upon a banner high above the barbarian horde. Yet perhaps they had worked instead towards this particular punishment, to have him try to strike an impossible bargain. To reason with a vengeful god.

There were others sharing the tent with him, men of his rank. One had come to him with a cup of wine, another flashing dice and a smile, the last two with a simple salute and a hunger in their eyes for stories from across the water. And one by one, as quickly as he could, he had turned them away. They left him alone, muttering to one another, no doubt cursing him as arrogant, aloof. They had not been his friends before, and they would not be now.

It did not matter. All that mattered were the words, the words that he would speak, the bargain he would strike. In silence, he sought to practise those words, time after time finding himself close to finding the right ones, the beautiful speech that might incline a god to mercy. But it was akin to remembering a dream – those rules and images that had once seemed so clear now impossible to recall. The longer he thought, the more the words seemed to slip away from him.

Footsteps drawing close, the hard rhythm of soldiers marching in step, and he knew that there was no more time left to think. Only to trust to a warrior's instinct, that when the time came he would do what must be done.

The rustle of the tent flap, the Praetorians standing there before him. The other centurions, previously seeming so eager for his company, drew away and busied themselves about their own errands, eyes to the ground. For the

Praetorians only came to summon a man to the Emperor, or to his death.

Their captain stood before him, eyes hard beneath the red-crested helm, the Praetorian symbols of wing and lightning upon his armour. 'Come,' he said. 'It is time to go.'

As they moved through the camp, all about him he could see the signs of the Legion readying itself for the march. Out from the stone walls of Aquincum and gathering upon the banks of the Danubius, the camp was alive with a terrible energy, of knowing that their Emperor was close enough to see, almost close enough to touch. Yet still Lucius felt a prisoner – his weapons stripped from him, marched in close order through the camp, feeling the eyes of hateful, envious men upon his skin as he was led to the appointed place at the appointed time.

Soon, the Emperor's high white tent was looming before him, like a marble monument of Rome carried out to its frontier, and the Praetorian centurion stopped them there, stared wordlessly into Lucius's face. A silent interrogation, looking for some mark of madness or treachery, the sign of the fanatic or the assassin.

Whatever silent answer Lucius gave, it seemed to satisfy the Praetorian. 'Walk five paces inside,' he said. 'No more, no less. Kneel before him, and stand only if he commands it. Even if you stand, do not look at him. Never look at him. Address him as "Caesar". Think very, very carefully before saying anything that is not "yes", or "no", or "Caesar". Is that understood?'

'I understand, sir.'

'Good.' The rustle of calfskin as the tent flap lifted, the scent of wine and incense flowing from within. And then, in a softer tone, the Praetorian said: 'Good luck.' One soldier to another, wishing good fortune before the battle.

Then another voice was speaking from within – speaking of him, calling his name, and it was time to step inside.

The first step was easy, from the cold into a place of warmth and brightness. Too bright, at first – the torchlight sharp against his eyes, the reflected glitter of gold like sunlight upon a polished shield, and so a moment's pause before the second step. The soldier's rhythm was gone then, wavering and wandering off the straight, parade-ground line he sought to walk.

At the third, some thick and cloying scent filled his nostrils – some perfume from a distant land, but to him the smell was redolent of the battlefield, and left the taste of death upon his tongue. Simple instinct sent him searching for the source, and his eyes went where they should not have. He saw greying skin, rheum-reddened eyes, a mouth twisted in pain. An old man sat in the golden seat of a god, it seemed at first. And it was only when he saw the purple cloak, the lines of the face so familiar from statue and monument, that he realised he was looking upon the Emperor himself.

Those dull eyes snapped to life then, a mad and brilliant gaze. And Lucius took his fourth step like a man gutted on the battlefield, already bowing forward, hands clutched close to the belly. At the fifth, he sank gratefully to his knees.

No words for a time. Perhaps he was meant to speak first
– had he forgotten some simple piece of etiquette? But just
as he thought he could bear the silence no longer, he heard
the words of the Emperor. A soft voice, speaking with care.

'It is always good to see a son of Rome come home.'

'My life is yours, Caesar.'

'You are like me – a dead man returned to life once
more. Let us hope you bring good fortune back across the
water with you.'

'Yes, Caesar.'

A shifting rustle of cloth. 'The barbarians, they shall not
give us much trouble?'

'They are worthy warriors, Caesar.' A little intake of
breath somewhere close, for it seemed he had spoken
something forbidden. 'But none may stand before Rome,'
Lucius added quickly. 'It will be a great victory, Caesar.'

'I am sure it will. And an honour, of sorts, for them.
We only destroy our truly great enemies. Perhaps such a
monument will not displease them.'

'It will not, Caesar.'

Again, he knew it to be the wrong answer. The creak
of leather as someone close by shifted from foot to foot.
Caius perhaps – Lucius knew that he must be there.

The Emperor sounded amused. 'Strange as it sounds, I
almost envy you your time amongst them. In a different
time, they would be worth a treatise. But what use is it
to study a dying people? They should be forgotten, don't
you think?'

The questions hung in the air, living and deadly, too
dangerous to touch. And so Lucius gave no answer.

'Ovid wrote of them,' the Emperor said, after a moment's silence. 'Briefly, but that shall be enough. No more words of Rome for them.'

'Yes, Caesar.'

'As for you, there is little to offer you. There can be no Crown of Valour given for a captured man. But we are grateful to see you return.' A pause. 'It is always good to see a son of Rome come home,' the Emperor said again, seeming unaware of the repetition.

Now, Lucius knew, was the time to stay silent. Soon the Sarmatians would pass into nothingness like a dream. In a year he would bear only scars and memories, and they would fade too, in time.

'We shall arrange some appropriate reward, I am sure,' said the Emperor. Again the rustle of purple cloth – some gesture of dismissal, it seemed. For once more he could hear the executioner's tread of the Praetorians coming forward, coming to take him away.

Always, Lucius had thought himself a brave man. He knew well the steady calm upon the battlefield that washed away all fear, where all that existed was the next action that must be taken – the turning of a sword, the bracing of a shield, half a step taken forward, one word spoken in command. Yet now he knew what a simple thing it was to be a coward, when it was necessary merely to say nothing.

'If my only request were to speak a little more,' Lucius said, 'would you grant it, Caesar?'

The air seemed to grow sharp about him, unseen needles prickling at his skin. And he heard Caius speaking, the Legate's voice cracking with a tremor of rage. 'The centurion is tired, Caesar, and has misspoken. Forgive him. He *will* go now.'

A dry chuckle. 'Oh, we must always mind the treasury, or so I am told. Words cost less than gold, most of the time, and this may be an uncostly reward. Speak then, centurion. There is little that surprises me now.' A little hardening of the tone then, as the Emperor said: 'But I am very curious as to what you will say next.'

Lucius did not answer for a long time. Kneeling before the Emperor, how easy it was to believe in Rome. For a god was power, nothing more, for all that the Christian cultists might whisper otherwise. Here, before him, was power. Nothing mattered other than that.

'I have been amongst the Sarmatians,' he said at last. 'Seen more of them than any other Roman, perhaps. And I think it would be a great pity to destroy them, when we might put them to better use.'

Silence, then. What was there to say? For it was a centurion's place to beat his men into order, to lead them from the front, to die as an example to others. It was not his place to think and speak, any more than a hunting hound would be asked for counsel.

The Emperor spoke again: 'What use is that?'

'They are the finest heavy horse in the world. The only cavalry who can break a Legion. They can make Rome more powerful than ever before.'

'And yet they have chosen to fight us, not surrender. I have offered them peace once already.'

'They wish for a war, Caesar. Grant them one against your enemies, and they shall fight for you.'

'You say so? You *think* so. Look at me, centurion.'

The old stories of myth, of looking upon the forbidden, of men turned to stone, dragged to the Underworld, immolated by a jealous god for looking at what they should not. But death to disobey the command of the Emperor, and so Lucius lifted his head and looked once more upon a god.

'You admire them, don't you?' the Emperor said flatly.

'Caesar, I—'

'There is no need to lie.' And the Emperor looked about himself irritably, at all the courtiers he was surrounded by. Something fell away from him then – the weary tyrant and conqueror was gone for a moment, and Lucius caught a glimpse of who he might have been had he not been chosen for the purple. Some bright-eyed scholar collecting stories of distant lands, noting ritual and practice, devising philosophies and writing epigrams.

'Do you admire them?' the Emperor said.

'I do, Caesar.'

'A failing in you, centurion. A corruption of the Roman spirit.' A pause. 'But tell me why, nonetheless.'

'Bravery, Caesar. They would rather die than be defeated.'

'Rabid dogs are brave, too. I would not spare them. And I hope that you do not doubt the courage of the Legion.'

'It is something different with the Sarmatians,' Lucius said. 'A kind of thinking bravery… forgive me, Caesar, I do not have the words.'

'A *thinking* bravery, is it? You believe it easier to be brave and not to think?'

'I do, Caesar.'

'So do I.'

Quiet, then. A Tribune gave a hesitant laugh, quickly stifled behind his hand when no others joined him. For most of the others seemed frightened, watching the Emperor. Only Caius kept his eyes on Lucius, his face blotched purple with rage.

'I will not spare them for being brave,' the Emperor said. 'That might earn them a place in my writings. But it is not a reason to keep them alive.' And there was a relief amongst those gathered as he spoke, for it seemed they would have their war. There could be comfort in butchery, if it were familiar enough.

'Yes, Caesar,' Lucius said.

A smile upon the Emperor's face. 'But perhaps they may be of use, as you say. And perhaps you may be of use, as well. For word came this morning, from Egypt.' A sound, then – the rapping of fingers upon a wax tablet. And once more, the stillness in the air. 'Gaius Avidius has rebelled in Egypt, and proclaimed himself Emperor.'

The air ringing with sound – men crying out their loyalty, calling for vengeance, sounding curses to the gods. The Emperor raised his hand, and just as swiftly there was silence once more.

'Yes,' he said, 'it is true. A single false report of my death goes to the west, and already the jackals think to pick at my corpse. If we had barbarians alone to fight against, that would be enough. So you will make one more offer to them, centurion. To bend the knee and enter my service at once. To fight against the enemies of Rome. Or we shall destroy them utterly.'

'Yes, Caesar. I will not fail you.'

'Perhaps you will.'

A heavy sigh, and Lucius saw that he was there once more – the tyrant, conqueror, killer. Rome's butcher. That was what a life spent wearing the purple had done to him, a life spent on the border, fighting a war without end.

'You spoke of bravery,' said the Emperor. 'I would like to admire *your* bravery, in saying what you have done. I would like to, but I cannot. It wearies me, and I do not like to be wearied.' A hard stare then, at Caius, the Legate. 'Surprise and reckless chances are for younger men.'

'Yes, Caesar.'

And the Emperor seemed to age before him – the skin almost translucent, the lips grey, the head lolling loosely. As frightening a thing as Lucius had ever seen, but the others must have seen it many times before, for they gave no sign of alarm. Perhaps it was this that had almost killed the Emperor – not sickness or poison, but the weight of one murderous decision after another. Perhaps there was a limit to the taking and the sparing of lives, before the gods grew jealous and gave a warning of their own.

The Emperor leaned back, closed his eyes, gave the slightest gesture of the hand. The audience was over.

Five steps out of the tent, each one lighter than the one before it. Lucius half expected to step into the air at the last, as the Praetorians gathered about him once more. A firm hand placed against the back of his neck, perhaps in case he were tempted to look like a hero escaping the Underworld, or a man who seeks to undo what he has done.

No more honours or glory for him. Only the worst of postings, rotten cohorts to command until he was spitted on some barbarian's spear, far away from Rome. All that he had fought for undone to save the barbarians across the water.

But perhaps it was finally true that he understood the Sarmatians – that reckless courage they had, to wager everything they had with no care for the future.

And the joy of them, too. That joy of one who has gambled so, and won.

When first Kai woke, he thought himself amongst the dead.

Still and silent figures around him on the ground. The smell of rot, the grey flesh. Darkness, too, and for a moment the choking feeling of being buried alive. Then someone moved close by – the restless stirring of one gripped with fever. Another man rolled over, slowly and with great effort, and when Kai saw the cast of the skin, the particular hollowness of the eyes, the lolling tongue, he understood where he was. He was not amongst the dead, but the dying. A tent filled with sickened men.

All but one. For a man sat on the ground beside him, cross-legged, head nodding with sleep. Hair plastered to the scalp with old sweat, the skin about the eyes dark and heavy, but these were the signs of weariness, not sickness. A little light upon the golden hair of the beard, sword-calloused palms turned towards Kai. And a smile upon the man's lips, when he saw that Kai was awake.

'Lucius,' said Kai, and the Roman nodded. Then: 'Water,' the word cracking and breaking even as he said it.

A skin of water opened and passed, the sweet clear taste of it flowing down his throat. And when Kai handed it back, he was surprised to find that his hand was steady.

'Where are we?' Kai asked.

'Not far from the Danubius. The Danu, as you call it.'

'You have spoken to the Emperor?'

'I have.'

'You have done it, then?'

'We have done it,' Lucius answered.

'And you have suffered for it?'

'No more than I am willing to suffer.' A shrug of the shoulders. 'But yes, I did. Or rather, I shall.'

'We go back now?'

'We do, as soon as we can. You are well enough to travel?'

'I am.' But it was a hollow voice that Kai spoke with – no strength to speak of the shame that gnawed at him, and no strength to hide it, either.

Another man might have mocked or goaded him. Or ignored the pain, or picked at Kai with words until he had all of the wrong answers. But Lucius simply waited. Hands clasped together, eyes soft. The posture of a man willing to wait forever and still receive no answer. A strength in stillness, that willingness to wait for the world to change.

At last, Kai said: 'What do your people think of fear?'

'All men are afraid,' Lucius answered. 'Except for the mad.'

'Do you think it a shameful thing?'

'Not of itself. It depends on what it makes you do.' Lucius hesitated. 'What it is that you are afraid of?'

'I am afraid every time I see a Roman. The banners, the weapons, the shields. I see them, and I cannot think.'

'It has always been this way?'

'No, only since the battle on the ice. Some curse. Or a message from the gods, that there is no use in fighting your people.'

Lucius did not answer for a time. 'I told my commander that you had been struck down by the fear of Rome. I did not know that it was true.' He looked at his hands. 'And I had wondered why you turned your horse away, when we fought each other.'

Kai closed his eyes. He had hoped that Lucius had forgotten, that the madness of battle and the pain of his wound had driven the memory away. But he had carried that knowledge silently with him all winter, the knowledge that Kai was a coward.

A hand was on his arm then, and Kai flinched at the touch. But once more, the waiting. And when at last he looked at him, Lucius said: 'You have nothing to fear from me.'

'I know.'

'And soon you will be away from here. We go across the water once more.'

'But that is the worst of it.' The words were easy now, a wound bleeding freely. 'I did not know I could be more afraid of anything than the Romans. But now I am more afraid to go back than to stay here.'

'Your sister? The others?'

'Yes. I am afraid to see them again.'

'Little chance of us running into them in open country.'

'Oh, I think that the gods do not mean to let me loose so easily.'

Lucius said nothing – once more, the waiting. Somewhere close, the sound of drum and horn calling a changing of the guard, and one of the sick men tried to answer it. Eyes mad with fever, and legs withered away to almost nothing, yet still he tried to stand, until an orderly hurried over and ushered him back to the ground.

'You can stay here,' said Lucius at last. 'A hostage. A prisoner. A guest. Whatever you want to call it. I told them that you are a prince amongst your people, a man they should keep alive.' He glanced around the tent. 'Here, at least, there are few signs of Rome. I will not make you go back across the water if you have not the heart for it.'

'Fear is not a shameful thing, only what it makes you do.' Kai echoed back the words. 'No. You shall need one of our people with you. And I will not send Bahadur or Arite.'

Lucius nodded. 'I knew an old centurion,' he said, 'discharged to a veteran's village. Lost his leg to an axe on the banks of the Rhenus. That unseen leg haunted him day and night, he was almost mad with that pain.'

'And you mean to tell me how he was healed.'

'They showed it to him in a mirror. All things reversed. He reached out and touched that missing leg, and the pain went away.'

330

'A good story,' said Kai. 'But I have seen Sarmatians thus afflicted. And our answer is simpler. We put them to death.'

'That *is* another way. But why not try the mirror first?' Lucius hesitated. Then he said: 'You have crossed the water on a hopeless task already. You were brave then. And I only ask you to do again what you have done before.'

A lightness then, a warmth like wine drunk beside a fire. Kai said: 'They will most likely kill us, you know.'

'I know. But I died once already, upon your sister's spear. I do not wish to do it again, but I will if I have to.'

'And I rose from the dead once before, after the battle on the ice.' And Kai felt peace settling upon him then, the feeling of all things in their right place. He stood, suddenly impatient, stirred by that beautiful restlessness that comes before a journey.

'You are well enough to ride?' Lucius said. 'We can wait—'

'I am ready. What need is there to wait?' Kai was smiling then – a half-mad smile, perhaps, but one born of courage, nonetheless. And whatever was to come after, he was grateful to have tasted that courage one last time. 'And so,' he said, 'let us do what we have done before, and can do again.' The smile fell away, then. 'But first, I must say goodbye.'

Arite had not thought they would live long, when first they were brought to the cages.

It was not because of the paltry food, for they were a people used to hard living. Nor the open air, for the winter was gone, the first warmth of spring already upon them. But the confinement itself – she thought that must be what would kill them.

Yet the Sarmatians had built a world of their own with what little they had been given. The food gifted to those who needed it most, rotten meat and mould-speckled bread tossed from cage to cage. Songs, too, from those who had the strength to sing them, the old stories of their people told over and over and over again. There was even love in that place – chaste courtships between the cages, unspoken for the most part, as women stared silently and men stretched their hands out into the empty air. And all conspired to sleep as well as they could, huddled together for warmth and holding their bindings still and silent. For it was only in dreams that they could roam free once again.

A world they had, and rituals, too. For the chanting that had greeted Arite and Tomyris had been no thing of chance or the moment. Few were the prisoners brought to them now, but each one was greeted in the same way – the rattle of chains shaken into percussion, the rapping of bowls upon the ground. Voices raised against the Emperor who had put them there, every curse that they knew of, the forbidden incantations of magic and witchcraft. All of them sat in circles, bound in iron, praying for the death of a god.

And so when once more she heard the roaring and the calling and the howls of grief, she paid it little mind. It was only when beside her, through the bindings at her wrists, she felt Bahadur tremble, then go still, that she knew who it must be.

But Kai did not come as a prisoner. No rope or iron bound around his hands, and dressed in borrowed Roman clothing – a man ready for a journey, it seemed. She understood then what it was that Kai had come to do. It must have been quite a price in silver that Lucius had paid, to give Kai this farewell.

She tried not to listen as he spoke to his daughter, and only in part to give them privacy. For she had brought five children of her own into the world, buried each of them in turn. Fever, stillbirth, the sword. Her sons and daughters all taken from her, and never again would she know that urgent, complete kind of love. But even as far away in the cage as she could go, she could still hear the little choking sobs, the whispers that passed between father and daughter.

Then the silence, the feet shifting outside the cage. She looked to Bahadur, hoping against hope that he might offer a farewell of his own to Kai. How many times had they sat together beside the fire, trading song and story. How often they had exchanged hot words, only to clasp hands and forgive. And, just for a moment, she thought she saw Bahadur begin to smile at the sight of his friend.

But it was more a baring of his teeth, the way a man may grin at mockery that he cannot answer with a sword. Then Bahadur turned away, and lay upon the floor of his cage.

Kai did not meet her gaze then – his body half turned from her, like a man guarding a wound. She found herself moving in the same way, a mirror to his shame, until there was anger, quick and sharp as battle fury. She leaned forward, her head against the wooden bars. He hesitated for but a moment, before he came close, close enough for them to whisper to each other.

'I do love him,' she said.

'As do I,' he answered.

'There is a madness in the blood between us,' she said. 'It is something that cannot be undone. But I will not be ashamed. I wish I had not given him this hurt. But I will not be shamed for it.'

He said nothing. She had spoken so softly that she wondered if he had even heard the words.

Then: 'I broke a promise,' he said.

'But did not lie.'

'No.' A little brightness in the eyes, then. 'That is true.'

'You go back across the water?'

'Yes. With Lucius. We shall win the peace.' He traced the borders of the bars with his fingers. 'And freedom for you all from this cage.'

'Live, if you can.'

'Keep them safe, if you can.'

'I wish…' she said, but let it trail away.

It was time then, for the parting. A longing to touch once more, a binding of fingers, a joining of lips. Any touch a betrayal, yet to part without it seemed treachery of a different kind.

He must have felt it, too. For he reached down, and took something from a pouch on his belt – one of the guards nearby stepping forward and raising a hand, until the Roman saw it was merely a strip of leather, nothing more. A worthless thing that a rider may use to repair a saddle, or bind about a sword handle. Kai laid it on the floor of the cage by her feet, as though it were something sacred.

She took a twist of cloth from the folds of her clothing, a rag she had kept in the way that a prisoner saves everything they can, and placed it beside his offering. After a moment, on some unspoken signal, each took the other's token.

One last brief touch, the back of her fingers passing against his. Then he was gone – away towards the horses, the river, the journey, and death.

28

Five days in the saddle, over the Danu and back across the plain. Lucius, Kai, and ten Roman cavalry sent to escort them. Their spears dressed with a branch and bound with twists of long grass, the marks of truce. A dozen men hunting an army.

Kai led them – in part from his knowledge of the mustering places and natural pathways across the plains, but also by a feeling, the unseen bond that pulled him back towards his people. The way that birds may make great sojourns across country and continent, through storms that may blow them countless miles off course, and yet still they find their way.

At night, about the campfires, the Romans whispered amongst themselves. Cursing him, no doubt, for they had little faith in the nomad's instinct. After the fourth day, with no sign of the army on the plains, even Lucius was beginning to doubt him. That night, as they made camp, he took Kai aside, quietly said: 'Are you certain of the way?'

'Not certain. But we shall find them soon enough.'

The Roman glanced back towards his men. 'We should have come across their scouts by now.'

'They will have no outriders. Just a single great warband, riding as one.'

'Why? It is madness for cavalry to move without scouts.'

'Because,' said Kai, 'they come to die, not to win.'

And on the next day, he was proved right. At a distance, past a copse of trees, they saw armour glittering in the light that danced across the scales of horn and iron the way the sun plays upon the sea. When they passed through the trees, they saw a second forest laid out before them – the tall spears tipped up towards the sky, the banners streaming behind. Upon the air was the war music of horn and drum, and before them the horses and their riders spread across the plain. A whole people hurrying towards their deaths, and for Kai there was pride at first, to look upon them once more, to see a courage and defiance that made him ashamed. Perhaps it was the way that his people were meant to die, standing together against hopeless odds.

But as they drew closer, he could see men lolling drunk in the saddles – not from the little wine and koumiss that most took to find their courage before a battle, but in the way that doomed men drink. Many of the riders were still winter-thin, skeletons in the saddle, while others rode fattened and content. Always before they had shared and gifted their food before the mustering, but what use was there in sharing anything at the ending of the world?

At last some invisible line was crossed. For a horn was calling in the air, drowned out at once by something else – a howling and screaming, as the army spoke with one voice. For here they saw the enemy, an enemy that they could kill. The Sarmatians were swarming forward then, seeming blind to the truce signs, spears levelled for the charge.

All about him, Kai heard the Romans speaking, panicking, making ready to flee. 'Do not run,' he said, and held the truce spear high. For he could see figures amongst the Sarmatians, riding across the lines and screaming at their men. The captains of the warband, those who would bear the dishonour of their men as their own, who were threatening and pleading with their warriors to stop. And so it was the swarming riders broke like a wave, through fortune or fate or the old habits of command, sweeping around and encircling the trespassers.

A strange silence, for a time, filled only with the heavy breathing of the horses, the clatter and rattle of arms and armour. Then, without speaking to one another, the captains broke away from the swarming riders, coming forward with their spears held low. Kai searched amongst them, hoping against hope to find a man or woman he might recognise and bargain with. And he did. The gods, it seemed, had a sense of humour.

For one man bore a familiar crooked smile, a scar across the face, his neck and arms dripping with gold that he had not worn before. And Gaevani leaned forward over the saddle, and said: 'So. It seems you did come back to die.'

'I keep my promises,' said Kai. 'And there will be time for that one soon enough.' He laid his hand to the twists of grass on his spear. 'But we come under the sign of truce.'

'No truce with the Romans. Not anymore. We have made our sword oaths for war.'

'Yet they would speak with—'

A chant from the crowd, drowning Kai out. 'No truce!
No truce!' as the swords beat against armour and lances
danced in the air. And Kai saw his people for the first time
as the Romans must have – blood-mad, blinded by their
honour. Murderers to be put to the sword, wild animals
on the border.

Kai lifted his spear towards the sky and held it there,
point tilted towards the earth, and the strangeness of the
gesture brought the mob to silence once more. 'Let us
speak, then, before you kill us,' he said. 'What harm can
there be in that?'

A voice from the crowd: 'We want to hear no trickery
from Rome.'

Kai answered. 'I did not ever think to see a Sarmatian be
afraid of words. Are you?'

Hisses from the crowd, moving and shifting like a
wave in water. But Gaevani was laughing then – a merry,
murderous sound.

'Let them speak,' he said. 'When they have emptied
themselves of the air, they shall be easier to skin. They will
make fine trophies for the hunt.'

All at once, the killing mood seemed to lighten, to pass.
The mob drifted apart. A few Sarmatians came forward
in the semblance of friendship, offering wineskins and
speaking what broken Latin they had – mocking the horses
that the Romans rode, asking questions about the women
over the river. The Romans took the wineskins doubtfully,
gave the briefest answers in return.

'What is this, Kai?' Lucius whispered to him.

'We are their guests now.'

'They meant to kill us a moment before.'

'And perhaps they shall before long,' said Kai, 'but we are safe until it is decided otherwise.'

Voices calling, the captains circling about them – an honour guard to lead them to the chieftain's fire.

'I have given you your chance, Lucius,' said Kai, before they were parted by the crowd. 'Do not waste it.'

'I will not,' he said.

It was Gaevani who led the way – some kind of champion he seemed to the Sarmatians now, and Kai set his horse forward until he was at that man's side, leaned close as they rode. 'I owe a great debt to you,' he said, 'for letting them go. Tomyris, and Arite.'

Gaevani went still. On his face was an expression that Kai had not seen before – the look of a man caught in something shameful. Then he smiled, and said: 'Shame to waste a handsome woman such as Arite. Perhaps I will have her for my own, when all this is done.' He leered at Kai. 'I have heard she is one who men may share, is she not?'

The feeling of hate rolling hot across his skin, his hand dancing towards the knife at his side – Kai took a hard breath, made himself be still once more. 'Always the testing with you,' he said. 'I wonder if it is that you find yourself so wanting.'

'Oh, that is not my way,' said Gaevani. 'I do love myself very well. But I grant you that yes, I do enjoy the testing. How else can you know if you are the best?' He swept his hand towards the army – the mad, straggling army, stumbling towards their death. 'That is what we are all here to do. That is why the chieftains will say no to you.'

'Does this seem a band of heroes to you? Do you think it will make a good death?'

Gaevani hesitated. 'No,' he said softly. 'I feel like an old man, wandering towards his grave, ruined and stupid. I would wish for a way other than this one.'

'That is what we come to offer,' said Kai. 'Another way.'

'Oh, I know. But it shall do you no good. And now, you will see why.'

For once more before them rose the great chieftains' fire. But four men now gathered there, not five. And one who sat raised above the rest upon a pile of furs, iron in his hand and gold at his throat, a mantle of scalps slung about his shoulders. There were fresh ones there now, gleaming wet in the light of the fire, and upon his brow something that no Sarmatian had worn for generations. A thin, battered circlet of iron wrapped about his forehead.

It was Zanticus, the man with whom they had come to bargain. But he was a chieftain of the Wolves no longer. This was a man who had made himself a king at the end of the world.

Lucius had thought that there could be no fear left for him, after his audience with the Emperor. He had seen this chieftain in the winter, from afar – heavy-set for a cavalryman, a thick braided beard and bright, hollow eyes, wearing the dead as trophies. An intimidating man to meet on the battlefield, but a warlord like any other, and what was a warlord compared to a god?

Yet there was something in the way that man smiled and laughed about the fire, even as he led a rotting army, a broken nation, towards its own destruction. And when Lucius saw the crown of iron upon his head, he felt the battle calm descend as though the swords were already drawn. For he knew all too well what men might do for a trophy such as that.

As they came beside the fire, Zanticus did not look upon Lucius at first. He stared at Kai, and he laid his hand to the fresh scalps on his cloak, fingers knotting into the hair, nails running across stitch and scar.

'What brings a man from a dead clan to my fire?' said Zanticus. 'Have you come to join these kinsmen of yours, here upon my cloak?'

Beside him, Lucius felt Kai quiver once, go still. A moment of waiting about the fire – half a step forward, an inch of iron shown, a single insult called in response, and the Sarmatians would swarm upon them and tear them to pieces. But Kai only breathed deep, and held his silence.

'Yes,' Zanticus said. 'A dog of Rome you are now. You shall not speak unless commanded. And what use is it to hear words from a dead clan? I do not bargain with ghosts.' He smiled, and inclined his head towards Lucius. 'We shall talk to those from a clan about to die instead. Speak then, Roman. What words do you bring?'

'Great chieftain—' Lucius began, but at once he was interrupted.

'A king now,' said Zanticus. 'King of the Sarmatians.

343

There never was anything that could unite us before, until you thought to come across the water.'

'Great king, I bring a message from the Emperor of Rome. He admires your bravery, salutes your courage. He has no wish to destroy such warriors as yourselves.'

Zanticus spat into the fire. 'This is all that you have to say? These words, we have heard their like before. Empty, and worthless. Surely there is more you have to offer?'

Lucius hesitated. 'Perhaps we might speak away from the crowd,' he said. 'The words of kings are not fit for the mob.'

'I am king of the people! We shall speak before the people!' A great roar answered his words, a chanting and rattling of spears, and Zanticus threw his arms wide open. 'Offer your bribe, if that is what you came here to do. Offer me gold and lands, a little kingdom of my own. Offer me iron and slaves. Offer it all to me, so I can say no.'

'I bring no iron or gold,' said Lucius. 'I come to offer you war. For Rome, not with her. A great journey, and glorious battle at the end of it, such as your people have never fought.'

Stillness for a moment. The crackle of the fire. Then Zanticus pointed towards the west, and said: 'Why travel far for a war, when we can have one there?' Once more laughter answered him around the fire.

'But against Rome, it is a war you cannot win.'

'What does that matter? You think us afraid to die?'

'No,' said Lucius. 'But that you might wish to see your children grow old. To enjoy the passage of the seasons, the spring flowers upon the steppe. That you would see ten thousand generations of your people ride free across the plain. It is a beautiful world that you have built here. Why let it end?'

A little sigh then, from somewhere close – a hesitance from the crowd. And a test for Zanticus to answer, whether he were truly a king of his people, or a tyrant leading them into the darkness. For a moment, the peace was there amongst them like a spirit, as hands unwrapped from sword hilts and eyes wandered towards lovers. And then the king spoke once more.

'There is no promise that you would give that we would trust,' Zanticus said. 'You are oathbreakers. You would have us throw down our weapons and let you butcher us. We will fight you, and destroy you. You are here because you are afraid. Why else would you come here?'

And all about them then, the blood-mad chanting, the words of a people who had chosen death. It would be no use to shout them down, to plead. But when Lucius laid a hand upon the hilt of his sword, the Sarmatians fell silent. And when he spoke again, he made himself speak lightly. The way a man might offer an idle wager, or ask a question of a child.

'You are not afraid to fight the Romans?'

'Of course not.'

'Then you would not be afraid to fight me?'

More laughter – uncertain now. For the crowd could feel that the words were changing, sharpening and hardening.

'Is it the way of your messengers,' Zanticus said, 'to insult a king?'

'I mean no insult. Our people will soon be killing each

other. And we may begin it now, if that is your wish. But I have not heard it said that a Sarmatian needed twenty men to kill one of ours. Or that their chieftains and kings lead from behind their warriors.'

'I do not ride at the back.'

'Prove it then. Fight me before you send your warriors to die for you. If you have the courage for it.'

Not a moment's hesitation before the king rose, standing nearly a head taller than Lucius and the iron war gear glittering upon him. Worse than that, a glitter of cunning in the Sarmatian's eyes. His gaze seemed to feel out old injuries – the spear wound in Lucius's side, the shield arm broken and reset three years before, the knee that he had wrenched when he first joined the Legion and still favoured in cold weather.

The first and last king of the Sarmatians came around the fire, threw his arm about Lucius's shoulder, almost brotherly. He leaned close – close enough for Lucius to smell the stink of wine and horse blood upon his breath. For a moment, for all that they were surrounded by a nation, they spoke as if alone.

'You are brave, Red Crest,' Zanticus whispered. 'I will give you the honour of a place on this cloak, and you will still be alive when I peel the scalp from your skull. That, I promise you.'

'You are a coward,' Lucius answered, 'not a king. Your people shall sing my name before the day is out, and you shall be forgotten. *That* I promise *you*.'

A slight widening of the eyes, a hint of grey to Zanticus's lips – whatever he had expected in answer, it had not been that. Perhaps he, too, had misjudged his opponent. Then the bloody smile spreading across the lips. And Zanticus turned his face to his people, and roared: 'Though our lives be short!'

And the Sarmatians answered, with one voice: 'Let our fame be great!'

29

It was no simple thing, to find the place for the killing. No use looking behind the encampment, the earth torn to pieces by the passage of cart and horse, and all before them the ground was treacherous and uncertain. And so together they went, Lucius and Zanticus pacing across the plain, testing the earth with their spears, stamping down long grass, probing the tussocks and reeds. And as he watched them, Kai thought he saw an odd companionship there, as they pointed out to one another the soft bog that might snare a horse, the tripwire of a root and the pit-trap of a watery hole in the earth. Perhaps, having made the decision to wager their lives, they now only feared a foolish death. A brief truce between them, as each sought to ensure that the other might die well.

All about the Sarmatians gathered – spreading across the rolling bank of the hillside above the campground, others climbing trees and roosting there like birds, while before them the seers and dream readers tore entrails from hare and horse, each one finding victory for the king of the Sarmatians in the bloody loops they cast upon the ground.

Kai sought to forget them all – Zanticus and Lucius, the Sarmatians and the Romans, Arite, Bahadur, and Tomyris in their cage over the water. There was only himself and the horse he tended, the horse that Lucius would fight upon. He led it back and forth to keep it limber, testing again and again the girth of the saddle, kneading the muscles with a horsemaster's careful love, whispering prayers to the gods of the battle and the hunt. For all his ministrations, the horse tossed its head and stamped upon the ground. It could feel the battle coming.

No horn called to the champions, no marked hour was reached. But something in the crowd grew tired of waiting, and a restless chanting began. A long spear raised into the air, as Zanticus silently answered his people and made his way to his horse.

As Lucius came to him, Kai searched for any signs of fear. Perhaps there was the slightest tremor in the fingers of one hand, that slowness to his steps of a man who cannot bring himself to hurry towards death. But a good blush of colour to lip and cheek, his eyes bright as he took the reins of the horse. It seemed unthinkable that a man so full of life might be about die.

'We shall see soon enough,' Lucius said, 'if I have wasted my chance.'

'You have not wasted it.'

'That I do not know.' A flashing smile. 'He is a big bastard.'

'Whatever happens, you have not wasted it,' said Kai. 'Courage is never wasted. You always meant to challenge him?'

'I did. I thought he could not refuse me in front of his people.'

'You do know us well.' Kai ran his hand one last time across the neck of the horse. 'Is it for hate or love that you fight?' he said.

'What?'

Kai smiled at him. 'I have always heard it said that one may only fight well for hate or for love. Better to choose now.'

'Let it be for love, then,' Lucius said. And he fell silent for a moment, searching. Many times before had Kai seen it, in friends and close companions, on the eve of battle and duel, or by those struck by fever or sickness who do not know if they shall see the sun rise another time. The search for the parting words, the ones that might matter most.

At last, the Roman spoke. 'Amongst my people,' he said, 'it is the worst of crimes to kill one's father. There is little that the gods hate more than that. I do not know whose gods speak true, yours or mine. But your shame is not fixed, it is not certain. My gods are not yours, but even so, perhaps that may mean something.'

'It does. I thank you for it.'

A calling then – a roaring, wordless challenge from the Sarmatian king across the field.

'I wish there was more time,' said Lucius.

'Go and earn it, then,' Kai answered.

'I will. For all of us.' And he was mounted in a moment, snatching up his spear and setting the horse to dance its way to the killing ground, sitting with the easy grace of a man born to the saddle. And though many Sarmatians howled their scorn, a few lifted their weapons in a warrior's salute, wished him good fortune, a brave death. For they loved horsemanship above all else, beyond the blood ties of clan, the feuds of nations, beyond honour or love.

They took their places, little more than a bowshot apart. The ground between Lucius and Zanticus was no clear horseman's run. Rough sodden earth, long grass that might still hold traps of bog and mire. Yet for all that, the light fell across it well, and the wildflowers fringed it with colour – perhaps, for all their searching for the best ground to fight upon, that was what had made their choice for them. A beautiful place to fight, and to die.

Zanticus set his horse stamping and feinting, trying to goad the Roman into charging first across uncertain ground. But Lucius let the reins go slack in his hands, leaned back and let the sun play across his face. He looked as though he would be willing to wait forever.

It began with silence. Not a sound, but the absence of sound, that moment where a horse's hooves are in flight but have not yet struck the ground. And then the horses tore across the plain, the light shining upon the spearheads, the great crowd struck to stillness. Kai saw it all so slowly – the careful placement of each horse's hoof, the shift in weight of the riders in the saddle. The spears weaving in the air, moving forward and back. But one of them was moving too far back, Lucius's spear drawing away from the mark, giving up all advantage of weight and reach. Then the weapon came forward once more and took flight into the air.

It was a heavy cavalry spear, not weighted for throwing. And so Lucius had waited almost to the last moment – thrown half a heartbeat before or after and it would have been for nothing.

For a single breath, the spear seemed to hang still in the air. Then all moved too fast to be seen – the rending crash of iron against iron, the screaming of a horse. Impossible, at that distance, but Kai thought he could taste blood in the air.

The horses together, then parted, slowing, still. Both men still in the saddle, but a cry from the crowd about them, the sound men made when they sighted a wound. And how frightening it was to know someone was wounded but to not know who.

Zanticus swayed in his saddle, the armour spiderwebbed with cracks from where the thrown spear had struck home. But the iron had held. There was blood upon the grass, and it was not his. For as Lucius turned his mount around, Kai could see the flank of the horse laid open, the quiver of muscle and meat in the open air.

A little sigh from the crowd, as Zanticus moved his horse slowly, carefully, finding the place for the next charge, the last one there would be. There was no urgency – Lucius had no spear, and a dying horse beneath him. It would be a careful, patient killing.

Then the Roman slipped from the saddle, stepped lightly upon the ground. He backed away quickly, for his horse knew of its wound now, and was apt to kick and kill any who came close. When Lucius was clear of it, he stood in a swordsman's even stance. The Roman cavalry sword in his hand, levelled in challenge for a moment, before it dipped back down again.

Zanticus cocked his head to the side, at a loss. A Sarmatian would choose to keep even a wounded horse under him, to be spared the shame of dying on the ground. But then, a smile upon his lips. Doomed men did mad things – no doubt he thought it no more than that.

The last charge. The long spear levelled, blood dancing from the iron head with every strike of the horse's hooves. And Lucius standing still, sword low to the ground, waiting.

Afterwards, long afterwards, the Sarmatians would tell stories of that sword he held in his hand. Mutterings of witchcraft and magic, a blade that made a man invincible and brought miracles with it. But it was the man and not the blade that brought a miracle that day.

For there was a scream from Zanticus's horse – it was rearing, stumbling, forelegs painted in thick black mud, the treacherous ground giving way beneath it. Lucius rushing forward, the sword lifting high, and the mere sight of the light upon the blade was enough to send the horse twisting and rolling, to set the Sarmatian tumbling from the saddle and beneath the hooves of his own horse.

A stumbling pursuit then, Lucius running and tripping across bad ground, clumsy and desperate, no time for honour or grace. Only the desperate race to be there first, before Zanticus rose from the earth. Kai alone willing him on, screaming his name, while the rest of the Sarmatians called for their king to stand and fight.

But Zanticus made no move to rise – lying on his side,

one hand cast across his face as though in shame at what had happened to him. When Lucius reached the king he rolled him over, lifted the sword high. The point trembled for a moment at the apex, and then slowly lowered once more. For the king's head lolled impossibly to the side, neck broken from the fall, sunlight glittering upon the dull iron crown.

Little sound from the Sarmatians who watched then. Only a whispering, passing like a wave from the front to the back of the crowd, giving the word to those who could not see. And Lucius looked about himself, a dreamer waking. The sword fell from nerveless fingers, and he was on his knees, bowing his head until he almost laid it upon Zanticus's chest, weeping and shaking as though he had killed a man that he loved. And even when Kai ran to him, lifted Lucius to his feet and spoke the words of victory, still he seemed weak as a child. He clung to Kai, for it seemed that Lucius had spent all his courage there upon the field. A lifetime's worth, perhaps.

They walked slowly together, and all about them the silence held, no one else moved. Perhaps the Sarmatians, too, were learning to wait – perhaps it was that Lucius could teach them the art of patience. Kai had the sense that if they could just get to their horses before the spell was broken, they might be safe.

But a figure stepped forward from the crowd before they could get there – the sun at his back, and Kai could not see his face. At first Kai thought it some son of Zanticus's coming forward for revenge, or another chieftain wishing to claim the kingship for himself. But there was no weapon

TIM LEACH

in the man's hand, and a smile upon his face – Gaevani, come to greet them, the one to break the silence.

'You knew the ground was weak there?' Gaevani said to Lucius. 'Too soft for the horse?'

'I did,' Lucius answered.

'That was done well.'

Lucius hesitated. 'What will happen now?'

'That depends. Will you really give them a war?'

Something like laughter from the Roman. 'After all this, they will still want war?'

'They will want it more than slavery.' Gaevani swept his hand in a circle. 'Tell them, if you can.'

For others were gathering about them – strangely shy and hesitant, chieftains and children alike. Kai saw a shadow cross Lucius's face, for perhaps he knew that it was not enough, all that he had given in courage. He felt the man leaning against the crook of his neck, the shallow breaths growing heavy. Then Lucius stepped away, standing tall, and spoke once more.

He had not the strength to shout – perhaps it would have done him no good. The words came soft and rasping, like a man speaking a secret. 'Fight for Rome,' he said to the gathering crowd. 'We have more enemies than can be counted. If it is war you desire, you shall have it. Iron, and gold. And if it is your homes you long for, know this. We do not keep our warriors in the warband for ever. Twenty-five years, and you will be free. Twenty-five years, and you go home.'

Silence answered him.

'You have shown you are not afraid to fight,' he

continued. 'Not afraid to die. Are you afraid of twenty-five years?'

It was almost enough. But still the Sarmatians made no answer – a sense of something missing, as when the storyteller finishes his tale too soon, and those at the fireside call for more, call for the true ending. Kai knew then what he must do, and he slid the sword from its sheath.

'Will you swear it?' said Kai.

'Swear it?'

Kai offered the point of the sword to him – a Roman sword, but still the iron would make it sacred. 'An oath upon the sword,' he said. 'That we shall have our war. That we will come back after those years, as you say.'

A shadow on the Roman's face. A hesitance that Kai could not understand. Then Lucius's hand was at the tip of the sword, and he said: 'I swear it.'

No cheers answered the Roman, no calling of his name. Someone nearby clapped their hands once, the way that seers sometimes ended a ritual, and it was done. The crowd breaking, drifting, beginning to reform in a different way. All about them Kai could hear word passing from one Sarmatian to the next – not spoken with joy or anger, but with a quiet acceptance. A trial to be endured, like so many before. A pride, perhaps, in having the courage to endure it.

Lucius's work was still not done. Kai watched the Roman speaking with each chieftain in turn – low, quiet, urgent. For the peace they held together was a fragile thing. It might not last the day.

Beside him, Gaevani said: 'A blow struck by the gods,

357

they shall call it. It will be sung of for a long time. Brave Zanticus, who made even the gods envious. Lucius and his spelltouched sword. Though perhaps they will make a Sarmatian of him, when the tale has been told enough times.' He chuckled. 'I begin to see why you look on him the way that you do.'

'He is a captain to follow,' Kai answered.

'He is a captain that will have you, I think you mean.'

'That too.' Kai turned, sword still in his hand. 'And what of us?' he said.

'What do you mean?'

'You promised to kill me when I returned. We may settle it now, if you wish.'

Gaevani said nothing for a time. Then: 'That time shall come. But not now.'

'Why not?'

'You entertain me, Kai. I never quite know what you shall do or say. I thought that there was little left in the world that surprises me. I shall have to kill you one day, for the injury you have done me. But I am not tired of you yet.'

Kai shaded his eyes, looked towards the sun. And he said: 'You shall not have another chance, it seems.' And he heard Gaevani curse, when the man saw what Kai did.

For there were riders to the west. The sun low at their backs, stretching their shadows long, making giants of them. Even at such a distance, he knew them. The slight figure of Tamura, hugging her spear close against her body as if for comfort. Saratos slouched low in his saddle, almost seeming a part of the horse he rode. The little gestures of the others that he knew from the long road they had travelled together, when they had kept company as intimate as lovers. And at their head, a rider on a one-eyed horse, red tassels dripping from the spear. Close-cropped hair, and a face that could have been a mirror of his own.

His sister, and her warriors. Come to claim their blood price at last.

30

They were a ragged band, the riders on the horizon, with the bandit look of those who have lived off the land for too long. Wolves at the end of winter, hard-eyed and hollow-ribbed. But the war gear was clean and well-tended, fresh scalps hanging from the saddles. And when Kai looked amongst the others once more, he saw that they too bore a single tassel of red felt on their spears. A mark from their new captain, a sign of their allegiance.

A mist spread across Kai's eyes, before he blinked to clear it and turned his face towards the sky – the gods had chosen a good day, at least. No stormtossed rain or lightning dancing on the plain, but the achingly clear light of a low sun. The gods wanted a fine view of what was to come, and perhaps they wanted him to feel, at the last, how sweet and beautiful it was, the world that he was leaving.

Lucius must have returned. For from his side, he heard the Roman say: 'How did they know where to find us?'

'They must have been following us for some time. Saratos is a good tracker, and Tamura was always soft-footed in the dark.'

'Kai, you must tell me. What does this mean?'

'Oh, Lucius. You have learned much of my people, but this is something you cannot understand.' Kai's horse and spear were close by – he took up the weapon, and carefully picked the truce leaves away.

'We must get our message back across the water,' said Lucius.

'*You* shall. They have not come for you.'

'There is an army at our backs. We can—'

'They will not fight for you here. They will follow you on the journey you have promised them, and fight and die in any war you give them. But this is my battle, not theirs, and they know it.'

At last, perhaps, there was an understanding – the orders died on Lucius's lips before he could speak them. The Roman's hand, trembling and weak, went to his sword once more.

'Perhaps it is worth the price I shall pay,' said Kai, 'to see this bravery from you. We always know these things too late, don't we?'

The Roman did not seem to hear him. 'We shall send one of my men back. Ferox, the fastest rider we have. The rest of us can—'

'No, Lucius. Stay here,' said Kai. 'And whatever happens, do not interfere. One last oath, can you give me that?'

The Roman said nothing, irresolute. For all that Kai had seen that man wounded to the point of death, kept as a prisoner and a slave, perhaps it was the first time he had seen him defeated.

'I swear it,' he said.

Kai set his horse forward, a steady, even walk. And he could feel the horse restless beneath him, longing to rush forward and greet its lost companions. For this was a feud it could not understand.

The feel of the sun on his neck and wrists, the spear smooth in the hollow of his hands. And the birdsong, the idle chatter and mating calls of a new season beginning. He tried to let his memories go, to think of nothing but the passage of one moment to the next, the fall of the horse's hooves, the beating of his heart, each single breath that he cast to the wind. Yet the memories came to him unbidden, all the same.

At some unspoken signal, as he came closer, the warband parted into two lines. A space opening between them, a channel wide enough for a single rider to pass through. Wide enough for the swords to swing and cut.

He was close enough to truly see them now. He tried to make them meet his gaze – they owed him that much, at least. Tamura was staring at the ground, hard-faced and sullen, some light lost from her eyes. Kai could not recall ever having seen Saratos without a smile, but there was no sign of it now as the old man looked straight through him.

Kai pulled the last branch of truce from his spear, the leaves flaking away beneath his fingers, and cast it to the ground. For there was no need to make them break taboo. He could spare them that, at least.

He passed close between them – close enough to smell the sweat of their horses, the stink of leather, the sour scent of men and women too long in the saddle. One of their horses snorted, and his horse's mane danced from the passage of the breath, so close were they. The rattle and clink of armour like a prisoner's chains around him, and he listened for the whisper of a sword leaving a scabbard, the sound of a spear cutting air.

He was past the first riders, and the second, and the third, until he was in the middle of the column, surrounded on all sides.

No stroke of sword or spear. No knife opening the thigh, or finding its place beneath rib or shoulder. They simply turned from him, one after another. The companions he had led, and fought for, the broken people that he had made whole once more, turning their horses to put their backs to him until only Laimei, at the back of the line, remained to face him.

A craving then for knife and blade, to scream like a madman and beg for the killing, to raise his spear and force them to it. For one always fears to die, until there is a glimpse of the broken life that lies ahead.

He made himself sit tall in the saddle, to pause and fix his gaze on each of them in turn as he passed. For even if they meant to abandon him, he would not cast them aside. And had one of them turned back, they would have seen Kai looking upon them with pride, and love. But none did.

And so he came, at last, to Laimei.

'You understand now?' she said.

He did not answer at first. Then: 'I understand.'

'What our father felt, when you would not kill him. You understand it now?'

'I do.'

'Perhaps it is that you do, at last.'

'You brought Bahadur across the water,' said Kai. 'No other could have done that.'

'And you brought Lucius to this place.' She looked away, towards the Sarmatians gathered upon the plain. 'You have done what you must, for the peace?'

'I have.' He hesitated. 'I did not know that it mattered to you. Whether our people lived or died.'

'How little you know me. After all of this. I almost pity you.' She fixed her eyes on him once more. 'Yet you broke your pledge. Abandoned your warriors. Once again, you could not do what was demanded of you.'

'No, I could not.'

She leaned forward over the saddle, and said: 'So I give you the choice that you would not give our father.'

Kai said nothing. He listened to the wind.

'A hero's death I offer,' she said. 'A good death upon my spear. I could not before – not for love of you, but for our people. I can do it now.'

He traced a finger across the haft of the spear. No trace of the truce leaves remained. 'You had to turn my people against me?' he said.

'That was not my work, but their choice. You abandoned them. What did you think that they would do?'

'I am a shamed man once again, it seems.'

She shrugged. 'It may be the Romans will find some use for you. They have always been great keepers of slaves and dogs, so I have heard. But you have no place amongst your own people.'

'I know.'

'I would not want to live so.'

'I know that, too.'

'And so what is your choice?'

'You have taught me much,' Kai said slowly. 'And I know, that from you, this is a kindness.' He looked to the west, thinking of the river beyond it, the people he had left behind. 'But I choose to live.'

There was pity in her voice, when she answered him. 'You shall regret this,' she said.

'That may be so. But in twenty-five years, I will ride once more with my daughter on the plain. I would not have her become as you are.'

A moment when there was something almost like pain upon her face. It had been so long since he had seen that. Then the lines of the face hardening, sharpening, twisting. Almost like a spell being cast, as though she had made a bargain with a sorcerer, to change the face that she hated, the face that reminded her of Kai. And at last, it was as though they looked nothing alike.

No great distance, to ride back to the encampment. Yet a journey taken alone always seems to be twice as far, and this was a kind of loneliness that he had not known before. The final bonds that held him to his people were cut at last. He had proved himself to be not of their kind, and so he did not ride back towards them, those who had been his kin and his people. He went to the Romans gathered at the edge of the plain, Lucius and his cavalry.

Some of the Romans were stifling laughter – amused, perhaps, by what must have seemed a barbarian's practice. But others were solemn, though they could not have understood what they had seen. They knew it for a warrior's ritual. And when he was amongst them once more, Lucius rode to him and laid his hands on the horns of Kai's saddle. Leaning forward, speaking softly, he said: 'You have paid more than I have, I think, for this victory.'

'It may be so,' said Kai. And it frightened him, how empty the words sounded, the need in his voice that he heard when he spoke again. 'You will keep your promise? Twenty-five years, and I shall see my daughter again?'

'I will keep my promise,' the Roman said.

'You hold my life with that oath, Lucius.'

A little dip of the Roman's shoulders, then, a weight settling upon him. 'Live, Kai,' he said. 'We go from this place soon. A great journey for your people. There will be a place of honour for you at the end of that journey. I will do all that I can to make it so.'

Looking back across the plain, its tall grass dancing in the wind and the first wildflowers of spring a brilliant scattering blue, Kai said: 'It is a beautiful land, is it not?'

'It is.'

'It will be worth those years, to see this place again.'

'It will.'

But for all those fine words, he could only think of the omen he had felt when he left the winter encampment. The whisper of a god, telling him that he would die in the west.

And he said to himself, in a whisper of his own that was spoken not like a prayer but a prophecy: 'Then I shall have to prove a god wrong.'

Historical Note

This is a work of fiction. Relatively little is known for certain about the Sarmatians, a primarily nomadic people with no written record of their own left behind and a minimal archaeological footprint. What we do know of them is pieced together from written Greek and Roman sources such as Strabo, Cassius Dio, Ovid, and Herodotus, as well as the archaeological finds that survive (mostly from grave sites). So what we have is limited in scope and unreliable in nature – frustrating for the historian, but exciting for the novelist (and, I hope, the reader).

We do know that there was a war with the Roman Empire in AD 175 or so, a battle upon the frozen Danube, and eventually a peace settlement which sent thousands of Sarmatian heavy cavalry to the north of Britain. Much more than that remains mysterious, but the Sarmatians are pleasingly connected to many myths, ranging from that of the Amazon warrior women to that of our own King Arthur.

If you'd like to read further, I recommend *The Sarmatians* (Tadeusz Sulimirski, 1970) and *Sarmatians* (Eszter Istvánovits and Valeria Kulcsár, 2017) as excellent summaries of the archaeological and written record, and *The Tales of the Narts* (John Colarusso and Tamirlan Salbiev, 2016), and *From Scythia to Camelot* (C. Scott Littleton and Linda Malcor, 2000) for more on the mythological links.

Acknowledgements

As always, enormous thanks are due to everyone who has contributed to the book.

To Caroline Wood for her insightful guidance and storyteller's instincts. To Nic Cheetham for his support and tremendous enthusiasm, and for setting me on the right path in the first place. To Wendy Toole for a careful copyedit, Mark Swan for the gorgeous cover, Clare Gordon for keeping everything on track, to Christian Duck, Lizz Burrell, Ben Prior, Avneet Bains, and Jade Gwilliam, and everyone else at Head of Zeus and Felicity Bryan for all they have done to help bring this book into the world.

To my colleagues at the Warwick Writing Programme for their wisdom, support, and good humour, and to my students for continuing to inspire me and to teach me the tricks of the trade (I hope that they occasionally feel they have learned something too).

To my parents, always, for everything.

To my friends, for at its heart this is a book about friendship. I suspect that those who are sceptical about the existence of the Amazon warriors have not met the climbing women of Sheffield – fierce, strong, and proud.

This book is dedicated to one in particular, a very dear friend who has fought hard for me in the difficult times of my life. She was strong when I was not, brave when I was afraid. May I swallow your evil days, Ness – courage to the champion, and victory to her spear.